The Runner and the Spare

Ruth Foster

To family, for as new join in, it only gets lovelier

Table of Contents

world, has most likely been through miners who are illegally trespassing or well-armed drug runners.

"Permission to enter was given in secret by presidential decree after the protestations of the Department of Indigenous Affairs. We were warned that the people of that area were dangerous, seeing all intruders as expendable."

"Expendable?"

"Killed, yes. With poison tipped arrows."

"And, circumstances being what they were, it wasn't possible to ask for DNA samples from anyone living in the reserve. We did ask around, and we were able to take some samples from people outside of the reserve who are of mixed heritage."

"What do you conclude?"

"There are two scenarios. The first is that the remains of the royal child were dragged off or eaten by a predator. The infant that was interspersed with the other bones was dropped there by an indigenous woman – perhaps she thought it would be a hallowed resting ground or appease some unknown deity when she came across the ruins while out to dispose of her own deceased child.

"The second scenario is that the baby was found alive and exchanged for a dead one. Perhaps a mother's child had just died, and she thought this was a fair exchange. She would still have milk and. . ."

"No." Lord Hampton's voice booked no uncertainty or argument. "There is no second scenario. No one survived that crash. And if by some miracle the baby lived, you know full well that no European, let alone a seven-month-old infant, could survive in that jungle under any circumstances. It is best to not even bring it up. The Princess Lilliana died with her parents on impact. They will remain interned as one. Let the dead rest in peace."

Three

23 years later

When Azim Shah got up that morning, he expected it to be a brilliant day. As usual, before rising, he had checked the weather app on his phone. A yellow sun showed up at all hours of the timeline. Just to be sure, he had opened his kitchen window to look up at the sky and to smell the air. His senses confirmed it, and as he drank his cup of warm tea and milk, he felt great satisfaction with what he had done with his life.

This very afternoon, at three o'clock sharp, he would be sitting on a white folding chair placed temporarily with several hundred others in precise and straight rows to watch his only daughter Aleena Jane receive her diploma. All that was missing was Aleena Jane's mother, his beloved wife, but Azim felt that the crisp blue sky was a sign of good omen. His wife had no fears of dying, certain even as she took her last breath, that Aleena Jane would be the first of their family to graduate from university.

"You were right, of course," Azim murmured to himself as he changed into his normal uniform for the day – a spotless and carefully ironed long-sleeved button-down shirt and just as carefully ironed pair of trousers. Azim was a taxi driver, and he was proud of the fact that he had never been late or missed a day of work. This very afternoon would be the first time he had ever deviated from his normal schedule. He was told that he could take the entire day off, but Azim felt that a half day was concession enough. If he finished by twelve, he would still have plenty of time to get ready for the ceremony of Aleena Jane's graduation.

Azim picked up his last passengers from the train station at 11:20. When he was told to take them to the Hotel Landress, the grandest hotel that was walking distance to the university, he felt a sudden jolt in his heart. Just as quickly he felt a searing pain run down his arm, but then it disappeared.

"You must have a child graduating," Azim said calmly as he seated his passengers in the rear of his car. "Congratulations."

Azim didn't mention that his own daughter was graduating. He had been an observer of his clients long enough to know that the slightest perceived equalizer – anything that lowered the separation between the servant (driver) and master (rider) – reduced the possibility of a tip. Azim also knew that if he spotted the couple whose luggage he had stowed and held the door for at the graduation ceremony, they would not recognize him. He was and would remain a faceless hired man.

Azim was wrong. Very wrong. He remained faceless, but he was not forgotten. He was remembered for what he almost did.

"Dear God! We're going to hit him!"

The shrill cry of Azim's female passenger seemed to come from far away. Azim felt he should respond. He should reassure his passengers that all was well. He should assure the couple in the back seat that he was a careful driver who had never once had an accident. He should let them know that he, too, saw the smiling child running toward them. First, he had seen the ball bouncing out between the two cars pulling into the hotel's *porte cochere*, and then he had seen the child, a boy who couldn't be much more than three years old, come darting out in pursuit.

But then had come the pain. The same pain in Azim's chest he had felt earlier, but this was ten, a hundred, no a thousand times, worse. It burned through his arms, and his brain become divided into two. One part telling him he needed to press the brake and to turn the direction of the wheel of his car, the other part noting how the sun reflecting off the child's golden hair seemed to set the curls ablaze. Then the two parts of Azim's brain came together for one final thought before he lost consciousness.

"Please God, don't let me kill him."

Four

No one, it seemed, could recount without garbled explanation exactly what had just occurred. Azim had been taken away by ambulance, still unconscious, monitors hooked to his heart and IVs started. Azim's two passengers, after being checked for injury and given sedatives to calm the nerves, gave contradictory stories of the child being there and suddenly not. The child's mother, arms around the child and unwilling to put him down, dabbed tears from her eyes as she repeated over and over, "He was in the street, and then just as I was screaming, he flew back."

The police were patient, as they knew that the brain is uncomfortable with things it does not understand. To tamp down cognitive dissonance, the brain fills in gaps. It uses past experiences and knowledge to make sense of what it perceives. A child may appear to fly backward and out of the way of a moving car, but someone or something made it happen.

For all the terrible things that police had come across in their line of work, they had also seen heroics. People who ran into burning buildings to save babies, strangers who recognized that someone was slurring their words because they were in diabetic shock rather than drunk, and children who recognized that an elderly person suffering from Alzheimer's needed a comforting hand while help was phoned for. Someone heroic had saved this child.

Someone had literally dived across the pavement and did a somersault on the hard, unyielding ground while keeping the child safely tucked in their arms. Everyone remembered the sudden appearance, the legs outstretched, the dull thudding sound as the body made contact with the asphalt. Everyone remembered the terrified screams of the mother as the child was thrust into her hands as well as the splintering crash of the taxi cab and the excited shouts of the hysterical passengers. But no one could remember exactly who it was who had handed over the child. Or where he or she had disappeared to.

Five

Once Xo Bosque had passed the child over, Xo's mind focused immediately on what came next. She needed to stop the bleeding. For that, she needed cold water. Although everything about this city was new, she knew that the hotel would have a bathroom.

Without hesitation, Xo pushed through the lobby doors and let the people rushing out to gawk pass around her. Although she appeared to stand motionless, invisible to the crowd passing by her, Xo was aware of everything around her. Years in the jungle had taught her to observe the whole at the same time as to note the slightest variation. A movement of a leaf when a breeze was not blowing might mean that the leaf was the head of a snake. A startled call of a macaw might mean that a jaguar was crouched on an overhead limb. A slight ripple in water might mean that a crocodile was slowing making its way along the muddy bottom. A slight variation in texture might mean that a green tree trunk was instead a sloth with four-inch-long claws.

It took Xo a fraction of a second to deduce where the bathrooms were located. She knew they would be discretely placed, most likely down a small hall so the door would not open directly into the lobby. All she had to do was see someone walk into the lobby from a far back corner at a pace not yet measured or with hands still held as if a little damp. Yes, there was a woman giving a slight tug on her jacket and adjusting her purse strap over her shoulder.

With her hand firmly held against her thigh to staunch the bleeding, Xo began to walk across the lobby. The fluidity from which she went from stationary to ambulatory was so gentle that once again no one seemed to notice her presence. When she pushed open the door of the restroom, no one in the palatial lobby would have been able to tell who it was that it had shut behind on.

Quickly, but with deep calm, Xo stripped off her shoes, shirt, and skirt. A quick cleaning and survey showed that her forearms were nothing to worry about. The blood would stop seeping once wet paper towels were plastered against them. The cut on the thigh, though, was a different matter. She picked some gravel out of it, but she knew it would need some stitching. Normally, Xo would press the two sides of the cut together while holding, one after another, a line of soldier ants up to it. Once each ant's jaws had clamped down, she would twist off its body, leaving the head and locked jaws to act as staples. But, of course, Xo couldn't do that here. Not in this strange place far away from where she felt most at home. No, not here in this foreign city where everything seemed to be made of dead hard surfaces.

There was a basket in the corner of the marble counter, and Xo reached over to it and began to look through its contents. There was an assortment of feminine hygiene products, combs and toothbrushes in individual cellophane wrappers, and at the very bottom, two small sewing kits. Xo opened one, removed the needle, and threaded it. Resting her leg on the counter, she stuck the needle in and carefully began to sew.

Methodically and without hesitation she pushed the needle through her flesh, pulling the threat taut with each stitch. The gash was almost closed when suddenly the door burst open. Xo looked up calmly, her fingers remaining steady on the needle that was embedded in her leg.

In an instant, she saw that it was a man, late to middle twenties or so, comfortable in his clothes, muscled, little risk to her because he looked completely out of his element. Shocked almost. Not with his surroundings, but with her.

"You can't read?" she said, her voice conversational.

The man was momentarily stunned, and his mouth opened several times before he actually spoke.

"Are you crazy? You need an ambulance!"

"No, and no, I don't," Xo said. She went back to her sewing, not looking up again until she had bent over to bite off the ends of the thread after completing the last stitch. Once finished, she calmly began to wipe the counter clear of any blood. The counter now clean, she gathered her clothes and began to get dressed.

"This is a woman's restroom," Xo said, as she pulled on her skirt. "It says so right on the door."

"Yes, I know that, but. . ."

"But what?"

"I thought you might need help."

Xo had finished buttoning her shirt, and slipped on her shoes before she responded to the man's comment, "I don't."

Then with great calm, Xo pushed past the man and exited the restroom. The man followed her. "I only wanted to help," he said. "I saw how you saved that child – great leap by the way – and when I saw you duck in here, I thought, when you didn't come out right away, you might have a concussion or worse. I was just checking that you were okay."

Xo ignored him, continuing to walk at a steady pace toward the lobby doors. "I've never seen anyone suture themselves up before," the man continued, "let alone without at least some kind of local anesthesia. You don't think you need some kind of antibiotic or anything?"

Xo shook her head, but then she paused. A reporter with a camera crew was standing just outside the lobby doors doing an interview with the doorman.

"This way," the man said, taking her arm. "I doubt if he will recognize you, but we can go out through the kitchen just in case."

Xo nodded and allowed the man to lead her back across the main lobby, into the restaurant off to its left, and through the kitchen where although they were met with inquisitive looks, the cooks and wait staff were too busy to stop them. When they stepped out onto the street, Xo said a simple thank you and began to walk away.

"That's all?" the man said, continuing to walk alongside her. "Aren't you going to introduce yourself?"

"Why?"

"So, we could get to know each other. Spend some time together."

"Not interested."

"That's cold," the man said, not seeming to be insulted at all. "I'm Christian, by the way."

"There is a man following us."

"I know. He's part of my security detail."

The answer surprised Xo so much that she stopped, only to examine then man's face more closely. "Is he protecting you or protecting people from you?"

"What?" the man looked very amused. "You think people need protection from me?"

"You're the one who burst into the woman's bathroom."

"Enough!" the man said laughing. "I truly thought you needed help."

"And you thought you could help me?"

"I'm a doctor."

"You're awfully young to be a doctor."

"Someone with a thicker skin would be hurt by your doubtful tone, but I'll pretend I didn't notice it."

"He wants to talk to you," Xo said, nodding her head forward and a little to the left. "Your security man."

The man who had introduced himself as Christian turned to look and then said, "No, I don't think so. He's just watching us." Christian turned back toward Xo, expecting to find her where she had been standing before he turned his head. Instead, she was quite a way down the street, almost to the corner, and when she reached it, she disappeared behind it without looking back.

"She left me!" Christian said in surprise when his security man came close. "I didn't even hear her move!"

"That's what happens when no one knows you are. No one special. That's what you wanted, isn't it? To be treated like everyone else."

"I wanted her name," Christian said, staring at the empty corner. "I want to see her again."

"Let's deal with the race first, and then I'll see what I can find out. Maybe she'll make it easy for us, and we'll see her on the course."

"Maybe," Christian said doubtfully. "But she won't be running. Not with that leg."

Six

"I'm sorry. At this time, only registered runners are allowed in this area."

Xo touched the numbered bid safety pinned to the front of her shirt.

The race official tried to hide her surprise. "Oh, I'm sorry. It's just that you don't look like. . ." the official's voice died away as she took in Xo's loose, flowing skirt that fell just below her knees and primitive looking rope sandals. All the other runners were wearing hi-tech sports shirts, shorts or tights, and shoes. Many wore camel packs on their backs with the drinking funnel tucked into their shoulder strap. Others wore light weight belts with fitted pockets for water bottles. Some were stretching, others nervously in line for the porta potties, others checking their watches or phones to make sure their GPS was working correctly. Xo was devoid of any kind of accoutrement that appeared race like. She had nothing on her back, there was nothing around her waist, and her hands were empty.

"You know this is an ultramarathon," the race official cautioned. It's not some simple 5k. It's more than 110 kilometers – 70 miles – long, over some really rough territory. And you can't walk it. You'll be stopped at the aid stations when you don't make the cut-off times."

"I know."

"Okay," the race official said, shrugging. "At least your entrance fees are going to a good cause. *Doctors Without Borders*. We had so many people try to enter this year that we tripled the number allowed, and we still had to turn people away. I think it was that huge amount of prize money being offered more than the matching donation for everyone who entered that did it, but hey, if some anonymous donor wants to encourage people to run and help doctors, then I'm all for it."

"I'm here for the prize money," Xo said.

"Right," said the official laughing as if Xo had just told a hilarious joke. "Now let me check your microchip. Yours is the first time I've seen it attached to a sandal strap instead of a shoelace. Don't take it off. It can only be removed by a race official after you stop or complete the course."

"You're set to go," the official said. "You can stand anywhere you want behind that group of elite runners. We let them start first so they can get ahead of the fray. That way no one gets tripped up while passing. The pack spreads out fairly quickly, so just be patient."

Xo nodded and moved to the side. She tucked her braid into her shirt, checked the tightness of her sandal straps, and when the gun went off, she waited until the elite runners had started before melting into the crowd and beginning to run.

Xo loved to run. Her earliest and best memories were running. She and her brother Koni would chase each other through the tangles and dense leaves of the jungle. Barefoot, they would have to twist and bend to avoid sharp thorns or poison vines. At the same time, they would have to keep careful watch of the ground, noting rocks that could bruise, roots that could make one stumble and trip, and even snakes, all too ready to strike with their sharp venom filled fangs. They had to learn to easily alter their stride, as sometimes they found it best to leap over a log or stretch of brown water, and always, always, they never wanted to be the one who admitted to being tired first.

Koni and she were inseparable. With him, in the damp heat of the jungle, she could forget that she was the only one of her people who didn't have perfectly straight black hair or skin that strangely lost its color if it didn't receive enough sunlight. She could forget, too, that there was something wrong with her eyes. With good humor, she had been told that her eyes were the color of a certain plant, but that didn't make sense because the leaves of that plant were a brilliant green. How could that be possible when the rest of her family and people had eyes so dark brown that they appeared black?

Koni and she could have run all day, melting into the jungle as silently and swiftly as night's arrival. They ran to where roots or fruits could be harvested, and once gathered, they run back to the village, their pace not slowing despite the banging of the baskets strung across their backs. If instead they had spent the day hunting, they ran to where they waited – sometimes for hours without movement – and ran back in tandem as they ferried their prey on a sling made of twisted vines.

It was a good and happy life. There were no years. There were only wet and dry seasons, marked by rivers that gulped down land, only to slowly, slowly, spit it back out.

It was a dry time when everything changed. She and Koni had run for half the morning. Once at a place where a bit of water remained in a shallow bit of forest floor, they melted into the nearby shadows. After they had prepared their bows and removed an arrow from their quivers, they stood motionless, ready, and invisible. It was then that they heard sounds that they had never heard before. Something heavy and ungainly was crashing through the jungle.

Willing their hearts to maintain an even slower beat, they waited for the unknown to be seen. It was only then that they would know whether to attack or to melt unnoticed into the shadows.

They were men, three of them, but men unlike neither Koni nor she had ever seen. Their bodies were covered in the strangest of layers. Pieces of material shaped to their arms and legs, and heavy clumsy coverings on their feet. No wonder they made so much noise when they walked! How could they know where to put their feet if they couldn't feel the earth?

The foreigners were also hampered by what they had done to their heads. They had covered them with a piece of shaped material that extended over their eyes, ears, and back of their head. Didn't they care that their vision was now obstructed? Didn't they realize that it would be harder now to discern where the sounds of animals came from? Didn't they know that the slightest breath of air on one's bare body and head could help one know what direction they were going to or when one might be nearing a clearing or waterside?

When the strangers passed by just inches from Xo, she could see beads of sweat pouring down their faces. Their clothes were damp where it had collected, discoloring large patches underneath their arms and down their backs. No matter they stank! A terrible smell.

Didn't they know that a single loincloth was what was best for survival? Bare skin made it easier to slip between tangles of vegetation and was less likely to be caught on sharp thorns. And bare skin didn't carry the stench that surrounded those men with an odor so revolting that it remained putrefying in the air for some moments even after they had passed.

When Xo and Koni had ran back to their people, yelling to all with great excitement about what they had seen, no one believed them. The women continued to work, those resting on hammocks remained in repose, and the children continued their games around the fire.

It wasn't until Rewe, one of the oldest and most respected of the people, returned from his foraging that anyone took interest. Rewe had journeyed over a full day to a site only he was familiar with to seek out a particular plant. The time of the plant's harvesting was crucial, for there were only a few days after blooming that the flower petals were useful for medicinal purposes.

Rewe hadn't even set down his basket before Koni and Xo were at his side regaling him with what they had seen. In direct contrast to everyone else, Rewe took immediate notice. His brow furrowed, and he asked, "How far had you run before you saw them? Did they see you?"

"Of course, they didn't see us," Koni had said, scoffing. "They moved like blind tapirs. They made as much noise as thunder, and they couldn't move through the world without first slicing it with a huge knife."

"You will take me there tomorrow," Rewe said. "But we must remain hidden."

Rewe's concern cast a sober mood on everyone, especially when he said that they might need to move the village. Moving the village was nothing new, of course, but usually a move was made after several seasons and the land had grown tired and needed to rest. Plants still grew, edible roots were abundant, and the thatch above their heads had yet to leak or be repaired. Moving meant extra work. Why would one go to all that extra effort when there was no apparent need?

Early the next morning they set out, Koni, Xo, Rewe, and two men Rewe has asked to accompany them who were skilled hunters. It was a simple task for Koni and Xo to find where they had first spotted the foreigners, and it was an even simpler task to follow where the men had gone after Koni and Xo had raced back to the village, eager to share their news. Koni had been apt in his description. The three strange men did indeed move like drunken tapirs, and their thrashing could be heard well before they were seen.

No one could understand what the strange men were doing except Rewe. "They call it mining," he said when he spoke to everyone around the fire that night. "It is when they wound the Earth and leave it scarred. They will make paths with hard surfaces and the Earth cannot heal itself. The animals that don't flee will die."

"But there only a few of them," one of the hunters who had accompanied them said. "We can kill them."

"They are like the mosquitoes," Rewe said. "They have tasted blood, and they will return and return and return and in even greater numbers."

The next morning, Rewe sent some men off to search for a new place to live. His instructions to Koni and Xo were to observe the miners. "Tell me what they do and where they go."

Koni did not think he had done anything wrong when he picked up the hat that one of the miners had lost. Of course, Koni and Xo could not understand what the men were saying. All the sounds that came out of the miners' mouths were so coarse and ugly that it was hard to believe they could mean anything. Yet as harsh and unintelligible as they were to Koni and Xo, they must have made sense to the miners, for when one started uttering his gibberish in an angry tone, the other two immediately came to him and started looking at the ground.

Koni and Xo almost started laughing. It was obvious that the men were all searching for the misplaced hat. The miner who has lost it kept touching his head and then kicking the ground in frustration as if, Koni described it later, he was a baby monkey wanting another suck from his mother's breast.

It was right in front of them! Couldn't they see it! It may well have been a dull green, its color helping it blend into the environment, but its shape was all wrong. It was too perfectly circular. And it stunk! It smelled of the men's noxious sweat.

"They gave up so easily," Koni said later as he picked up the hat and examined it closely. "They're as blind and deaf as a baby bamboo rat. Why do you think Rewe is so worried about them?"

Before Xo could respond, Koni said, "I'll take this back to the village to show everyone. The children will have a lot of fun playing with it. And then they'll understand how truly odd these men are."

It was a simple act of kindness – a desire to share with tangible proof some of the intruder's strangeness to the people who had only heard Xo, Koni, the two hunters, and Rewe speak of them. Koni naively only wanted to share. He had no idea that by fingering the hat and then returning with it to the village so that all could examine or play with it, that he had started what was to become the end.

It was only a few days after the hat had made its rounds in the village that a baby grew ill. The baby's nose began to run, he developed a low-grade fever, and he began to cough. He died in his sleep. It wasn't long before everyone became ill.

There were many kinds of monkeys that the people were familiar with. The howler monkey was one that even the youngest child could identify unseen due to its unique call – a whooping howl that could be heard from over a mile away.

The baby had stopped breathing while asleep, but the suffering lasted much longer for many of the others. Their fevers became higher, they vomited, and they coughed so violently that they broke ribs. And the sound that followed their fits of coughing? A whoop that before they had only imitated. Now it became a sign of death.

Even when Xo learned that the more common name of the illness was the onomatopoeic whooping cough, she still thought of it as the Monkey Sickness. It was pure evil, and her people had no way to fight it. They had never come across such an unseen enemy, and they had no idea how to battle it. They couldn't. Their bodies were not equipped. Death followed death. The only two who did not succumb were Xo and Rewe.

Xo was so numb with anguish and exhaustion that she could not cry. She had been so busy trying to take care of others, wiping them clean of vomit and bodily excretions, bringing water, keeping the fires lit, that at first the enormity of what had passed and what she had lost did not register. It wasn't until Rewe insisted that they burn the village, and all the dead within, that Xo knew that her life would not and could not ever be the same.

They walked for miles, that first day after they had turned their people to ashes. When they made camp next to a small river and Rewe handed Xo some fish he had cooked on their fire, she could not eat it. "You must," he told her.

"Why didn't I die?" Xo asked in anguish. "How can I eat when Koni and no one else is here to eat with us? How come the evil didn't take me? It would have been better if it had."

"You and I couldn't die. We have something to finish."

Seven

At first Xo didn't understand what Rewe was saying. His words describing a distant past seemed as unreal as the immediate tragedy that caused the annihilation of her people.

Rewe had been far away from where the people usually traveled. He had been in search of a particular fungi that grew on trees closer to where there was more sunlight. It was the fungi he used when he mixed his potions needed to offset the venom of the bushmaster snake. It had to be administered quickly, and it was the only thing that stopped one from bleeding to death.

Rewe had been about to turn back, when suddenly he heard a loud strange whistling. It was high in the air, above the canopy, but he could hear it coming closer and closer. It only stopped when it changed to a thundering crash as it hit the topmost branches and vines. He could then hear it coming even closer as the air shook with the sound of breaking branches and falling limbs as it fell, crashing to the forest floor.

Cautiously, Rewe had made his way to what had left a hole in the forest cover. "I heard a happy gurgling, and I wondered what creature could make such an innocent sound after such a roaring and thundering destruction. It was you. Lying in a bowl of moss. You were kicking your legs against its sides, and you liked the way it kept popping back in shape every time you lifted your feet.

"I brought you home."

"But how did I fall from the sky?"

"I don't know."

"But my mother. . ."

"When I got back home, with you in a sling — you couldn't walk yet — Manula took you. Her baby had died just that morning. I took its body back to where I found you, as I knew I had to return to the forest what it had given us. I meant to put Manula's baby back in the moss bowl, and I did, but then I looked all around the area to try and find out more about what had happened. That was when I found other bodies. Big ones. Strange looking. One was a young woman. I could tell because she had breasts. She was your first mother, but now Manula was your mother. I went back to the moss bowl and picked up Manula's dead baby. I put her in the arms of your first mother, for that was the right thing to do. Mothers take care of the young. That is what they do."

Xo didn't question why she hadn't been told this before. It didn't matter. It didn't take away the pain or depth of sorrow that she was feeling now.

"But why didn't we die? Why didn't the Monkey Sickness kill us? What do we have to finish?"

"I don't know why we didn't die. But you and I were the only ones who ever had contact with Outsiders."

"Outsiders?"

"People who don't live in the forest. Like the dead mother."

"You've been outside of the forest?"

"Many years ago. When I was younger and would travel looking for plants. At one time I thought I would walk to the end of the world. Instead, I came to a place where they had killed the forest. So many people lived there they were like termites, all crowded together and living on top of each other. But dirtier."

Xo shook her head, unable to even conceive of such a thing. How could there be no forest?

"I'm going to take you there."

"No, you're not!" Xo's reply was instant.

"To finish," Rewe said. "You need to go back. You have no family left."

"But I have you!" Xo protested, tears forming in her eyes.

"There must be a reason why we did not die. It must be that it is time for you to be with your own kind."

"But you're my kind! My mother Manula . . ."

"Manula is dead."

"So is that other woman," Xo shouted. Xo was so angry she stood up and took a threatening step toward Rewe. Then she stopped, aghast at what she had done. Rewe was an elder, the most revered man of the People. Never before in all her life had Xo raised her voice in anger to an elder. It simply was not done. It just wasn't.

Bowing her head, she stepped back in shame. Before she could apologize, Rewe spoke. "I understand. It is a hard time. It is a difficult time. But you lived when so many died. The forest is telling you that you are no longer welcome. At least for a while."

"But how will I know when I can come back? There is nowhere else I want to be!"

"You will know. But for now, I need to get you ready. I cannot leave you unprepared. I am old and am ready to meet the ancestors. But I will not go dear child until you are ready to start anew."

Eight

Rewe was true to his word. Every day that followed in the seasons that came after the annihilation, he taught her everything he knew about the forest. Xo already know how to read animal tracks and the calls of birds, and which frogs one could use to lace one's arrows with poison, but Rewe knew the jungle so intimately he could breathe with it. He knew its secrets – what days in a lunar cycle one should harvest medicinal flowers, how to make pink dolphins rise to the surface, and when one could enter water and be safe from piranha, anacondas, or crocodiles.

They were lonely years, but they were good years, too. Xo knew they were over when one afternoon she spotted blood on her upper thighs. She didn't have to tell Rewe. She knew he would sense it when she came close.

"It's time," he said that night when they sat around their small fire. "You're no longer a child. It's time for us both to go home."

Xo never thought of the missionary school she spent four years in as home. But she did what Rewe had taught her: observe, learn, and keep hidden how much you know about and your opinion of those around you. The customs, those of housekeeping and sitting behind a desk for hours each morning, were the hardest for Xo, but she never complained.

One would think that the language barrier would hold her back, but in truth, learning to understand what people were saying was easy. Perhaps it was because Xo was used to paying attention to the subtle differences of sounds in the jungle. Ignoring one soft note, a single pop of a bubble of water coming to the surface, or a slight rustle of a leaf might be cause of death. They were all a warning of something on the move, whether it be a deadly wasp on the wing, a caiman rising from its bed in the mud, or a jaguar extending its paw on a branch overhead.

After Rewe left Xo at the school, she never saw him again. He did not look back once after he took her to the door stoop, but she did not knock on the strange building as he had instructed her to do until she had watched him become a smaller and smaller speck in the distance and then finally disappear. Although Xo felt a piece of her would never heal, she knew that Rewe, at least, was whole again. He was now with Koni, Manula, and all the rest of the people.

Reading didn't especially interest Xo, as she couldn't understand the joy of fiction. When given a copy of *The Jungle Book* by Rudyard Kipling and told that she would especially enjoy it, she was shocked that anyone would consider it of merit. Animals didn't congregate and have councils. The only part that struck a chord was that Mowgli, the boy raised by wolves, initially didn't want to leave the jungle and live with humans. That she could understand.

Nonfiction, on the other hand, was useful at times. Architecture, art, history, and the social sciences had little interest for her, but biology and nature were a different matter. When she read about vaccines, she finally understood what had caused the extermination of her people. The Monkey Sickness – whooping cough – was pertussis.

Highly contagious, pertussis was a bacteria that was easily controlled by a vaccine. Most people received the first of several doses for it starting at two months of age. More than likely, she had been vaccinated. As she read and investigated further, she was sure of it. After all, the scar on her upper left arm – a small round indented circle – matched almost exactly the photograph in the book of what a healed small pox vaccination looked like. If she had been vaccinated against small pox, she had surely been vaccinated for tetanus, measles, mumps, rubella, and all the other diseases she was reading about that came from outside the jungle.

Koni had only meant to entertain with the hat he had so innocently brought back to the village. He had no idea that it was harboring death. To people who had never been exposed or had a chance to build up immunity to the foreign bacteria, it was lethal. Why did Rewe survive? Perhaps he had been exposed in earlier travels. Or, some of the strange potions that he was forever making and ingesting had protected him. Not that it mattered now. They were all gone.

Xo never made a close friend at the mission, but that was her choice. She was never unkind, always stepping in to help before being asked. But she felt no kinship to anyone. Now that she was dressed like everyone else, the fact that she more closely resembled some of the missionaries in appearance than she did other students at the school only made her feel more alien to everyone else.

Despite how Xo felt, the truth was that it would have been nigh impossible for Rewe to have found a better place to leave Xo. Leticia may have been in Colombia, but Brazil was just across the street, and Peru across the river. The entire area was known as the *Tres Fronteras*, and it was a mix of cultures, people, and languages. No one stood out, as all three countries had an agreed upon policy of not checking passports or asking for documentation in the surrounding vicinity. Drug traffickers mingled with legitimate suppliers of tropical fish for the aquarium trade, and tourists flew in and out of the small airport, happily paying to spend days drifting on the colossal Amazon river and nights in luxury jungle camps.

Once Xo became fluent in Spanish, Portuguese, and English, as well as the two most common indigenous languages, no one would have any cause to think that her background was anything special. Everyone had a story and for many, it was a recent of the old ways meeting the modern. Hand-made canoes floated down the river next to motor driven craft or large supply boats. The heat was inescapable, and under the sweltering sun, no one would think of asking Xo questions about her past. The few times when the nuns had tried, Xo would not offer any information.

It was by chance that she found a way to support herself. A tourist had come to the mission school asking for help in spotting birds. He wanted to see more than the massive flock of white winged parakeets that descended in a deafening mass each day at dusk in the town square. He wanted to take photographs of the birds that secreted themselves farther in the jungle, and for that he needed a guide. Did the nuns know of someone reputable and knowledgeable?

Without hesitating, Xo stepped forward. She had found several old bird guides among the donated books in the school library, and she had found the familiar pictures soothing. One of her favorite teachers, Sister Teresa, had helped her learn the Latin names as well as the ones in the local vernaculars. "You'll have to pay me," she said.

"I'll pay you what you're worth," the man said.

Xo nodded, but she didn't argue. She instinctively knew she would be paid more if she didn't quibble or try to negotiate. She arranged to meet the man the next morning in the lobby of his hotel before the sun came up.

She found it so easy that she thought the day bordered on the absurd. Despite the man's pair of high-powered binoculars, camera with huge lenses, and the app on his phone of Colombian birds and their calls, she was able to find bird after bird for him. The man had gotten nervous when they reached the end of the road and she continued into the undergrowth, but when she named the varied species he would be sure to see, he followed.

When she took him back to his hotel after the sun had set, he was as munificent with his praise as well as his cash. Word got around, and it wasn't long before people were coming to town asking for Xo, specifically, to guide them. Soon, she earned enough to purchase her own pair of binoculars. She made it a point to hire local people to ferry her and her clients around when needed, as well as take them down, up, or across the river in their small boats. She paid her workers generously, and they became loyal and dedicated to her in providing the best service possible.

She could have moved out on her own, renting a room or place in town, but she preferred to stay at the missionary school. The location of the school suited her better, as it was at the edge of town, and it served to keep interested suiters away. She paid the nuns rent, and she continued to help where ever she was needed whenever she was on the premises.

Xo still ran. Every day. No matter the time and no matter the weather. She ran when the rains were so heavy that the roads were turned to streams, and she ran when the sky blazed so hot that the only birds visible were raptors circling on updrafts. She had stopped during the time of the great dying, but a few weeks after she and Rewe were together, he had said to her, "It is time for you to run again."

"Without Koni?"

"Koni is still running. You are to join him."

Xo didn't think that possible, but she wasn't going to argue with Rewe. When she started to run again, the ache for Koni was so great that she had to stop and wrap her arms around her rib cage because otherwise she felt her heart would break out in sorrow. Koni wasn't there to be chased, and she had no need to try and stay ahead. Rewe had made her continue. Xo was angry, but because Rewe was her elder, she continued to do what he insisted she do. And then one day she understood.

A group of white-fronted capuchin monkeys had begun to follow her, swinging from the branches and calling to each other with great excitement, as she made her way down a path that led to a watering hole. Suddenly, one of them dropped on her head. It wasn't a baby, but it was still so small that most probably its mother had just recently stopped carrying it on her back. Xo continued to run as the monkey held on to her hair with one hand and her ear with the other. Meanwhile the monkeys in the trees above continued to screech, moving airily through the tangled foliage above at the same pace as she was making on the ground. The monkeys following Xo didn't seem upset or worried. It was more like they were laughing, taking great pleasure in the predicament that the little monkey on Xo's head had found itself in.

That was when Xo felt Koni's presence. She felt it so strongly that she stopped running. The moment she stopped, the monkey leaped from her head onto a hanging vine and scampered up to rejoin its companions. As the monkeys began to toss twigs and small fruits down on her, teasing her to start running again so they could continue their game of chase, she knew that Koni was enjoying the spectacle as much as she was. Yes, running was healing.

On some of her early runs during those first horrible weeks after Rewe had left Xo at the school, Xo didn't want to turn around. She wanted to continue to run straight ahead, never circling back and returning to the place with the confining walls, strange food, and incomprehensible customs. Paradoxically, it was the running away that gave her the strength to return.

Rewe knew it would, she thought to herself. That's why he made me run.

Nine

Sometimes it is a simple twist of fate that can alter one's direction, and that is what happened with Xo. She had been hired by someone not as a bird guide but as someone to spot monkeys for his children. The children were spoiled, as Xo expected. One child, a girl about ten years old, actually threw a temper tantrum when the monkeys would not come out of the trees and allow themselves to be petted. "But in Australia we got to hold the koalas! What good is a monkey if I can't take a selfie with it?" she cried. "I hate this place!"

Masking her emotions, Xo simply said, "Problem fixed! Let's go!" She then took the children to a man named Gustavo who had a home a few miles down the river on the Peruvian side who had several monkeys.

Poaching was illegal, but it was still big business for many. Money was the only goal, and the animals' well-being meant nothing. Birds, monkeys, cats, even snakes and frogs – size or type didn't matter as long as a private collector or dishonest zoo would pay. Often, when it came to the larger mammals, the mothers were killed. Smaller animals were easier to handle and ship.

Gustavo had been on the river when a boat ferrying cages of captured animals had flipped. The driver was drunk, and he was going too fast to note the change in water surface that warned of an underwater blockage or mass of vegetation. Gustavo had saved what animals he could. Knowing that the monkeys were too young and sick to live on their own, he took them to his house and cared for them.

The visit was a success. It was also very profitable, as the father casually handed Gustavo a hundred-dollar bill and said, "Great show."

He had been just as generous with Xo with her payment, and as he nonchalantly handed her a pile of bills, well over the amount she had quoted him as her price, he said, "I don't suppose you know someone I can run with. Running on the hotel treadmill is getting a little old."

"You need a running guide?"

"Yes, I'd pay, but only if it someone who can keep up with me."

"How long and how far do you want to run?"

"Do you know what an ultramarathon is?"

When Xo shook her head, the man explained. "A regular marathon is 26.22 miles. Ultramarathons can be anywhere from 50 to more than 100 miles. Some are held over really tough courses. We're talking incredible elevation changes, uneven surfaces, fording streams, and the race doesn't stop when it gets dark or the weather goes bad."

"I'm an ultramarathoner," he said, unable to mask his pride.

"You want to run 100 miles?"

"Of course not! But I'd like to run about 15 on a jungle trail. It would be good training."

"Now?"

"Good lord, no! It's been a long day. Tomorrow, at seven, before it gets too hot. My wife can sleep in, and the kids can spend the day at the pool."

"Seven then," Xo said, nodding.

Ten

"You know who is going to show up," the man's wife told him that night as they sat on their balcony drinking glasses of wine. "Some young kid without shoes who thinks you won't last the length of a soccer field."

"Well, that guide seems to know people. Xo, that's her name. She's more competent than anyone else we've met on this trip. But whomever she gets, I'm going to enjoy seeing their dismay as some white man leaves them in the dust."

"Just don't go stepping on any snakes," laughed his wife as she tilted back her head and drained her glass.

"We'll go side by side on the road until I know your pace. Then I'll lead. I'll slow down when you need me to."

The man nodded. He masked his feelings of disdain and disappointment. Disdain because did Xo in her loose skirt and rope sandals really think that she could keep up with him? She wasn't even carrying a water bottle for God's sake. Disappointment because even though he was sure no one could best him when it came to stamina or distance, he had hoped that someone might show up who could at least push him for a good mile or two. Now it didn't even seem possible. Resigning himself to once again running on the hotel's treadmill to enhance his workout after they returned, the man simply said, "Let's go then."

When they returned, sometime later, to the road by the hotel, Xo altered her pace so she and the man could run side by side. The man didn't seem to notice. Instead, with a grim look on his face, he cut across the grass and made his way to the hotel swimming pool. Once there, he stumbled off the edge on the deep end. When he emerged, water sloshing from his shoes, he walked straight to Xo. She was standing at ease, nothing in her bearing showing surprise that someone would walk into a swimming pool fully clothed.

"That was one of the greatest runs I have ever had in my life!" the man said. "You're amazing! The logs, the bending, the sliding, the leaping! I had no idea how you knew where we were going. And you just kept going. I've never had such a work out in my life! You didn't even break a sweat! When can we go again?"

"Fifteen minutes?"

The man put his head back and laughed uproariously. "As if!" he said.

It wasn't until the man had showered and drunk copious amounts of water and fruit drinks that he said to his wife in a shocked voice, "My God, she meant it. She would have gone again in fifteen minutes!"

The man extended his family's stay so he could run with Xo for the rest of the week. After their last run, he asked Xo if she could meet him to discuss a proposition he had for her. "Nothing wayward," he assured her. "Bring a friend if you want."

Xo didn't accept, but as she didn't decline either, the man said, "Okay then, please come at three to the hotel. They serve a great high tea, and we can sit on the balcony overlooking the river."

When Xo arrived, she saw the man sitting at a table with a woman who quickly stood as Xo approached. Putting out her hand the woman said, "I'm Lara Tran, Tom's wife, and you, of course, already know my husband, Tom Winters. I can't thank you enough for taking such good care of my family. First my children and those animals you showed them, and then all the running you've been doing with Tom. Truth to tell, I've never seen my husband enjoy a vacation more. It is a pleasure to finally meet you."

Xo didn't respond, but she stood quietly, observing Lara. It wasn't until Lara motioned to a seat and said, "Please sit down," that Xo spoke.

Her voice was poised. "Yes, ma'am."

Lara laughed and said, "Don't you ma'am me Xo! And stop this calling my husband *señor*. He's Tom. Got it?"

"And trust me, dear," she said pouring Xo a cup of tea and sliding the tray of scones and finger sandwiches toward her plate, "Tom is much smarter than he appears. He has thought this through, and to put it in simplest terms, he would enjoy it.

"And you, too!" Tom said, patting his wife's hand affectionately. "You would enjoy it, too."

"Get on with it, then!" Lara said laughing. "Tell her!"

It was not what Xo expected. Tom and Lara would sponsor Xo to run. They would be willing to fill out applications, pay entrance fees, take care of travel costs, and support her in any way that was needed.

"Shoes are optional," said Tom, his eyes twinkling. "I'm sure Nike, Hoka, Mizuno, New Balance, Saucony, and everyone else will be begging you to wear theirs, but of course you've got to win a few big races first. For now, I'll provide you with what you want."

"Nothing is free," Xo said.

"I'm not giving you money," Tom said. "I'm providing opportunity." When Xo didn't respond immediately, Tom sat back in his chair. Grinning widely, he said, "And I wouldn't be honest if I didn't tell you that I can't wait to see the reaction on people's faces when you come out of nowhere and cross the finish line."

"Only if there is prize money," Xo said.

Tom looked surprised, but Lara somehow knew what we behind Xo's desire for money. "Land," she said softly. "You need to buy as much as you can before it disappears."

Eleven

Xo ran a marathon with Tom in Bogota. Easily accomplished, but she didn't win because she stayed by Tom's side, matching his pace as he explained aid stations, trail etiquette, and how timing chips worked. Tom suggested another marathon for training purposes, but Xo told him no.

"There's a race in England," she said. "It's only about 70 miles. Runs along some ancient wall. But there's a huge prize. Enough to pay you back airfare and for me to start buying land."

"Only about 70 miles," Tom said looking at Xo strangely as he slowly repeated her words. "And how can you be so sure you will win? That race is going to attract some of the greatest long-distance runners in the world. Remember, you don't have elite status yet. You'll be starting back of the pack."

"Bet on me," Xo said. "You'll make your money back and more."

The race started out in Cumbria at Carlisle Castle. It followed pretty much the remains of Hadrian's Wall, a Roman fortification built in 122 AD to mark the north-west frontier of its empire. Xo waited until the first street crossing before she started passing people. "Slow down!" she was told good-naturedly.

"You're going to burn yourself out."

"Pace yourself."

The comments kept coming as Xo continued to overtake runners in front of her. When someone said to her, "Hey, we're all in this for fun," Xo just smiled and kept on running.

"Let her pass," one runner admonished to another who didn't want to move aside. "We'll catch her at the first aid station."

"Or on the first hill," laughed another.

Xo was soon out of the pack, and she sped up to decrease the distance between the competitive runners who had been allowed to start first. Once she had caught up with them, she began to methodically pass them one by one.

"What the hell!" said a man.

"Where did she come from?" muttered another.

"Is she for real?" said another dismissively.

Xo didn't answer anyone. She just continued to run. When Xo came across the first aid stations, she didn't see a reason to stop. She didn't slow her pace one iota, either. Who would need food or water at this point? By mile 25 there were only four runners ahead of her. She could see them, two sets of two, making their way up a steep, grassy hill. She caught up with the first set, passed the one in fourth place, and was about the pass the one in third when all of a sudden the runner turned his head so he could take a look at who was catching up with him.

"Hey! It's you!" The surprise and delight in his voice was palpable. "How's the leg?"

Running at his side, Xo spoke for the first time since the starting gun had gone off. "Christian," she said.

"You remembered my name!" Christian said, feeling a strange jolt of excitement strike his chest.

"You did make quite the entrance," Xo said, the briefest of a smile curling the edges of her mouth.

"Honestly, first time in a women's bathroom," Christian said. "Well, as an adult," he amended. "I'm sure I was taken into one at least a few times when I was a baby."

"I'm guessing the leg is fine," Christian said. "It certainly isn't slowing you down."

"Why do you need a babysitter?"

"What?" Christian, almost lost his footing as he sputtered in surprise. He then had to speed up a little to catch back up to Xo.

"The security man," Xo said, tossing her head back to the man who had been right behind Christian and was now carefully maintaining a five-foot gap.

"How do you know he is my security man?"

The look Xo gave Christian bordered on contempt. "You told me he was yesterday."

"But you never got close to him, and he's in completely different clothes."

This time Xo's look was one of total condescension. "And why would that make him unrecognizable?"

"Do you have a name?" Xo asked, calling back to the man behind them.

Xo didn't miss the almost imperceptible nod of assent Christian made to the man before the man answered her.

"Jack. Jack Robinson."

"I'm Xo. Pleased to meet you."

"He's not my babysitter," Christian said. He couldn't explain why he felt irritated that the conversation wasn't solely with him. Christian liked and respected Jack. They had been together many years, and it made no sense that Christian would feel that Jack was overstepping his bounds.

"Now what type of doctor needs a security detail?" Xo said in a teasing voice. "What, are you afraid of being kidnapped or something?"

"Ma'am, I would prefer it if you ran behind us," Jack's stern voice cut in before Christian could respond to Xo's teasing.

"Ma'am? Jack, are you kidding me? My name is Xo."

Christian started to say something but Jack said, "Sir, I have this under control."

Xo looked at Jack, and then she looked at Christian. Xo had merely been teasing, but she saw that she had touched a nerve. Kidnappings were a well-known practice in Colombia. Guerilla groups like M-19, FARC, and ELN had started kidnapping victims in the early 1970s, and criminal groups and drug cartels soon joined in. Present day, of course, it wasn't that great of a problem, but it still happened enough that there were plenty of wealthy people who maintained security patrols as preventative measures.

"No worries," Xo said. "I spoke thoughtlessly. But run behind you? I think not." She was unable to keep her eyes from twinkling as she picked up her pace and moved ahead.

"Jack! What the hell is wrong with you?" Christian said angrily. "She's harmless!"

Jack looked at the figure who seemed to be effortlessly increasing the distance between them as she moved ahead. "She's awfully fit and quick. She's the one who mentioned kidnapping. I'm just doing my job, sir."

"You think. . ."

"I'm being cautious. I told you I was going to check her out yesterday, but I came up with nothing. She wasn't staying at the hotel, or at least no one fitting her description was. Now that I have a name, I might get a bit further."

"Xo. It's an unusual name."

"Xo Bosque."

"She didn't say her last name. I thought you said you came up with nothing. How would you know her last name? What aren't you telling me?"

"I'm not hiding anything from you. I know her last name because I went through the sign-up roster before the race. I always do that. Her name stood out because as you said, her first name is quite unusual. There was only one Xo. Last name Bosque."

"Do you remember anything else about her?"

"What do you mean?"

"An address, age. . ."

"She's from Colombia."

"Really? I would have never guessed it, not with those green eyes."

"Right," Jack said brusquely. "Colombia. A country where kidnapping is quite a lucrative business."

"You know I'm the one who followed her into the restroom."

"Right," Jack said, even more brusquely than before. "And even with a leg that she stitched herself she's going to beat you. That makes for unusual circumstances. And I've been in this job long enough to know that anything out of the ordinary is cause for concern."

"You're not concerned that you're going to be beaten by a girl?"

"You're the one setting the pace," Jack said.

Christian let out a yelp of laughter. "Well said," he responded good-naturedly, "but I have to tell you Jack, you can't blame this on me. I'll bet that woman sets a course record that we won't come close to. She'd shame you even if you were running alone. Admit it, despite what you're saying, you can barely keep up with me."

Twelve

The buzz had spread about the runner in a skirt who was now in second place. People began to line the course close to the aid stations to get a look at her. The man in first place kept looking back. He wouldn't admit it, but he was unnerved by her presence. She maintained a twenty-foot distance, so that he couldn't accuse her of drafting, and she seemed as fresh at mile 50 as she did at mile 30. He wondered why she didn't pass him.

Xo could have. She was biding her time. She didn't care about setting a course record. She only cared about winning. If she stayed in sight of someone the entire time, it would be harder for someone to accuse her of cheating. No one could accuse her of having an accomplice who drove her on some of the uninhabited rural sections on an off-track vehicle, or even riding some miles on a bicycle that she had previously stashed hidden in bushes. Tom had warned her that people would be suspicious. Newcomers just don't pop up on the scene and win — especially on races where there was a substantial winner's purse.

"They may even ask for a urine sample," Tom had told her. "It's a competitive sport, and people cheat. It's human nature."

At the last mile, when they were once more in the city, and spectators lined the taped off streets, Xo moved ahead. She made sure to cross the finish line only about five feet ahead of the man who came in second. Immediately, she turned to him and said, "You were amazing!"

He looked in terrible pain, but he reacted the way true athletes should. "You made me run faster," he said.

They both set course records he, for men, Xo for women.

"Do you have a phone number yet?"

"For Cinderella?"

"Very funny," Christian said.

"She did disappear. Not at midnight, I admit, but just as soon as she got that winner's check."

"Jack, I've never asked you for anything before. Just get me her phone number."

Jack looked at Christian somberly. He and Christian had a good relationship. It must have been hard for Christian to always have someone following him, but Christian knew Jack was only doing his job and respected him for it. There were a few times when Christian needed to let lose, and Jack didn't say anything, only putting a stop to it there was a chance of Christian being in danger or someone was trying to take opportunistic photographs.

Never once, though, through all the years of Christian growing up, attending college, and then laboring through medical school, and working for *Doctors Without Borders*, did Christian ask Jack for information about anyone. Of course, he never had to. Women were always pressing Christian notes with their phone numbers or trying to sit next to him in class or where ever he went. Jack's job had always been to keep women at a distance, and Jack couldn't help but find it a bit humorous that after all these years, it was Christian who was asking for a phone number rather than discarding the slips of paper covered in them.

In fact, Christian had started running while in undergraduate school because it was a way to work out without being constantly accosted. He could run early in the morning or at night. He never wore headphones, as he would spend the first miles going over course work in his head, solving problems, or going through the steps of an upcoming surgery. Then, as he covered more distance, he would clear his mind. He would fall into a tranquil state and despite the physical exhaustion, he was left only with a sense of serenity and rejuvenation.

Christian found runners, and especially long-distance runners, to be a wonderful community. They all sought the same kind of solitude that Christian did, and usually, if someone recognized him on the trail, they tried to mask their surprise. "Great stride," was all they would say.

Jack felt lucky that Christian was such an athlete. Jack had been a competitive runner starting in middle school, and he considered that fact that he had to keep watch over Christian while Christian ran, a real perk to the job. Jack had expected Christian to be somewhat egotistical and self-absorbed, as many who were born to privilege and wealth were prone to be. Yet Christian had taken to his own path early on, insisting on going to a university and undertaking a hard science degree. No one expected him to continue, especially in medicine.

"The phone number, Jack. I want it," Christian repeated.

"I'm going to give it to you," Jack said, "but first you have to hear me out."

"Agreed," Christian said, crossing his arms against his chest.

"Her full name is Xo Bosque."

"Yes, you told me that before."

Jack continued as if he had not been interrupted. "She is from Colombia. Her passport says she is 23 years old and she was born on June 1 in the city of Leticia."

Christian was instantly alert. "Why are you saying her passport says, and not that she is? You're not telling me you still think she's involved in something nefarious, are you?"

"I honestly don't know what to think. The passport is legitimate. Colombia has been issuing biometric passports since 2015, so hers has an embedded chip. Of course, one can still forge a passport, but I would say hers is up and up."

"Then what's the problem?"

"It's just a feeling. It was enough that I went deeper. Her birth certificate wasn't issued until she requested one – right before she applied for a passport. The names listed for her parents are names from an indigenous tribe that no longer exists. The school she attended was a missionary school in Leticia. Records there say she arrived alone, almost naked, and completely illiterate as well as unable to speak Spanish at – the nuns took a guess – about the age of 13 or 14."

"You know this isn't making me lose interest in her," Christian said. "If that's what you're trying to do."

"She doesn't look like an Indigenous person, or even Latina."

"She's beautiful, but it's more than that. It's the way she carries herself. She's. . ."

"No one today doesn't have a history, Christian. She has no backstory – there's too much information missing. No one suddenly appears at the age of 13 or 14. Spontaneous generation was proven to be false way back in Pasteur's time."

"What are you implying?"

"Christian, she leaped in front of a moving car. She stitched her own leg. She ran. . ."

"Effortlessly."

There was silence for a moment and then Christian started to laugh. "Dropped from outer space? Or perhaps a robot?"

"I don't find anything about this amusing. She might be. . ."

Christian put up his hand. "Enough," he said. "Give me her phone number."

Jack nodded. "You know I disapprove," he said, but then he recited the number.

After putting it into his contact list, Christian looked up at Jack, unable to hide the impatient look on his face.

"I'm leaving! I'm leaving!" Jack said, his grin hiding his concern as he made his way to the door.

As soon as the door swung shut behind his bodyguard, Christian punched in the number. It rang and rang, but no one answered. When he finally heard Xo's recorded voice identifying herself and saying she would get back to them when she had time if they would please leave their number, he suddenly realized he didn't know what to say. Without thinking, he pushed the end call button.

"I've never done that before," Christian thought as he stared down at his phone in disbelief. When it suddenly started ringing, he almost dropped it. Unfortunately, it wasn't Xo. It was only the Queen of Norway.

"Mother," Christian said, careful to mask the disappointment he was feeling.

Thirteen

With a watch cap pulled low over his forehead and a ragged backpack slung over his shoulder, Christian achieved his practiced goal of anonymity. Jack walked a pace or two behind, discreetly scanning the crowds hurrying past in every direction. He hated that Christian insisted on public transport. To Jack, airports were never safe.

First class passengers had just been called when Christian ambled up to the correct terminal door, but much to Jack's dismay, Christian didn't go in. Instead, he stopped abruptly. Jack turned to see what Christian was looking at, and all his senses of something not being right shot up. Xo was sitting in a seat by the window, and cradled in her arms was a baby.

Christian stared, his body rigid.

Let's get on the plane," Jack said. "Let it go."

Ignoring him, Christian walked up to Xo. "You didn't answer my calls," he said. "Jack is afraid you're a secret agent because you have no past."

"I figure," Christian said, making himself comfortable as he moved aside some baggage in the seat next to her so he could sit down, "You must be pretty good at it if even Jack didn't know you had a baby."

"Good at what exactly?" Xo asked, unable to hide the start of a smile breaking out.

"Being secretive," Christian said. "Cute baby," he said, leaning over and looking at the face of the sleeping child. "Boy or girl?"

Xo let out a little laugh. "I don't know."

A second or two passed while Christian digested what she had said. "Let's hope it isn't yours then."

"You sound tremendously relieved."

"Oh, I am." "But for the baby, of course," Christian hastened to add. "It would be a terrible thing if its mother didn't know what sex it was."

Just then a harried looking woman with a toddler in tow showed up. "I can't thank you enough," she said to Xo. "We made it to the bathroom just in time. Another second, and it would have all been in his……oh, you got her to fall asleep! How did you do that? She never falls asleep! I was sure she was going to scream the entire flight. Now that she's down, she'll sleep for hours. You're a godsend," the woman said as she took the infant back and expertly placed her in a body sling.

"Ouch, that hurts," Christian said as the woman left for the boarding gate.

"What hurts?" Xo cocked her head inquisitively.

"That you're a godsend and yet you didn't return my phone calls."

"Or respond to your text messages."

"Now you're just being mean," Christian said laughing. "I'm fully aware that you were giving me the brush off."

"But here you are."

"Here I am." There was a moment of silence and then Christian said, "I hadn't given up. I don't give up that easily on things I like."

"I have a plane to catch," Xo said standing.

"Are you being coy?"

"No. I have a plane to catch." Xo nodded to the last of the line of the embarking passengers. "I don't want to miss it." She couldn't hide her smile as she stood and took a step toward the attendant checking tickets.

"Who is following whom, I wonder?" Christian said as he joined her. "That's my plane."

"Jack," Xo said, nodding as she stepped in front of him to have her boarding pass scanned.

Xo's seat was in the economy section of the plane, and looking down the aisle, she could see that hers was the last remaining empty seat. To her surprise, Christian stayed right behind her as she continued down the aisle. When she got to her row, she turned, prepared to ask him what he was doing, but she never got the chance.

"Allow me," he said, taking her bag and putting it into the overhead storage bin.

Surprised, Xo voiced her thanks and then began to sidle her way past the two seated passengers so she could get to her window seat. When she sat down, she expected to see Christian making his way back toward the front where she had seen some empty seats in the first-class section. Instead, Christian was talking to the passenger cramped in the middle seat.

"I have a proposition for you," Christian, his smile disarmingly charming. "My ticket for yours. I'm in first class, if that helps sway you."

The solicited passenger snapped up the offer with an emphatic "Yes!" Then, almost as if afraid the proposal might be rescinded, he rose quickly, snatched Christian's boarding pass, and raced down the aisle to where the first-class passengers were seated.

Xo looked on with amusement as Christian, after knocking the passenger seated in the aisle seat and apologizing profusely, attempted to make himself comfortable in the middle seat. When he was finally situated, seatbelt on, legs uncomfortably crammed against the seat in front, he turned to Xo. With a huge grin on his face he said, "I can't wait to rub it in Jack's face that he isn't sitting by my side. Slipping up on the whole keeping close and under his watch kind of thing."

"Oh, he's doing his job all right," Xo said trying hard to hide her amusement but not doing a very good job. "You're just not very observant. He's sitting in the row right behind you, but he did one better than you. He at least has the aisle seat."

"Maybe I prefer the middle seat."

Xo scrunched up her face thoughtfully and said, "You don't even look as if you fit in the middle seat."

"I've been in worse," Christian said amiably. "And the company is worth it."

"I was planning on sleeping the entire flight."

"That's too bad. Well, at least I'll get your meal."

"This is not first class. There are no meals."

"Well, your little bag of pretzels."

"You won't save it for me?"

"Now you're asking too much of me," Christian said. "Rules are, the pretzels always go to those who are awake."

"Well, then, I guess I can't sleep."

"That's good news," Christian said, his eyes twinkling. "Why are you going to Norway?"

"There's another race."

"Ah, the one where you run through the Lyngen Alps. 140 km, 9,000 meters of positive elevation. You know that one's self-supported so you have to carry a backpack of compulsory equipment and food."

"But I'll have the midnight sun, so no worries."

"Right, no worries." Christian looked at Xo with an amused look on his face.

"Are you running?"

"Not this year."

"Before you said you were only running for money. There's no prize money being offered on that one, so why?"

"I heard North Face is sponsoring a runner. If I can best him, they might extend an offer to me." When Christian didn't comment, Xo continued. "North Face pays big. Some of their elite athletes get over 150,000 a year. I've got a few races in the US lined up next, and that should get me more attention if this one isn't enough."

"Have you ever been above the Arctic Circle?"

Xo shook her head. "It will be my first time. In fact, this trip is my first time abroad. England, Norway, and then a place in the US called Colorado."

"How's the leg?"

"Healing."

"You don't want to show it to me?"

Christian could only laugh at the face Xo made at him. "Don't even think about giving me that line about being a doctor again."

"It wasn't a line. I really am a doctor."

"Of medicine? License off the internet?"

"Ouch! Yes, of medicine. University of Oslo. Very reputable."

"And your patients? Where are they? Are they happy with your office hours?"

"Very funny. I don't have regular office hours because I work for *Doctors Without Borders*. My assignments are usually for eight weeks at a time. I just finished up in Lebanon, and next I'm off to Sudan."

"All the safe spots."

Christian shrugged. "I enjoy my work. It's challenging and a reminder of how fortunate I am." "Your turn," Christian said, continuing in a lighter tone. "Tell me something about yourself."

"Like what?"

"You said you were running only for the money. That is not why most people run. What's the deal?"

"I want to buy land. In Colombia, the southern part in Amazonia. Miners and loggers are just decimating the forest. And poachers, too. I want to buy as many tracts as I can to keep it safe. I'll hire local people to protect it, and I'll live right smack in the middle of it."

"That's a good reason," Christian said soberly. "And in a location quite a bit hotter than 350 kilometers north of the Arctic Circle."

"It's your turn now," Xo said, "to tell me something about yourself. Why the bodyguard? Did you get some warlord angry by healing the wrong person? And why Norway? Why are you going to Norway if you're not running?"

"A family matter."

Xo looked at Christian appraisingly. "You don't sound particularly happy about it."

"Would you come with me? It would make things easier."

"What?"

"Yes, you'll come with me. Xo, I'm going to owe you!" Christian's face lit up with happy relief. "It will go so much better with you there. That lady was right. You are a godsend!"

"But. . ."

"No but's. I know there's no connecting flight to Tromco until tomorrow. You'll get a dinner out of it! And a place to stay if you want."

The sideways look Xo gave Christian made him burst out laughing. "Just dinner then."

Fourteen

"He says he's bringing a friend."

Juliana put down the paper she was reading. "Male or female?"

"He didn't say."

"For dinner?"

"Yes, for dinner."

"Didn't you ask?" Juliana couldn't keep a slight tone of exasperation out of her voice.

"I couldn't. He didn't tell me. You know our son. He told the majordomo to set an extra plate. The butler informed me."

Juliana picked up her phone and pushed the name Jack Robinson on her contact list. After a brief conversation, she hung up. Looking at Haakkon, her husband, the King, father of her two sons, and said slowly, "He's bringing a girl."

"There's a first time for everything."

"You know it doesn't mean anything," Juliana said in an irritated voice. "He's doing it just to aggravate me."

"And I would say he has succeeded." Haakkon came over to his wife and put his hand fondly on her shoulder. "We've never been able to control him. We just need to be grateful that his rebellion has been to become a doctor. Most parents would be content with that decision."

"Yes, but he puts himself in constant danger. The places he goes!"

"It would be difficult for anyone to be the second son when it comes to royalty. If this is the way Christian deals with his older brother getting all the attention because he is the heir apparent, then I would say we are very lucky parents."

Juliana sniffed. "I just wish he wouldn't be so wayward. Every time I introduce him to a lady who will strengthen the monarchy, he laughs at me. At least Oscar married someone with royal bloodlines."

"I think you've forced enough introductions on him," Haakkon laughed. "I don't think there are any princesses left. Just be glad that the people love him. What was he voted as again? Ah, yes, Norway's sexiest man of the year. For four years running, no less."

Juliana finally laughed. "I don't think Oscar has ever gotten over it! And of course, Christian always trying to disguise himself with all those scruffy clothes he wears doesn't help. Oscar doesn't understand anyone wanting to hide from attention."

It was Haakkon's turn to become serious. "If he's bringing a girl, then it's going to make your matchmaking a little uncomfortable. A small family affair and then two single women – one a princess of England?"

"And the other a commoner. I can't have Princess Carolina feeling put out. I've heard she's very temperamental. Still, worth putting up with because of the accord it will bring. A marriage between Christian and Carolina will really strengthen the bond between the two countries."

Haakkon didn't have time to ask if the marriage would make Christian happy because Juliana was already dealing with how to deal with the situation of two unattached females at the dinner table. The solution, she decided, was to invite more than Oscar and his wife and child to dinner. Now, she was inviting every relative and in-law currently in country. "We have to make it a party," she said, "so that girl he's bringing will get lost in the crowd."

Fifteen

Christian had texted when he was a few minutes away, and Xo responded that she would be waiting outside. Xo was staying in the extra room that a recently widowed woman was letting out. It was close to the airport, and Xo had previously met the couple when they had hired her to identify birds two years before. The husband was too infirm to walk, but Xo had arranged for them to sit at a picnic table at someone's *finka* along the river in the early morning hours when the birds were most active.

The couple had been overjoyed, and the man had sat with tears flowing down his face. "They're so beautiful," he kept saying. "Thank you, thank you Mr. and Mrs. Macaw. Thank you, thank you, Miss Yellow-tufted Woodpecker," he would say, naming each bird that Xo would draw close to them by imitating their sound. The man had died soon after, but his wife had sent Xo a note thanking him for the pleasure she had provided for her husband during his last days as well as an invitation to spend the night if she ever found herself in Norway.

"You look amazing," Christian said as he held the car door for her.

"It's not my dress," Xo said, smoothing the material over her middle. "Or my shoes. Do women really wear these spikes all day?"

"I've never understood it," Christian said. "But honestly, it's hard to take my eyes off you."

"You don't have to say that," Xo said in a matter-of-fact tone. "I said I would go with you. I'm not backing out."

Christian wanted to tell Xo again how incredible she looked. He had heard the expression, "She took my breath away," but he had never believed it possible. Now he knew otherwise. But Xo seemed not to care, and once again, Christian found himself in a novel position. He didn't know what to say. He wanted her to believe that his complements were real.

Xo spoke before he could think of how to convince her he meant what he said without sounding like a sycophant.

"Rigitza, the woman I'm staying with, it's her dress. She made it herself years ago. She didn't make the shoes, of course, but she had them dyed to match the fabric."

There was a moment of silence and then Xo broke out into a small giggle, "She told me what I was going to wear before was unacceptable."

"Was it?" asked Christian curiously.

"Not to me. I could run in it," Xo said.

"I wouldn't have minded. Do you want me to go back so you can change?"

Xo told him that was very kind of him, but thank you no. For the remainder of the trip, Christian pointed out facts about the places and buildings they were passing. The history, the architecture, the cultural details, Xo found it all fascinating.

"Now, this family matter," she said, when Christian pulled onto a little lane behind an enormous building. "Are we going to be late?"

"No," Christian said, as he waved to a guard who allowed them continue down the lane. "We're right on time."

"Then what are we doing here? Isn't this the back of the palace?"

"Yes."

"Your family lives here?"

"Yes." Christian looked at Xo hoping to see a different reaction from the swooning and almost hysterical fawning that most women gave him when they discovered he was a prince.

Christian's hopes were well met, and even exceeded, as Xo didn't comment at all about his being royal. Instead, all she said, was, in the most matter of fact voice, "Now, this family matter – if you don't get it resolved, what are they going to do? Chop off your head? Or are you offering up mine instead?"

Christian broke out laughing. "It won't come to that, I promise. Trust me, the evening will be spent on me being told I need to come home and cut ribbons and do more of all that ceremonial stuff that my older brother loves."

"What do you need me for then?" Xo asked curiously.

"Oh, I need you," Christian said as he parked the car. "I need your protection."

"Protection from what?" Xo asked as she stepped out of the car door that Christian was holding open for her. Christian didn't answer her until they had gone up some steps and through the door that had been opened by a formally dressed servant.

"From my mother's matchmaking," Christian said, unable to contain an impudent smile. "I'm sure she's brought yet another royal lady here whom she considers an appropriate match."

"And I'm not that," Xo said calmly. "An appropriate match."

Christian kept Xo by his side. Even when his mother tried to separate them, telling Xo there was someone she wanted to introduce her to, Christian prevented it. "I'll introduce Xo to them in a moment," Christian would say, intervening. "We'll circle the room, mother. Don't worry."

Christian was true to his word. "You're making this easy," he whispered into Xo's ear at one point. "I can't get over how calm you are," he added, not realizing he spoke the last words at a more conversational level than he meant to until he heard someone say, "Yes, her poise is remarkable."

"I'm Carolina," the woman continued, addressing Xo, but purposefully not extending her hand.

"And how are you related to Christian?" Xo asked.

Christian tried hard to smother the laugh that had come up into his throat. He had never officially met England's Princess Royal, but he, along with most of the rest of the world, knew full well who she was. She was the Queen of England's 25-year-old second born. A constant presence on the party circuit, photographed in skimpy bikinis on dazzling white sand beaches as well as in elegant haute couture gowns at elite galas, Carolina was known for her attention-grabbing antics and ever-changing list of current suitors.

After a startled pause, Carolina answered in a sultry voice. "Maybe related one day," she said, hiding not at all a languid appraisal of Christian's form.

That evening, as King Haakkon and Queen Juliana sat in the dark outside on their favorite bench, Haakkon said quietly, "She held her own."

"What do you mean?" Juliana asked.

"You know what I mean. Christian's friend. Xo. She held her own. Carolina was like a dog on a bone, and no matter how hard she gnawed, Xo answered with poised diplomacy. She never let on that she knew that she was being insulted. And that way impossible to insult."

"Maybe she didn't know?"

Haakkon looked askance at his wife before he responded. Haakkon knew that his beloved wife's chief concern was the monarchy, but he also knew there was no hiding from the truth. Carolina was a spoiled socialite filled with silicone. She would not make Christian happy.

Speaking slowly, he said, "At the dinner table, Oscar asked if Xo had met Christian during medical school. Xo said she wasn't a doctor. Oscar then asked if they had met at university. Xo said that she didn't go to university. Carolina, who everyone in the world knows barely passed her O levels, has no standing when it comes to making fun of someone's education, or lack of. Despite that, she said loudly, "Why would he be interested in you?""

"And Xo answered, 'I can run faster,'" Juliana said, breaking into a smile.

"And then Carolina asked, in an acid tone I might add, 'What good is that?'"

"And Xo said, 'I won't be the one eaten by the jaguar.'"

Both Haakkon and Juliana laughed. Laying her head on Haakkon's shoulder, Juliana mused, "It might possibly be the first time in her life that Carolina didn't have a snappy reply. It was a good thing that everyone laughed. Thank goodness for your segue into a different subject. It was quite masterful, my love."

"I've had years to practice my diplomacy," Haakkon said, kissing the top of his wife's head. "And as for being diplomatic, next time you play matchmaker, at least now we know Christian's type."

"What do you mean?"

"You must have noticed! I know you did! The similarity between Carolina and Xo. Something in their structure and coloring, though of course Xo was much more striking. Next to her, Carolina just seemed like a paler, washed-out version."

"Would you say it that way? That seems a bit harsh. How about we just say Carolina is a softer version."

There was silence for a moment and then Juliana continued. "I'm going to get the two of them together again soon, if need be. But first we need to send Christian to the Netherlands. If I remember correctly, Madeline, Queen Henrietta's daughter, is quite the athlete. And she's just turned of age. A tennis player, right?"

"Green eyes?"

Juliana swatted her husband's arm playfully. "One can't have everything," she said. "But if some jaguar comes around, rest assured that Madeline can smack it with her racquet."

Sixteen

"Do you ever do any doctoring?"

"Ouch!" Christian laughed. "Usually when people answer their phone they say, 'Hello,' or, 'I'm so glad you called.'"

"It's just that you seem to call me an awful lot. And, you didn't answer my question."

"Yes, I do take care of people. I'm between surgeries right now. I'm training people here to operate on obstetric fistulas. It's something I shouldn't be doing."

"Then why are you wasting your time?"

"That isn't what I meant. I probably should have worded it differently. Of course, I should be teaching people here the procedure, but the truth is that this kind of fistula happens very rarely in the developed world. It's considered a disease of poverty. If women were given adequate maternal care or treated early, surgery wouldn't be needed. Instead, all because of that hole in their birth canal, they become incontinent, leak feces, and often become infertile, depressed and rejected. And if that isn't bad enough, it's no small occurrence.

There's something like two million women already suffering from it, and despite all the medical knowledge we have, about 75,000 new cases every year."

"Then you should keep at it."

"I will, but I miss you."

Christian wasn't aware that he was holding his breathe until Xo answered. He had been hoping for words of the same sentiment, but whatever Xo was feeling, she continued to mask it. She answered in a matter-of-fact tone.

"I have one more race to run, and then I go home."

Slowly freeing the air he had contained in his lungs, once again willing himself to sound as dispassionate as Xo, Christian asked, "To Colombia?"

"Yes."

Christian looked around at the desolate landscape he was working in. The ground was hard and dry, and the tents set up by aid workers were ragged and stained with filth. Children sat wearily by their mothers, seemingly as desiccated as their empty surroundings. They looked at Christian who had walked a few steps from the corner of the operating tent to gain a bit of privacy with little interest.

It was the phone calls to Xo that had kept Christian going. She always answered, and even without endearments, somehow, he always felt invigorated. He would lie on his cot at night and think about what they had discussed. She was slow to reveal anything, but he would dissect everything she had said, looking for clues that would help him understand how she had become the woman that she was.

"You could come visit me."

"Are you serious?" Christian couldn't keep the surprise from his voice.

"Why wouldn't I be?"

Christian didn't bother to answer that question. Instead, he just said, "Yes. Yes, I'll be there as soon as this stint is over." Later, when he walked back into surgery, his step was so light that for the first time since his arrival to this war – ravaged drought-stricken land he didn't feel the scorched earth's heat burning the bottom of his soles.

"Usually fewer than half the runners finish the race within the 30-hour time limit," Tom said to Xo as they waited for the start. Take your time on this one. It's definitely the hardest race you've been in yet. Don't be disappointed if you don't do as well as you expect."

Xo nodded. She didn't bother to tell Tom that she knew exactly what she was getting into. 50 miles in, 50 miles out, climbing and descending 15,600 feet.

"The Leadville 100," Tom went on, unable to hide the satisfaction on his face. "The Race across the Sky. Through the heart of the Colorado Rockies. Starting at over 10,000 feet. Did you know that some of these runners showed up two weeks early just to adjust to the altitude?"

Once again, Xo didn't verbally answer. Instead, she just nodded. Xo was grateful to Tom for introducing her to ultramarathons and helping her get there, but she had no interest in the social aspect that Tom was enjoying. Tom liked being the center of attention, and he enjoyed telling the story of his "discovering" Xo.

Xo almost knew it by heart. "I was so disappointed when she showed up to run in that skirt," he would say, and then he would proceed to tell them how he was so exhausted after their first run that he walked fully clothed into a swimming pool. Several writers had asked to interview Xo, but she had silently shaken her head. It only added to people's curiosity, especially as she had so easily won all of her previous races.

Xo knew that words have power. Use too many of them, and the message becomes diluted. For now, she knew that Tom and his wife Lara were sufficient. Tom, for all his talk of her innocent provincialism, and Lara for telling everyone that all Xo wanting to do was buy land in order to save the rainforest. It made great copy.

When Xo was asked to submit a urine sample before the race, she willingly acquiesced. When Tom found out, though, he threw such a fit, that it soon became common knowledge what had been asked of Xo. So, too, was Xo's response, "Before, during, after. Just ask."

At the aid stations, it was Xo people were looking for. They clapped and cheered, snapping photos and videos with their cameras and phones as she ran past, usually without stopping. She ran just as she did on her other previous four races. About twenty feet behind the leader, passing him near the end of the course so as to cross the finish line first.

When asked what race Xo was going to run in next, Xo said simply, "I want to go home. To Colombia. I am going to buy land that can't be logged or mined." It all went viral, and Lara very cleverly started a go fund me type of account. Lara seeded it with five thousand dollars, and it grew from there.

After the race, while waiting for Tom to finish, Xo sat quietly with her eyes closed away from the crowd. She could hear people coming close, and she knew they were taking her photo, but she paid them no mind. But when someone came and sat beside her, she turned to look. It was a fellow runner, and she took the bottle of water he extended out to her.

"Lara said you're going back to Colombia. "Are you going to continue racing?"

Xo smiled and made her usual noncommittal shrug she gave to anyone who asked a question.

"I'm Raul Van Maarten," the man continued in a conversational tone. "I'm a writer. A runner, too, and I'll be writing about this race."

When Xo didn't respond, he went on as if she had asked him to continue. "Lara says I should do a story about the reserve you want to start."

"To see if I'm a thief?"

"I wouldn't put it that baldly," Raul laughed. "But people are fascinated by you, and there's a lot of money being added to that fund. And you're a phenomenal athlete. Coming out of nowhere. I'm sure you've got quite a backstory."

"Lara says you should do the story?"

"Yes."

"In seven months," Xo said. "Come to Leticia and visit me. You can see what I have accomplished."

"You'll tell me how you train, too? And all about your racing?"

"No. My history is my own."

Raul said, "Then why should I write the story?"

There was no false bravado when Xo spoke. "Because I'm not going to race again for six months. And when I do, I'll win."

Lara had done her homework before asking Raul to speak to Xo. Raul had won several prizes for his journalism, and he was known for his careful reporting. Raul didn't rely on hyperbole, as he was able to write about his subjects with such depth and understanding that the reader felt they were being personally introduced.

Raul, on his part, had done his homework, too. He already knew the few public details Xo offered up, but he knew there was something missing because he couldn't find more. No one just appeared. Especially when one was such a superb athlete. And, Raul could say this with an impartial journalist's perspective, Xo was beautiful. There was something about the way she held herself. An unkind or insecure person might describe her as cold or stand offish, but Raul, after studying what photos of her showed up on the internet, had decided that the correct word for her manner was regal.

Raul had been especially intrigued when Lara had advised him that Xo was not as simple as she appeared. "She's goal-oriented. Tom may have introduced her to ultramarathons, but they have only been a means of getting what she wants. She wants land. And she wants to keep it safe. Don't underestimate her."

"So, you'll remain a mystery woman?" Raul said slowly, thinking about what that meant.

"You'll be the only reporter welcome in my home. You can observe, take photos."

"Of you?"

"Just one. Running. But I'll be training and hiring local nature guides, so you'll get some incredible animal and bird photos."

Raul already had phrases running through his head he could use in his stories: wild Madonna, Tarzana of the Amazon, Mystery runner of the rainforest. Lara was right. Xo was clever. She would garner great attention simply because news was limited. And if she truly did use all donated funds for rainforest preservation, giving a reason for the local population to keep the forest from being destroyed, his articles would only increase the donations. Of course, that would happen only if she continued to win. It was as if Xo could read his thoughts.

"I'll win."

Raul made a very wise move. He agreed.

Seventeen

Xo stopped and stared. She couldn't help but notice the blazing headlines and the front cover full page photos. Leticia may not have been a grand urban metropolis, but it did cater to tourists. And for that reason, many of the little shops sold, along with sunscreen, insect repellent, and mosquito nets, gossip magazines. Often the magazines were out of date, the pages well-thumbed, but still there was always a traveler that wanted to catch up on celebrity happenings or to have something light in hand to read on the plane.

The headline *Princess Carolina Meets Her Match*! wasn't what drove Xo's interest. It was the photo. It was of Carolina, dressed in tailored safari garb. Carolina was in front of a dingy canvas tent with a red cross on the door flap. Her head and body were slightly turned, as she was kissing Christian on the cheek.

Xo picked up the magazine and quickly scanned the article. Carolina had surprised Christian when she showed up with cases of medical supplies. Did this mean that the doctor prince was the one to finally catch Carolina's heart? What a royal match they would make!

What a younger, modern, and more stylish edge they would give to the stodgier monarchy. And the uniting of two royal bloodlines was not only a monarchist's but a true royalist's dream.

It went on and on, with flashy photos of Carolina, past and present, liberally sprinkled throughout.

Xo put the magazine down. She wasn't happy. The magazine was over a week old, but she had talked to Christian several times since then. It was true that they both had to wait till they had decent internet connections, but still, you would have thought he would have mentioned that Carolina had visited. According to the article, she had stayed for four days! Worse, when Xo calculated dates in her head, those four days were some of the times when Christian didn't answer his phone.

Xo was not going to ignore the story. She was going to ask Christian about it. But first she had to go make her way through the open-air airport and stand on the tarmac where Christian's plane was just landing.

"Xo!" Christian flung down his duffel and swept Xo into his arms. "I missed you!" he said, holding her close. Instinctively, Xo started to pull back, as she had never been greeted in such an exuberant or familiar fashion before.

"Uh-uh," Christian said softly, "I'm not letting you go yet! Xo, you don't know how good it is to see you! Oh, you smell good! And feel good, too!" He nuzzled her neck, holding the back of her head with one hand, his other hand circling her waist.

Xo couldn't help herself. She burst out laughing. "Enough," she finally said, "enough!"

Christian picked up his duffle bag, swung it over his shoulder, and then grabbed Xo's hand. "Where to? Wow, this is a different kind of hot than the desert. Just as, but it's so humid. I swear if I tipped my head back and opened my mouth wide enough, I could drink the air."

As Xo led him out to the road where she had parked her scooter, she tried to pull her hand away. "Uh-uh," Christian said again. "I'm still not letting you go. Really, Xo, you don't know how good it is to see you. I really missed you! It gets lonely out there in the middle of the Sahara."

Xo waited until Christian had climbed onto the seat behind her, his duffle bag strapped to his back like a backpack, before she said, "Lonely? With Carolina and all those reporters?"

Christian started to answer, but Xo revved the engine, drowning out his attempts at speaking. Wisely, Christian decided to wait. Meanwhile, he held on, his arms tightly circling Xo so he would not be jolted off. Christian was used to undeveloped roads, but this was incredible. It seemed there were more potholes than roads, and he had no idea how Xo could go so fast and zig back and forth between them. As they left town, the road got narrower and narrower. Xo didn't stop until sometime much later when the road had become a single rut between looming vegetation.

"Are you leaving me for the jaguars? You do know that I didn't invite her?" Christian said, picking up the conversation where Xo had left it as he carefully disembarked, gingerly shaking his limbs to make sure they were all intact.

"No," laughed Xo, as she pushed the scooter into the brush so that it was covered. "Not if you're willing to walk."

"Where are we going? We're in the middle of nowhere!"

"Home," answered Xo. I though you wanted to see where I live." She hesitated for a moment and then said, "You can stay in Leticia. At the Mission School where Jack's staying, or a hotel if you want."

"No, no, I didn't mean that. It's just that this is incredible. It's like we are the only two people in the world. We could just disappear and no one would ever know. We would never be found."

"Not even by Carolina?"

"Not even by Carolina," Christian said. "Do I detect a bit of jealousy?" he asked, a wide smile breaking across his face. "I can only hope!"

When Xo didn't reply, Christian reached for her hand and pulled her into an embrace. "She did bring medical supplies, and she brought a lot of attention to the cause. That's the only reason why I didn't send her away."

When Xo remained stiff, Christian moved his head back a little so he could look down on her. "Are you still angry?"

"Why would you think that?"

"You're awful tense."

"I'm not used to being hugged."

"Right," said Christian just a bit sarcastically. "Or your hand being held. Xo, whatever you think happened with Carolina, I assure you, it didn't. There's no reason to be upset."

"Nine years, give or take." Xo spoke softly, but her gaze was steady.

Christian had no idea what Xo was talking about. But then, he was finding that was often the case when it came to Xo. With any other woman, he would have assumed it was some strange attempt at seduction, but he knew Xo well enough by now to know that she didn't flirt, at least not in the inane coquettish way so many other women came on to him.

Christian met Xo's gaze, but he gave a simple nod of encouragement and waited expectantly.

"Since I've been hugged," Xo said again. "I'm not used to it."

Whatever Christian was expecting to hear, it wasn't that. For a moment Christian was too shocked to speak or even move. Flashes of Jack telling him that no one comes out of nowhere went through his mind. How Xo appeared at the age of thirteen or fourteen, an age that the nuns simply guessed at. Nine years, give or take. It was all beginning to make sense. Or not make sense exactly, but pieces were beginning to fit together.

"Then we have a lot to catch up on," Christian said tenderly, pulling Xo once again into an embrace. He held her gently for a moment, and then he kissed her. Her lips were soft and warm, and though she stood quietly, tasting and feeling a man's breath for the first time, Christian felt as if he too were being initiated into something new. It was as if he was standing at her door, his feet firmly placed on the welcome mat that she had put out. She would answer soon, inviting him further in because she had to. She had to because although there had been so many kisses before, with oh so many women, never had he felt like he did right now. Never had it felt so right. Never had it felt like part of him would become missing if it were to stop.

Christian's kiss was unexpected, and although Xo felt pleasure at the feel of Christian's mouth against her own, she was able to remain conscious of the moment. She was aware of the damp heavy air, the tiny rustle of vegetation as hidden animals scurried by, the cacophonous calls of brightly colored macaws and other birds. Yet something strange happened. She felt it coming, and she could not stop it. She couldn't control it. And perhaps most importantly, she didn't want to. It started as a softening of the shell she had surrounded herself with for her own protection for so many years. Then it became a gentle disarming where she felt herself exposed. Ordinarily that would have meant time to hold her shield higher and firmer, but now, as unfamiliar sensations traveled through her nerves, she only wanted to let herself further in to whatever door Christian had suddenly opened.

Unable to stop herself, not wanting to stop herself, Xo began to respond. At first tentatively, shyly, hesitantly, but as Christian became more demanding, the burning feelings racing through her limbs and stomach took on a life of their own. Her legs felt weak, but it was of little matter, for there were Christian's arms around her, keeping her close and safe.

When Christian pulled away, Xo did not see his eyes wide and confused because of his own shock at how deeply he had been affected by a single kiss, for she stood still, eyes shut, allowing the trembles she felt along her nerves to settle into calm. When she finally opened them, she saw Christian looking at her with a serious expression. "Xo," he said gently, as he traced her jaw and underneath her chin with one hand. "Xo," he said again, for that was all that was needed to be said.

Eighteen

Christian felt his heart pounding against his rib cage. He was equally terrified and electrified. The only thing keeping him from thrashing wildly was Xo who seemed completely oblivious to the danger they were in.

"Stay on your back," Xo instructed, her voice as calm as if she had asked him to pass the salt at a well-lit dining table. "Keep your arms at your side and just gently kick your feet to stay afloat."

Christian was too nervous to answer, as he was afraid that his voice would startle the sleek brown animals swimming around him. There were five of them, at least, as far as he could tell, and one of them had to be at least six feet long. The smaller young ones were playing some type of game where they were swimming under him and coming out on the other side, and it was hard for him not to ball up and turn over when he would feel them brush against his back. When he saw one actually jump out of the water and skitter across Xo's belly, he thought Xo would finally understand the danger they were in, but instead, she just laughed.

Just as suddenly as the animals appeared, they disappeared as quickly. "River otters," Xo said, as she made her way to the shore. "They love to play. Nothing to be afraid of."

"I'm used to otters being a bit smaller," Christian said as he followed Xo onto a sandy bank. "That big one must have weighed over 50 pounds. My God, Xo, I've never seen or been as close to anything like that in my life. I didn't even know things like that existed, and I still can't get over how close they came to us."

"There are only a few thousand left," Xo said, "if that. They're being hunted to extinction. But it was unusual for them to swim around us. You were very lucky."

"I think I prefer the pink dolphins. Less ferocious somehow."

Christian followed Xo to where they had left their picnic supplies under the shade of a tree edging the sandy bank. He helped her spread a large cloth, and then he sat down beside her.

"I have to leave tomorrow," he said quietly. He waited for Xo to say something, but when she didn't, he took her hand. "I don't want to," he said, bringing her hand to his mouth and kissing it gently.

"Jack will be relieved."

Christian burst out laughing. "I don't know if he is going to hate you or love you, but I actually think he is beginning to like his time in Leticia."

"The nuns are taking good care of him."

"Right," Christian said, once again laughing. "Big strong Jack Robinson being take care of by nuns."

"Perhaps," Xo said, her eyes twinkling mischievously, "This is the first time Jack is being watched more closely than you. The students won't leave him alone, and according to Gustavo, Jack is like a little kid when it comes to fishing and catching all those piranhas. And then of course there is all that handy man fixing that the nuns have him doing. They're not going to want him to leave."

"Do you want him to leave?" The words were nonchalant, but there was something deeper in Christian's voice. Xo knew what it was.

Jack would be staying as long as Christian was. If Christian left, Jack would leave. Christian was asking Xo if she wanted Christian to stay. His way of inquiring was light and gentle, designed so as to make her feel no pressure, but Xo knew from the way Christian's body had stilled that her answer was of great import.

Quietly, she withdrew her hand from Christian's, and she placed it, along with her other hand, in her lap. "Christian," she said, looking at him directly, "I've never been happier. You know the answer."

"Xo," Christian said gently. "Xo," he said again, this time with yearning, and then he moved his hands to her face and drew her close.

They had touched each other over the last few days, gentle strokes in passing during daily activities, a hand on a small of the back, a nuzzling on an upper arm while laughing, a lingering stroke of a hip, but there had been nothing as intimate as their first kiss. Perhaps it was the intensity of what they felt the first time their lips had met, the sharing of a tiny bit of soul, that was holding them back. Neither one had been prepared for such a physical stirring, and both found the unexpected response a reason for reserve. Christian because he was afraid that rushed intensity would give Xo cause to withdraw, and Xo because she had to think about the new sensations that had coursed through her veins.

This time, however, they were ready. Under the shadowy coolness of the trees, with the feeling that all the time in the world was theirs, they embraced and kissed. Hands explored and stroked, and it was without shyness that each helped the other disrobe. Christian, in part due to experience and in part due to a doctor knowing the body's anatomy so intimately that he was fully aware of all the pleasure points, at first led, but Xo was a leader, too. She was not afraid to respond, and as Christian took delight in her moans of pleasure, so did she when it came to eliciting a response from Christian.

When finally, the leisurely explorations were no longer enough, their bodies expectant with wanting more, Christian rolled Xo onto her back. The intensity of feelings quickly went from controlled to uncontrollable. Each felt a new world of feelings before them, and their bodies could not help but respond with heightened fervor. When at last they could no longer contain themselves, unable to remain on the edge of what was to overtake them, they joyfully, willingly, uncontrollably gave in. Not to each own, but to each other.

Nineteen

"I'm so sorry Lord Hampton, but there will be a slight wait. The dentist is dealing with an unexpected emergency right now."

"Is any emergency expected?" Lord Hampton asked, his tone brittle. Unsure of how to respond, the receptionist meekly looked down at her desk. She didn't look up again until Lord Hampton had moved away from her desk and took a seat next to a table with a stack of magazines. Then the receptionist couldn't help herself. Although she tried to be surreptitious about it, she kept looking over at Lord Hampton.

A real Lord! A man who had talked and drunk tea with the Queen! A man who had met the Queen's daughters Princess Rose and Princess Carolina! Oh, how the receptionist wished Lord Hampton would tell her what they were like. Share a detail, no matter how small. She would love to know. She so wanted to ask, but she knew not to.

The receptionist was new. She had been hired a mere two months before. During her training, she had been told explicitly to not make any personal comments to Lord Hampton, ask about the Royal family, or to even mention his connection to them. "He will bite your head off," she was told. "He has made us all cry."

The receptionist knew that if she ever suffered such a caustic tongue lashing, she would melt. Dissolve into a puddle of tears. Yet she couldn't help herself. She couldn't stop peeking glances at the storied man just a short distance from her. She wanted to soak up every detail, for she knew this was most likely the closest she would ever get to anything Royal.

"His face is like a stone," the receptionist thought, as she saw him turn his head so as to peruse the magazines beside him that had been bought to entertain patients while they waited. The cover of the magazine on the top of the stack wasn't pristine, but the receptionist had placed it there regardless. She did this because it was the most popular magazine they subscribed to, and this week's copy was especially sought after. The well-thumbed pages were proof of that. The receptionist herself had read the story several times. How could she not with such an amazing photo and catching title?

Princess Carolina Meets Her Match in bold black type, and then the photo of the princess and the prince she was kissing! He was so handsome! And a doctor! What a different world those royals lived in. To have such exotic adventures and to dress so stylishly!

Momentarily forgetting her place, the receptionist gushed. "That story is a real favorite. One lady stayed after the doctor had seen her just so she could finish it. We're all hoping there will be a royal wedding. It would be brilliant, it would!"

Lord Hampton didn't verbally respond, but he showed his disinterest in carrying on a conversation by lifting up the other magazines in the stack one by one. Most of them were earlier editions of the same entertainment magazine, stories about Princess Carolina in all of them, and Lord Hampton's face remained stony with indifference. With a queasy feeling in her stomach, the receptionist nervously turned back to her computer screen. She couldn't quite believe that she had spoken to Lord Hampton. It hurt that he didn't respond, ignoring her as if she didn't matter or exist, but perhaps that was better than being excoriated until she cried.

Inwardly sighing, the receptionist kept her eyes glued to the computer screen until she heard the door open. Despite not expecting any patients, she quickly finished the line of the invoice she was working on so she could look up and greet whomever it was who entered the room. The words died in her mouth as there was no one to utter them to. The waiting area was completely empty. And the door that she had heard open? It was swinging shut on Lord Hampton. As the receptionist stared in astonishment at the exiting figure, the receptionist thought she saw something tucked under Lord Hampton's arm. A magazine, perhaps? No, that wouldn't, couldn't make sense. For if one was to purloin a magazine, wouldn't it be the one with the story about Princess Caroline meeting her match? And that magazine, the receptionist noted, was still sitting on top of the stack.

Twenty

"What would that old fuddy-duddy want with you at this hour?"

"I have no idea," Sir Reginald Cooper replied. "But he said it was imperative."

"Everything is imperative to Lord Hampton," Princess Carolina said as she moved her fingers languidly through the hair on Reginald's chest. "Our stalwart protector of the Crown, that he is. You'll let me know as soon as. . ." Carolina never finished the sentence, instead putting a trail of kisses that moved from Reginald's neck downward.

"I could, we could. . ."

"No," Carolina said lying back coquettishly. "When you come back."

Carolina waited prone, with eyes half closed until Reginald left the room. Once the door shut behind him, she immediately sat up and picked up her phone. After commanding it to dial "Big S" she lit a cigarette as she waited for a response.

"What's up Lil S?"

"Not sure. Something big. Lord Hampton beckoned, and Reggie ran out."

"At this hour?"

"Do you think it's about getting naked at that party last week? Bollocks! I thought all the phones had been collected. You don't think anyone uploaded a photo. . . I was so tanked up I don't remember anything that happened."

"No, I don't think that's it. If any photos were out, we'd be the ones being called."

"Okay. Bright side is no long sermon about how we don't respect the Crown. You don't think mother's going to finally step down, do you? Wouldn't that be a blowout!"

There was a moment of silence while both princesses thought about how their lives would change if Rose became queen. "Oh, Big Sister," Carolina said, "Let the merriment begin!"

"First thing to change," Rose said giggling, "is to lock Lord Hampton out of the castle! Too bad beheadings aren't allowed anymore! We could get rid of the pesky bugger with a stroke of the ax! Oh well. We all have to adapt to change, even the Crown! Let me know, Little Sis, what's up as soon as you know."

"Why else would I be here?" Carolina said, exhaling smoke. "What I do for the Crown!"

❦ ❦ ❦

"Here at last," Lord Hampton said icily as Reginald entered. Reginald knew better than to offer an excuse. Instead, he silently made his way to the empty one of two wingback chairs upholstered in herringbone gray in front of Lord Hampton's desk. As Reginald took his seat, he took a quick look at the person sitting in the opposite chair. Reginald didn't recognize him, and that, to Reginald, was cause for worry.

"At your service, Lord," Reginald said as soon as he was seated.

Lord Hampton gave Reginald a piercing glance, and then he nodded at the man sitting adjacent to him. Without saying a word, the man opened up a folder he was holding on his lap and handed Reginald a magazine.

"Trail running?" Reginald said reading some of the words on the cover. "Is Her Majesty intending to sponsor another charity?"

"Page 23," the man who handed Reginald the magazine said tersely.

Reginald gave a quick glance at Lord Hampton, hoping to get a glimmer about what was going on, but Lord Hampton's countenance remained as stony and unrevealing as ever. Trying to keep his own face as expressionless, Reginald opened up the magazine to where he had been directed. Reginald was a speed reader, used to quickly summing up situations and weighing facts. It was this particular skill set that Lord Hampton had recognized and utilized him for. Lord Hampton looked at Reginald expectantly, but Reginald felt a stab of fear in the bottom of his belly, for he had no idea what was expected of him.

"The woman in the photo. . ." Lord Hampton said, finally breaking the silence.

"Xo Bosque, from Colombia," Reginald said, relieved to show that he had gleaned pertinent information from his quick examination of the pages.

"I would like you to make her acquaintance."

Reginald wasn't sure he had heard correctly. "Excuse me?" he said, looking at Lord Hampton and the man sitting next to him. "You'd like me to. . ."

"Make her acquaintance," the man said calmly.

Reginald remained silent, unable to think of what to say or ask. It didn't make sense. Slowly, he sat back in his chair.

Lord Hampton spoke bluntly. "Yes or no."

"Yes, yes, of course yes, but..."

"Good," Lord Hampton spoke with finality. "This is Colin Smith. He will make the arrangements."

"To. . . to where?"

"Colombia."

Despite the years of servitude and diplomacy under Reginald's belt, Reggie could not control the ripple of surprise that crossed his face. He opened his mouth to say something, but nothing came out.

"You will keep this to yourself," Lord Hampton said calmly. "You may go now."

Reginald wanted more information, but he kept silent. Reginald had worked hard to get to where he was. He planned on going higher. He would be patient. He would find out in good time, and he would use what he discovered to his advantage. Knowledge was a source of power. It was a means.

After the door closed behind Reginald, the man who had been introduced as Colin Smith asked, "Can he be trusted?"

Lord Hampton gave a dry laugh. "I have no doubt that Princess Carolina will extract the few details he has been given as soon as she puts her fingers under his shirt. Just get him down to Colombia. He's a perfect decoy. And you. You know what to do."

"No paper or electronic trail. Report verbally to you in person only."

"The monarchy. That is all that matters," Lord Hampton said. "We will erase anything that gets in its way."

Twenty-One

"I never knew that a minute could be a day. A second an hour."

Xo was so struck by the sweet poetry of the words that she didn't answer. Instead, she repeated themselves to herself so that she wouldn't forget.

"You're there? Xo, can you hear me? Do you have a signal?"

"Yes," laughed Xo. "I'm at my usual spot. I'm on the roof of Hotel Leticia, all for that one special bar of service."

"And I thank you for that! Though I don't want to think about how you get up there."

"I told you. I climb the mango tree next to the hotel."

"I appreciate it Xo, but be careful. I look forward to these calls every day. They keep me going. I'm counting the seconds until I can see you again."

"Because each second is an hour and each minute is a day," Xo softly repeated.

Christian laughed. "See what you've done to me? You've turned me into a lonely poet."

"You spoke for both of us," Xo said softly.

Christian felt a wave of possessiveness wash over him. Not to control or to wield power. Only that he wanted it for himself. He didn't want to share Xo's feelings with anyone else. He didn't want her to long for anyone else as much he yearned for her.

So many women had told Christian that they loved him. When he didn't respond in kind, Christian had seen it all – sobbing, accusations of cruelty, threats of revenge, and honest to God down on the floor full on pounding of limbs temper tantrums. Christian had never believed any of them. He thought all their histrionics were a ploy to manipulate him. What all those women really wanted was to be a princess. They wanted a crown. What was it about royalty? How could marriage to Christian make them a princess if they didn't already feel like one inside?

Christian had never hesitated in telling all of these women that they had misconstrued his words or actions. He did this even though he knew he had never misled them. He knew that their perception, driven by their want, was their reality. He apologized for any misunderstanding, but inwardly, he seethed. It was only to Jack that he vented his anger. "I never initiated it," he would say. "I never said there was a future. I always said I was going to be a doctor. And you know they never loved me. They only wanted my title."

Xo was completely different. Her strength – both physical and mental – astounded him. She lived a life like no other women or person he had ever met. And yet, despite all that had happened to her (Christian could only guess and surmise. It could not have been easy and most probably traumatic. No one shows up alone at a mission school unable to be understood what is spoken to her, and when able, unable or unwilling to speak of the past), she did not look back. She judged a person on actions based on where they were, not where they had come from. Titles and degrees meant nothing to her.

"Visit me!" Christian said impulsively.

Xo didn't answer, but Christian was not to be deterred. If Xo would ever consent to Christian being the man at her side, it would only come about because of his own actions. It would have to be *despite* having been born in a palace. A challenge Christian would not turn aside from.

"Not to Afghanistan, of course, but to Norway. I'm about done with my stint here – I was only filling in for someone short term, and I've got to go back to Norway for some family thing."

"Another match making attempt?" Xo asked.

"I wish you sounded jealous!" Christian said. "But I certainly hope not. Please come, Xo. We've been apart too long."

This time when Xo didn't answer, Christian said, "I'm booking you a ticket. I'll send you all the info."

"I haven't said yes."

"I'm buying the ticket anyway. If you decide to leave an empty seat on the plane, then so be it. But I want you to know you will be missing out on a lot. I can't promise you giant otters, and you won't want to swim in any of the fjords here, but I can promise you whales. Humpbacks, sperm, minke, and orcas…"

"No."

"You're making me want to throw a temper tantrum," Christian said. "I want to lie on my back and pound my legs and arms on the floor while I wail and scream. Instead, I am going to book you a ticket and send you photos of all the things you will miss out on."

Xo couldn't help herself. She started to laugh. "I'm warning you," she said before hanging up. "I'm going to turn in your ticket and use the money on my reserve."

Xo sounded so certain that Christian felt it wasn't going to happen. He sent the ticket and all the information, regardless. He kept waiting for Xo to talk about it, or to at least comment on, but she never mentioned it in their nightly phone calls.

It took incredible restraint on Christian's part not to ask about it, but somehow, he knew he couldn't. He knew that if he delved into it, Xo would draw back. She would not come. He had shown that he wanted to be with her. It was her turn to choose him. He would be patient. Relentlessly so.

Three days before the departure date on Xo's ticket, Christian phoned Xo. "I'm in Kabul," he said. "Just arrived at the airport. Only to find out that my flight back home is delayed. That's to be expected of course."

Christian paused, hoping Xo would say that she, too, would soon be on her way to Norway. Instead, as the silence lengthened, Christian began to feel anxiety pulse with every heartbeat. "Xo," he started to say, but before he could finish the sentence Xo spoke.

"Is Jack there with you?"

Surprised at the question, Christian almost snapped his response. "You know he is."

"I would like to talk to him."

Christian's hand tightened around the phone as he felt a wave of emotions wash over him: rage, jealousy, bewilderment. Christian had woken up nights dreaming of Xo, yearning for her touch and caresses, aching for her ardor, wanting her to need him as much as he needed her. Desire for her was like a drug, and he needed her sooner than now. He had hoped beyond hope that she would meet him in Norway, but already he had prepared for her absence by purchasing tickets to Colombia the day after his presence was required in Norway. She had left him in agony, and now she was asking for Jack? When she knew he was in a place where calls could be and were suddenly dropped with more frequency than not?

"Why?" Christian said, struggling to keep his voice calm.

"Christian, I need to talk to him. If we lose service have him call me back."

"Here he is," Christian said, but without telling Xo and before handing the phone to Jack, he put it on speaker.

After Xo finished speaking, Jack said calmly. "I'll get back to you. You were right to call. Stay out of Leticia."

Jack handed the phone back to Christian, but when Christian held it up to his ear all he heard was the dial tone. Christian didn't say a word. Instead, he walked over to the ticket counter and asked to speak to the man in charge.

It took some time as well as most of the cash Christian kept hidden for emergencies and bribes, but he got what he wanted. Tickets in hand, he turned to Jack who had stood silently close by.

"Colombia, then?" Jack said.

Christian didn't answer, but he nodded and then started walking at a rapid pace to a gate different from the one they were waiting at. Jack kept pace, but he spoke calmly in a measured tone. "I wouldn't be doing my job if I didn't remind you that the Queen expects you there on Constitution Day."

"You don't have to come," Christian said, not lessoning his stride.

Jack didn't say another word until the two of them were sitting on the floor cramped together between boxes strapped to walls of a cargo plane. "You know she might be on the way to Norway. She has the ticket you sent."

Christian was blunt. "She's not. And quite possibly she won't stay out of Leticia. I just know it's bad if she asked you for help."

Christian didn't say more, but Jack had been with Christian so many years that he knew his charge almost better than Christian knew himself. Jack knew that Christian didn't understand why Xo had asked Jack for help and not Christian. Jack knew that Christian was infuriated.

"She wouldn't ask me for medical help," Jack said, breaking the silence that stood heavy between them.

"What's that supposed to mean?"

"She asked you for help. You just can't see it."

"She asked me to put you on the phone. She asked you to investigate Reginald Cooper. She told you that there was something wrong with him. She didn't tell me."

"But she asked you to get me. She wasn't hiding anything from you. She knew I would tell you everything, or even more likely, she knew you would put the phone on speaker."

"But. . ."

"There are no buts. My job is security. Like I said before, if she wanted medical help, she would have gone to you."

The two men were silent as they both shifted uncomfortably, trying to find a more comfortable position between the boxes. "We'll have seats on the next two flights," Christian said. "At least I think so."

"What I would do," Jack said, "is start thinking about what you are going to say to Xo when you show up. Are you sure she's going to be happy to see you?"

"It will be a surprise."

"Not all surprises are good."

"You know what's going to be good, Jack?" Christian said in a fierce voice. "When I dispose of Reginald Cooper, or whoever that bastard really is."

Jack couldn't help himself. He began to chuckle. "You know," he said. "You sound more upset right now than you did when we were getting shot at on our way to Kabul. Bullets whizzing by, and you're as calm as a clam. But now, just the thought of another man pursuing Xo, and you're acting like a hotshot jumping into what might be a real hornet's nest."

"It's not a hornet's nest," Christian said in a determined voice. "It's piranhas in a feeding frenzy. The first course – Reginald."

"I really like my job," Jack said, a grin washing across his face. "Keeping you out of trouble is more entertaining than I ever thought imaginable. Still, if you don't show up in Norway and Xo does, can you imagine how the Queen is going to react? We'll both be lucky if we don't lose our heads."

Christian cracked a smile for the first time in hours. "Who do you think will take the first whack? Xo or my mother?"

Jack didn't answer, but his laugh resounded throughout the back of the plane.

Twenty-Two

"You're a drug dealer, now?"

"What? Xo! That's not how it is at all! Goddamn it, why do you always make me forget what I was going to say. A drug dealer?"

"You look pretty rough, and," Xo gave a discerning sniff, "you smell."

"You would too if you hadn't washed or slept for 48 hours!"

"48 hours?" Xo sounded doubtful.

"13 hours getting to Kabul in the back of an open-air truck, then hours waiting in airports, three different planes, only one of which had seats for us, and then here, to Leticia, specifically where Jack told you to stay out of."

Xo wrinkled her nose. "Aren't you supposed to be in Norway? Wasn't there some family thing you couldn't get out of? Why are you here?"

"To save you."

For the first time Xo didn't snap back a reply. Despite her stillness, something flashed quickly across her face. She stood a few feet from Christian, having turned to face him when she heard him coming up behind her and calling her name. Her eyes had widened at the sight of him, but her voice had been calm when she asked him if he was a drug dealer. Christian knew he looked rough and unkempt. Dirt from Afghanistan was embedded into his clothes, he hadn't shaven in days, and his hair was so windblown and stiff that it looked like a crushed and dented crash helmet. Still, the last thing Christian had expected to be called was something so nefarious as a drug dealer. Dammit, would he ever know what to expect from this woman?

"I thought. . ." Xo said slowly, and then she paused.

Christian waited, his heart thudding inside his chest despite his exhaustion.

"I thought you came here to accompany me to Norway."

"That, too," answered Christian, his voice steady. The two of them stood, staring at each other, and then just when Christian began to think with sinking feeling that he had misunderstood – that Xo saying she thought he was going to accompany her to Norway didn't mean that she was actually going to Norway – everything changed. With graceful fluidity, Xo covered the distance between them and jumped into Christian's arms, wrapping her legs around his waist. Christian held her easily, his arms supporting her weight, as Xo cupped his face with her hands and brought his lips to hers.

To Christian, it was a long drink that quenched a powerful thirst. Her lips were soft and warm, and her body pressed against his was like a home he had never known and never wanted to leave.

"Xo. . .Xo. . ," he murmured each time their lips began to part, but then before he could utter another word, he or she – it was impossible to say, for the both of them were so eager – was silenced as once again they shared each other's breath, a little bit of their soul.

It was Xo who finally pulled herself back. "How about we bathe in the river, and then . . ."

"And then," Christian agreed, reluctant to put Xo down even though he knew soon he would be holding her even closer and more intimately. "Then, and then, and then."

Afterwards, both sated and exhausted in the most wonderful way possible, Christian stroked Xo's back as she lay cupped again him, her head on his chest.

"Tell me about this Reginald Cooper," he said.

"That's not what I thought you were going to say," Xo said languidly.

"What did you think I was going to say?"

"That we're going to miss our flight to Norway if we don't get going."

"That, too," laughed Christian, but then in a sudden motion he moved Xo up so he could look directly into her face. "I'm more concerned with your safety first," he said. "Tell me why you asked Jack about that Cooper man."

"What does Jack know?" Xo's voice was guarded.

"He's working on it. Service has been sporadic and sometimes unavailable, but ever since you called, he's been calling contacts, going through data bases, and doing all that he can. By the time we landed in Leticia, Jack already knew where Reginald was staying, and he went there while I came here, to you."

"I could have told you where he was staying," Xo sniffed. "The most expensive hotel, of course. But he's not paying for it."

"How do you know that?"

"He keeps asking for itemized receipts. It's obvious that he's going to be reimbursed."

"But what is it about him? Why do you want to know about him?"

"There's something off about him. It's as if he thinks he is an expert on frogs because he can identify them by their color, but he's forgotten that the color is only there to let you know what type of poison to put on your darts."

"That doesn't exactly give me a better understanding."

Xo said slowly, "He's just a little too eager. And though he has a pair of binoculars, and he said he was a birder, he didn't know anything about birds. He didn't write anything down, and when I told him a different name for one kind that we saw several times – very distinctive by the way – a turquoise tanager – he never noticed! He acted as if he was taking photos of the birds, but instead he was secretly taking photos of me. With his phone, no less. If he really wanted photos of birds, he would have a better camera or a fancy lens."

"Not so secretly if you know."

"He doesn't know that I know."

"Is he a journalist? A freelancer trying to make some big bucks?"

"I don't know. All I know is that he keeps asking questions about me to everyone he comes into contact with, and he keeps pressing the people at the main desk to get another guide day set up with me."

"Why doesn't he just call and ask you?"

"He can't."

"He can't?"

"He's having difficulty with his phones." Xo didn't bother to hide the satisfied smile that spread across her face.

"Phones, as in plural?"

"He's gone through four," laughed Xo, "and is currently without."

"Four?" Christian said incredulously.

"Two just happened to fall in the water; two I'm pretty sure he thinks were stolen."

"Were they?"

Xo didn't answer Christian's question directly, but she answered it. "I want Jack to look at them. There is no one in his contact list, and I think he tried to delete the number of every call he made. There is a high probability that he never got any photos out, just because he was never in a place with enough service before. . ."

"Before you stole them," Christian said. "Xo, I can't believe you. . ."

Xo said, "I didn't steal anything. I just happen to have them in my possession."

Christian said, "Are you going to return them?"

"After Jack sees them. Maybe." There was a long silence, and then Xo spoke again. "He never went to the police. That's one of the things that bothers me."

"Maybe he was embarrassed. Maybe he doesn't want to admit that he's an easy mark."

The look Xo gave Christian was so disdainful that Christian could only laugh. "Not so fast," he said as Xo began to get up. Christian pulled her back with one arm while caressing her hip with another. "You've got something of mine," he said.

"Do you think I stole it?" Xo asked, curiously.

"No, but you made me lose it."

"What? What did I make you lose?"

Christian didn't answer until once again they lay exhausted, the single sheet that once covered the bed in a tangle at their feet.

"My heart," he said. "But you don't have to return it.

"I won't," Xo said laughing. "At least not yet."

Twenty-Three

"You can't. I won't allow it."

Christian's inability to hide his indifference only infuriated Queen Juliana more. Fighting to control her temper she said as calmly as she could, "The balcony will be crowded enough as it is. What with all the family and the other guests. Constitution Day and the Children's Parade is a sacred tradition. The Royal Family has stood together on the balcony and greeted the Children's Parade for over 100 years. I won't allow you to miss it."

"I never said I wouldn't be there."

"You're not bringing that woman!"

"She's not that woman, Mother," Christian said. "Her name is Xo." His voice was pleasant but steely as he continued. "She's my guest, and either she stands by my side, or I won't be there."

"She can't be." Queen Juliana said, exasperated. Looking at her husband, she said, "This would be a good time for you to help me out, Haakkon. Tell him that she can't be there. Princess Carolina is going to be there. It would be too awkward – only three single adults – you and two women. The press will go crazy. The speculation will be wild. No one will focus on the children. It will be all your fault."

"Carolina isn't my problem," Christian said.

Juliana started to say something, but King Haakkon put up a hand to silence her. "You were born a prince, and with that comes privilege," Haakon said, addressing Christian. "But it also comes with obligation. You will be there on the balcony. You will be there to support your older brother. It is disappointing that you would be so immature as to threaten your mother with a lack of attendance."

Christian stood abashed, for he didn't remember a time past his teenage years that his father had ever rebuked him. Christian was furious, but he tamped down his anger enough that he didn't answer back. Instead, he stood, his body taut and ramrod straight.

Juliana looked pleased, almost smug, especially as the king continued. "Your mother extended an invitation to Princess Carolina, and you will treat her, as we expect you to do with all our guests, well. Remember that it is beneficial to our people that we maintain international relationships. Need I remind you that Great Britain and the entire Commonwealth are valuable allies and trading partners? I will not have a diplomatic scandal due to whom your current infatuation is with."

Christian stared at his father in shock. Never had Christian been lectured about obligation to the crown. It had never been needed. Christian had always accepted that he was the "spare" when it came to the applicable and prudent notion of the royal line needing an "heir" and a "spare" to continue. Not once had Christian expressed jealousy when Oscar was fawned over or given special attention. When Oscar has asked Christian to stand beside him when he married Brigitta, Christian had felt it was an honor. And when both Oscar and Brigitta asked him to be godfather to their first child Alexander, he took the responsibility of being a mentor to the crown prince seriously.

To be accused now by his beloved father of not thinking of the crown, of purposefully doing Norway harm, pained him. Belittling Xo by calling her nothing but a current infatuation only added salt to the wound.

One lesson Christian had to learn while doing surgery in war torn nations was that one could not show fear. If his voice trembled as he asked for a scalpel, or if looked nervously up every time the tent rattled from an artillery shell, then the nurses and all those in attendance would flee in terror. Christian could show no fear, no matter how poor the odds for survival. His remaining calm and optimistic gave those around him confidence. Good leaders didn't need to yell and curse. So, when Christian next spoke to his father, he showed no fear or sign of suffered insult. With the same measured tone that he used when he wanted to instill confidence in his surgical team, Christian asked a simple question.

"Father, would you have married the Queen of England if your mother asked you to?"

Julianna made a strangled sound with her throat, but she silenced herself with a hand over her mouth when Haakkon stood up so abruptly that the chair he was sitting in tumbled backwards onto the floor. Despite the carnage of the crashing furniture, Christian didn't move. He continued to stare steadfastly into Haakkon's eyes as Haakon glared at him. The seconds ticked by, each one seeming to be longer by far than the last, and then Haakkon finally spoke. His words insured that Juliana could not object when Haakkon said that there would be enough space on the balcony for everyone, even an unexpected guest.

"Nothing would have kept me from marrying your mother. I would have gone to the ends of the world to find her."

After a moment of silence, the king and the spare staring into the eyes of the other, Christian gave a single nod of his head. With no other sign of acquiescence, Christian turned and walked out of the room. As Haakkon looked at his youngest son calmly making his way out of the room, as if all they had conversed about was the weather,

Haakkon had a thought that would forever remain unsaid. "He is the son who should have been king."

Christian had initially been irritated that Xo wouldn't stay at the palace with him. She had insisted on once again staying with the elderly widow Rigitza.

"I'll let Rigitza dress me," Xo said. "It will please her, and I'm not going to let you deprive me of the pleasure of making her happy. She's expecting me."

"She's expecting you? So, you were planning on coming all along! Here, you kept me guessing, but you already had decided! Xo, you were playing me!"

"No," Xo said laughing, "Honest. I wasn't sure I was coming until you showed up. That's when it became a sure thing. And that's when I texted Rigitza and asked if I could stay with her. Then she told me to pack light, as she would make sure I wasn't a sartorial embarrassment."

"A sartorial embarrassment?" Christian couldn't help but burst out laughing. "She really called you that?"

"She didn't call me that exactly. She just said she would make sure I wouldn't be. There's a difference."

"Maybe the answer is not to wear anything."

Xo made an exasperated gesture, but before she could say anything, Christian grabbed her hand and brought it to his mouth for a quick kiss. "Whatever you wear, I won't be able to take my eyes off of you."

"I guarantee you along with everyone else there if I'm not wearing anything at all," Xo said dryly. Christian had burst out laughing.

"Then we'll have to trust Rigitza," Christian said, when he could finally control himself.

Christian replayed that conversation again in his mind as he drove to Rigitza's home to pick up Xo. The recollection made him feel better, as he was still disturbed by how his mother and father had reacted when he told them Xo would be joining the family. He was used to being ignored, all the attention and focus on Oscar, and now Christian realized, perhaps he preferred it that way.

He was going to tell Xo that he owed her an apology. She had been right to take care of her own accommodations. Xo was astute enough that she would have quickly picked up on how his parents, and especially his mother, felt. And now that he knew Princess Carolina had been staying with Oscar and his family for a few days and would soon arrive with them to the palace, he was especially glad.

Just the thought of Carolina made Christian clench his teeth. How clever of his mother to have her stay with Oscar at the summer palace beforehand! Oscar got a rise out of being followed by the paparazzi, and there were sure to be new photos of Oscar and Carolina plastered everywhere. Oscar would play it safe of course, always having a child in hand or his wife at his side. Then, when photos of just Carolina and he hit every media outlet, Oscar's press corps could reveal the uncropped photos. Both Oscar and Carolina would come out looking like innocent victims of unrelenting gossip mongers. And, of course, once Carolina was sighted on the balcony next to Christian, rumors about the two royal families joining together would be rife.

Christian was also going to tell Xo that his mother had invited Carolina, and that she was currently staying with Oscar and his family. It was not that Christian felt Xo needed to be warned, it was that he didn't want Xo to think that he knew anything about Carolina's visit in advance.

All these things Christian was going to say, but when he walked into the back garden where Rigitza told him Xo was waiting for him, he couldn't. Instead, he stood, staring like a star-struck teen catching sight of their idol heart throb.

Christian was used to elegantly dressed women. He had attended enough ceremonies and balls throughout his life that ladies in long dresses, long white gloves, and jewelry heavy with diamonds and precious stones was nothing out of the ordinary. Yet Xo, in a simple bright red linen wrap dress, took his breath away. As she came closer, he saw that it was patterned with small white shaped emblems of Norway: the moose, the dipper bird, the cod fish, and the heather plant.

"I refused Rigitza's stilettos, so we compromised," Xo said grinning, lifting a foot so Christian could see her creamy off-white espadrille wedges tied with a ribbon round her ankle. "I'm also forgoing the hat, but Rigitza insisted that she put up my hair, as she objected to my pony tail."

"You're always beautiful," Christian said, unable to take his eyes away, "but . . ."

"But what?"

"You take my breath away."

"As I would do if I had no clothes on," Xo said, laughing.

Christian went over to Rigitza who was standing by the door. "You are a true artist," he said, hugging her. "You captured her essence." When Xo saw how overcome Rigitza was with Christian's compliment, Xo felt a wave of unfamiliar tenderness. Only Christian would have taken the time to compliment Rigitza. Xo could tell by the way Rigitza had reacted that it was moment that Rigitza would treasure for the rest of her life.

With eyes shining, Xo gave a slight lift to the soft folds of material that fell below her waist. "I can run in it, too," she said. "If need be. It's perfect."

The first thing Xo asked as they drove to the palace was, "Has Jack spoken to you? Why isn't he with you?"

"You don't want to ask about me?"

Christian took a quick sideways look at Xo and laughed at the face she made at him. Then looking back at the road, he said, "Jack's meeting with me later this evening."

"With us," Xo corrected him. "He's meeting with us."

"I'm sure he knew you were going to be with me."

Xo was silent for a moment, and then she said thoughtfully, "There's something wrong."

"What do you mean?"

"If there wasn't something wrong, he would have cleared it all by now."

"Xo, I think you might be overreacting."

"No, I'm not."

It was Christian's turn to be silent for a moment. Then suddenly he laughed. "Okay," he said. "I'm willing to wait and see. I apologize in advance for saying out loud you might be overreacting."

"But you can think it?"

"Yes. And I won't apologize for that."

"Okay," Xo said. "Okay."

"One more thing," Christian said as he was waved through the entry gate at the back of the palace. "Carolina's here. My mother invited her. She's been staying at my brother's, and she'll be with us on the balcony. I didn't know."

As Xo stepped out of the car, not waiting for Christian to open the door at her, she turned and spoke to Christian over the top of the car. "No worries."

"Good!"

"In fact," said Xo, "the day has just gotten a lot more interesting." Then, with a deliciously naughty smile, she slammed the door and started walking toward the palace.

Christian quickly caught up to her, grabbed her arm, and leaning down, whispered, "What are you up to? You're not jealous, are you?"

"Jealous of what?" Xo was so surprised by Christian's question that when she asked her own in return, she stopped walking and came to a complete stop.

"Of Carolina." As Xo continued to stare at Christian, perplexed, Christian began to feel foolish. "That my mother prefers her. She wants me to marry her."

Xo let out a bubble of laughter. "Not today, you aren't. Now let's have some fun."

Christian started to say something, but then he realized he didn't know what to say. Instead, he took the hand that Xo was offering him. Once he had it, he took a few steps with her, but then he stopped and pulled her close and hugged her tight. "I love you," he said.

"Right," Xo said. "That's what all good sons say before they watch their mother feed their current infatuation to the lions."

Looking down from their bedroom window, King Haakkon and Queen Juliana observed their youngest child. "He seems quite taken by her," Haakkon said quietly. "I wonder if . . ." He let his voice trail off.

"You wonder what?" Juliana almost snapped.

"If he's met his match."

"He has, but it's not her," Juliana said, sniffing disdainfully at the couple below. That girl, she's not royal material. She never will be."

From a different window, one story below, someone else looked down onto the back courtyard. It was Princess Carolina. When Christian pulled Xo back to him so that he could hug her, Carolina had seen enough. She continued through the hall and into the restroom where she quickly called her sister Rose.

"That damn woman is here. Where the hell is Reggie when we need him? I want him to find out everything he can about that her. The faster we sink her the better."

"Reggie hasn't gotten back to you?"

"No, if you can believe it. Not since Lord Hampton sent him out of the country."

"And you still don't know why?"

"No. He just texted me and said he was going straight to the airport but that he would catch me up later. I left him a few messages, but I think his phone was stolen because all of sudden my messages wouldn't go through so I immediately stopped calling."

"You didn't leave your name or. . ."

"Seriously, Big S? Do you think I'd leave any way to identify myself?"

"Just being careful. I just don't want anything to happen that keeps mum on the throne. The faster the old biddy abdicates, the better for us."

"I know. I know. Why else do you think I'm here? If I marry this spare and you marry a fighter pilot or some other royal commander, she'll think it's safe to step down."

There was a moment of silence, and then Carolina said, "It's just a little unfair. You get to pick a hot dish, and I end up having to spend time with the crown prince and his nerdy wife and child, all to keep my prospective mother-in-law happy. Now that woman, she's a real. . ."

"Careful!" laughed Rose. "But remember that I'll give you permission to get a divorce as soon as the throne is mine."

Twenty-Four

King Haakkon tried to hide his amusement as Juliana threw down the newspapers in anger. Putting down his cup of coffee, he leafed through the pile and read the headlines out loud. "Mystery Nanny," "What Did She Say?" "Nanny with the Magic Cure."

"I don't know why you're upset," he said. "These are harmless."

With a sigh so exasperated that it was theatrical, Juliana tapped her manicured fingernail on a paper near the bottom of the pile. The words "Nanny Lust!" were blazed across the top of the page. When Haakkon simply shrugged, Juliana snapped. "There's more. All these filthy articles on my news feed about how the nanny swooped up Alexander when he was having that temper tantrum, and the minute he was in her arms, he just started to laugh. How amazing she was, and how everyone wants a nanny just like her."

"You were the one who made sure she stood in the back," Haakkon said bluntly, "and you were the one who handed Alexander to Carolina, who promptly handed him off to Xo when he started to flail."

"This isn't my fault!"

"You wanted Carolina to look like a beloved aunt. It didn't work. You should be grateful that Xo stopped Alexander's temper tantrum and made him laugh. We would have all looked ridiculous if he had to be removed from the balcony. We're lucky that the headlines aren't about how spoiled the son of the crown prince and one day heir to the throne is."

"In fact," Haakkon said, his eyes twinkling as he took a sip of coffee, "I only wish that Oscar and Brigitta had a nanny as good as Xo."

"Oscar would just lust after her," Juliana said, and then she put her hand over her mouth in horror. Quickly, she looked to see if any waitstaff was close enough to have heard.

"We have the same concerns," Haakon said, "but it's best not to speak of them."

"I know," Juliana said softly. "I'm so sorry." Then she took Haakkon's hand and spoke in a much lower voice, "It's been an upsetting time. What with all that is going on in Spain. To think that an illegitimate child can now claim the title of princess all due to a DNA test. We have to be much more vigilant than ever before."

"Don't make Xo your whipping girl. Christian will do what's right."

"Oh, dear God, Haakkon, is she pregnant? Is there something you're not telling me?"

"Well, marrying the nanny certainly would make the populace feel closer to royalty!" laughed Haakkon as he set down his cup and left the drawing room.

Princess Rose could barely contain her anger when her sister Carolina entered her apartment at Kensington Palace. "It's all over social media," Rose said, smacking her phone down on the table. "All this crap about the sexy nanny with the magic touch. You buggered everything. Why the hell couldn't you hold that screaming kid? Bollocks I wish you had just thrown him over the balcony!"

"You and me both," Carolina said. "What was the brat doing up there in the first place? That's why there are boarding schools for fuck's sake."

"He's a little young for boarding school don't you think," Rose responded, her anger abating now that she could see that Carolina was as frustrated and upset as she was. Rose lit a cigarette and handed it to Carolina before lighting one for herself.

"I detest children," Rose said between puffs. "I plan to be just like Elizabeth when she was queen. My children will be raised by nannies just like hers until they are old enough to be sent to boarding school. That story about Cousin Charles not recognizing his mother when she returned from one of her tours wasn't heartbreaking. It was proof that Auntie did it exactly right when it came to children – keep them far away and out of your life. If I could have it my way, I'd go with a surrogate. Oh, if only the crown could be so modern!"

"I was just so surprised when Juliana handed that boy to me." Carolina whined defensively. "And then he bit me! Just because I pinched him when he wouldn't stay still. And when I pinched him harder to punish him, he goes all ballistic. I thought it would make that friggin' Xo look bad if she had to hold the screaming pox, but no, he shuts up for her! Gets her all the good press."

"Maybe she didn't pinch him," Rose said dryly. "What did you call her? Xo? What kind of name is that for a nanny? And why the hell wasn't she dressed properly? My nanny is going to be some aged crone whose uniform is a sack. All the style sites are going crazy over her dress. Wasn't she a conniving minx to have all those emblems of Norway on her dress? That was no accident. That was planned."

"She's not the nanny."

"Who then?"

"The woman I told you about before. She was the one who was there the last time I was there. She was the reason I couldn't get Christian alone. She wouldn't leave his side."

"Hmmmm," Rose said thoughtfully. "She hasn't been named yet on anything I've read. The influencers are getting more mileage out of calling her the nanny."

"The stodgy news people are the ones who would find out who she really is, but they don't care."

"Which is why they're all going out of business. They can't accept that the world has changed. Well, we're already a step ahead since you know her name. Now it's time to find the dirt on her so we can bury her."

"How are we going to do that?"

The look Rose gave Carolina was one of contemptuous superiority. "Reginald of course. How soon can you see him?"

"All this attention isn't good."

Xo picked through the papers that Jack had carried in and had placed on the table in front of she and Christian before he sat down. "I'm the nanny?" she asked curiously. "That makes no sense."

"Welcome to royalty," Christian said. "It's all a demented picture show."

Xo shrugged. "No worries. I'll go home, and everyone will forget all about me. I'll just be one of those extras that dies in the first scene of the movie. What do they call them? Extra in a Red Shirt. Doesn't even have a name when the credits are listed."

When Jack and Christian didn't say anything, Xo said, "Trust me, I can melt into any crowd. No one will recognize me. I'm fading already! Lighten up!"

Xo grinned mischievously, but Jack and Christian remained serious.

"Reginald Cooper," Jack said.

Immediately, but so subtly it was almost invisible, Xo's entire demeanor changed. She remained in the same position, but her body became tighter, as if every muscle and tendon was on high alert.

"You're right, Xo, he was ordered to go to Leticia to find out everything he could about you."

"Why? Who ordered him?"

"Lord Hampton."

"Who?"

"Lord Hampton? Lord Hampton, Knight of the Garter, Knight Grand Cross of the Royal Victorian Order, Military Award after military award ad nauseum Lord Hampton of Great Britain?" Christian asked in disbelief. Unlike Xo, his reaction was quite visible.

"Great Britain?" Xo asked, surprised. "Why would some Lord I've never met want to know about me?"

"He is the one who asked Reginald, Reggie, familiarly, to check up on you."

"You've not made anything clearer," Xo said. "You still haven't told me why. Or don't you know?"

"There is a reason Lord Hampton has the string of letters after his name. His entire being has been focused on protecting Great Britain, and to Lord Hampton that means not just its lands and inhabitants. It means protecting the monarchy and the one who sits upon the throne. Lord Hampton feels royalty is not granted. It is a divine right."

"Got it," Xo said. "I get the danger."

"What are you talking about," Christian demanded. "Jack, what is going on? What did you find out?"

Before Jack could speak, Xo started to laugh. "Christian," she said, "this is all because of you. Lusting after the nanny. You're the one that got me into this mess. Lord Hampton wants you to marry

Carolina. He's like your mother. It makes for a perfect political match. I'm in the way."

Jack put up his hand for silence. "Xo, it isn't funny. I don't think you fully understand what kind of man Lord Hampton is. Don't underestimate him. He feels it is his God given duty to protect the throne. Not only to protect it now, but to ensure that nothing ever takes it down. He will do anything to protect it. Anything."

"But I'm just the spare," Christian said dryly. "As is Carolina. I'll never ascend to any throne, and the likelihood of Carolina doing the same is just as faint. There is too much interest in Xo. Something else is going on."

"Perhaps I'm not being clear," Jack said. "Lord Hampton feels he is an instrument of God. The throne is sacred. No manmade law will get in the way of him preserving what he perceives as God's will. Am I making myself clear?"

"So, God wants you to marry Carolina?" Xo asked Christian with an innocent expression her face. Then, when she saw the look of dismay on Christian's, she couldn't contain her laughter. "And you thought I was the one that could help you with a family matter! Seems not!"

"Reginald is sleeping with Princess Carolina."

Both Xo and Christian looked at Jack with astonishment. "What did you just say?" Christian asked.

"Reginald is sleeping with Carolina," Jack repeated.

"Does Lord Hampton know?" Christian asked.

"Does Carolina know that Lord Hampton knows?" Xo asked at the same time.

"Yes and no."

"Yes to what, no to what?" Christian snapped at Jack.

"Yes, Lord Hampton knows Reggie is sleeping with Carolina. No, Carolina does not know that Lord Hampton knows she is sleeping with Reggie."

"Does Reggie know that Lord Hampton knows he is sleeping with Carolina?"

"No. Reggie has plans for advancement. He wants power. Knowledge is power. It can be used to coerce. But Reggie is young and arrogant. He has greatly underestimated Lord Hampton. He thinks of Lord Hampton as a doddering fool who is past of prime. He doesn't understand that Lord Hampton has only grown wilier and more determined as he has aged."

"So," Christian said in a thoughtful voice, "Lord Hampton sent Reggie to Colombia to get him away from Carolina. And diabolical man that he is, Lord Hampton knew that Reggie would try and seduce you, Xo. To Lord Hampton, Reggie was a problem. A problem, but a problem he could use to get rid of another problem. If you and Reggie hooked up, then I would lose interest in you, and be free for Carolina. And if Reggie was with you, Carolina would be free for me."

Xo started to laugh again. "I'm a problem, am I? This gets crazier by the minute! But it's Lord Hampton who has underestimated me. I would never sleep with Reggie. Or anyone like him. I'm much more discerning."

"As am I," laughed Christian. He smiled tenderly at Xo before asking Jack, "Where is Reggie – Reginald, whatever he wants to call himself – now?"

"Meeting with Lord Hampton."

"Wouldn't that be quite the conversation to overhear," Christian said.

"No," Xo said as she stood up. "I could care less. I'm going back to Colombia. Carolina is all yours."

Twenty-Five

"I think you're going to die."

"Well, hello to you, too," Xo said, her voice pleasant.

"This is madness. You should not be doing this. I don't think you know what you are getting into."

"I told you that I would not race again for six months. It's been six months. I'm racing."

"You also told me you were going to win. You can't possibly win. This is not your normal ultramarathon. This is the Badwater 135. Starting point lowest elevation in the entire United States. Death Valley, 280 feet below sea level; ending point Mt. Whitney portal, 8,300 feet above sea level, 135 miles away. Xo, temperatures are going to hit 127 degrees. The asphalt will get even hotter. Your shoes are going to melt."

"I know all about the course," Xo said, her voice just as calm as before. Three valleys, three mountain ranges. I know my shoes will melt. I have extras."

"You know there are no support stations. You have to provide all your own water and ice and food."

"And even bags for human waste. Yes, I know. My support team has them."

"Support team? Everyone else has the maximum four. You have only two, Prince Christian and his bodyguard. One has to drive the car, and the other can't last as a pacer. In this extreme heat, five minutes max, and they are going to have to get back in the air-conditioned car to recover. You're going to have to drink incredible amounts of liquids to prevent overheating, and if you don't replace the salts you lose with all your sweating, you could die, Xo. You could die!"

Raul van Maarten was so upset he turned off his recording device and put it down. "Xo," he said, "You've kept your side of the bargain. You haven't talked to any other reporters. You've invited me to Colombia after this race for my exclusive, but this is not the story I want to write. I don't want to write about what the world has lost.

"I know you're hoping to get a lot of publicity because of people posting things about you and it going viral on social media, but this isn't the way to do it. It isn't worth it. When you drop out – which you will – people are going to draw blood. They'll crush you the way chickens go at those in the yard who show any weakness."

Xo cracked a smile. "How can you be thinking of chickens now? Think about that runner with the one leg who had to drop out after her bone broke through her skin inside her prosthesis. She didn't quit. Entered again and finished."

"Amy Palmiero-Winters," Raul said quietly. "I've met her. I've written several articles about her. Her prostheses heated up to 160 degrees, and she suffered third degree burns. It was years before she could make a second attempt. And yes, she finished, but it took her over 46 hours. 46 hours, Xo. That's well over any of your finishing times. You're can't last. You can't do it."

"I'll finish a bit faster," Xo said, "But I'll think of her when I get tired. For inspiration. You, you just plan on buying your ticket to Colombia."

"I'll do that," Raul said, "but only if you allow me to on your crew."

Xo didn't respond. It wasn't until Raul said quietly, "It will make the story I write all the more powerful," that Xo consented.

It was harder than Xo had expected. The heat was relentless. Breathing hurt. Breathing, inhaling a life-giving source, was supposed to sooth. Instead, each intake of breath felt like she was adding red hot embers to the fire already blazing in her lungs. Xo's skin felt just as hot. Xo wore a white long-sleeved shirt and loose white track pants, but they didn't seem to offer protection. Instead, they gave Xo the uncomfortable and terrifying feeling that she was trussed like a turkey in a baking bag. Her skin was crisping.

"Why don't you call him? He wants to race. Why aren't you calling him?"

Xo stared in astonishment. Rewe was in front of her, maintaining a distance of about twenty feet between them. His feet seemed to melt into a lake of smooth water. His body was defined, in stark contrast to the hazy background behind him. "Heat haze and mirage," one part of Xo's brain explained. "Science can explain it all."

Rewe shook his head a little, looking at Xo with amusement. "You were always slow to accept," he said, though his lips didn't move. "Call him. He wants to run with you. He's been waiting."

"You can't be real," Xo said. "I'm hallucinating. You left me in Leticia. At the missionary school. All alone. You didn't look back." She sped up slightly, her anger at her abandonment driving her forward, but despite her acceleration, the distance between she and Rewe remained constant.

"Hallucinations are real," Rewe said. "You know that."

"But. . ." Xo could not put her thoughts into words. Instead, she only saw images flash through her head. Of feast times and celebrations before the Monkey Sickness. Of Rewe carefully mixing up a special porridge. Of Rewe carefully metering out portions to chosen ones. Of Rewe sitting by their sides talking to them and calming them if they began to tremble or shout. And of afterwards how the entire village would listen as the potion drinkers recounted to Rewe where they had been and what they had seen. And how then that evening, as they feasted, Rewe would remind them how privileged they were to be able to have seen a small part of the unseen world surrounding them.

"I didn't drink. . ." Xo said sadly, feeling an overwhelming sadness. "You never let me."

"Because you were unprepared. But now you're ready. Obviously. I'm here." Despite the distance between them, Xo could clearly see the twinkle in Rewe's eyes.

"He wants to run with you. He's been waiting. Call him." Rewe said before disappearing. "Call him."

"If you can keep this up, you're going to set a course record."

Startled, Xo turned her head to take a quick glance at the man who was running next to her. It was Christian. Or at least it seemed to be. "What world are you in?" Xo asked.

Christian looked over at Xo, assessing her medically. He couldn't get over how unaffected she looked when he knew what a toll this race should be taking on her body. Had to be taking on her body. "Seriously, Xo, are you okay? What world are you talking about? Are you hallucinating? That's a common symptom of dehydration. Do you need another power drink?"

When Xo didn't answer, Christian continued to talk. "Hallucinating at this point isn't that uncommon. One marathoner on this very course saw some green lizards. He said they were fantastic, and they ran with him for quite a while. He also saw a mysterious woman wearing a silver bikini. She rollerbladed in front of him for miles."

"You're not wearing a silver bikini."

"Would you like me to?"

Despite her dry and chapped lips, Xo cracked a small smile. "No," she said. "It's not a good image."

"Somehow, I just can't feel insulted by that comment," Christian said, feeling tremendous relief that Xo was engaging in conversation. "I will never wear a silver bikini, so I have no worries about how I would look in it."

"Christian, I'm fine," Xo said. "I wasn't sure I was going to make it, but now I know I will. Go away please. I need to talk to someone else."

"Raul? You can't. He hasn't recovered from the last five minutes he ran with you. I like him by the way. He's a good reporter. I think he'll do right by you, but then again, with reporters one never knows."

"Christian, you're talking too much," Xo said impatiently. "It's not Raul. It's Koni. He's waiting. We're going to run together. Go," Xo waved a hand at Christian dismissively. Christian started to say something, but he was stopped by the impatient look on Xo's face as she turned her head toward him. "Now," she said. "Step aside."

"What did you say to her?" Raul and Jack, almost in unison, asked Christian after Christian opened the car door and got in.

Christian didn't answer right away. Instead, he guzzled the sports drink Jack had handed him. Even though Christian felt closer to Jack than his own family, he didn't want to admit how readily Xo had dismissed him, especially after what Jack said when he put down the empty bottle.

"Whatever you said, it was the right thing."

"Yes," Raul agreed, his voice almost reverent. "It's like she's gotten a second wind. She's floating. Doesn't look stressed at all. Unbelievable. F-ing unbelievable."

"She's hallucinating," Christian said. "She thinks she's running with someone named Koni."

The three men looked at the road baking in front of them. Xo was the only person in all of its stretched expanse. The heat made the surrounding air shiver, but somehow Xo seemed to be in a different world. She was focused, her legs moving at a steady pace, and she moved with graceful ease. She showed no sign of dehydration or exhaustion.

At Raul's request, Jack moved the car alongside of Xo so Raul could take some photos. "She's laughing," Raul said in disbelief. She's ninety miles in, and she's laughing. Whoever this Koni fellow is, he knows how to make her happy."

Christian tensed. Jack had been with him long enough that he saw the almost imperceptible change in Christian. Raul didn't notice at all. "I'll have to ask her who he is," Raul said. "When I visit her in Colombia. He obviously means a lot to her. Do you think they were lovers?"

Twenty-Six

"He did a good job," Christian said as he handed Xo a copy of the magazine with the article Raul had written. The photograph of Xo laughing on the Badwater course graced the front cover. It was the perfect shot, for it captured the pure joy that comes from running, even when the surrounding world is harsh and lethal.

"You're going to get a lot of donations," Christian said. "It's great publicity. All these photos of local people caring and rehabilitating animals, especially the ones of all the children helping care for them are amazing. And his writing is riveting. How does he describe you? Oh, in so many glowing ways, but my favorite? My absolute favorite? The one that I am sure is going to stick? *Tarzana, Ballerina of the Amazon.*"

"My Tarzana, my Ballerina of the Amazon," Christian said in a too reverent voice to be taking seriously.

Xo threw the magazine down. "Stop it," she said laughing, while at the same time hitting Christian playfully on his upper arm. "You're mocking me."

"Maybe I'm deadly serious."

"No," Xo said, pulling Christian's hand to her chest. "I see that smile you're trying to hide. And I don't care what he called me. He sent enough magazines for everyone he mentioned or photographed for the article to have a copy of their own. He didn't have to. And he wanted to put in more photos of me here in Leticia, but he stuck to our bargain. Only one."

"He picked a great photo," Christian said. "Seriously. You look fantastic. Bare feet, jumping that log, bending so your head doesn't hit the vines hanging down."

Xo shrugged. There was a moment of silence, and then Christian looked at Xo intently. "Raul told Jack and me that he was going to ask you about Koni. He wanted to know if you were lovers."

Xo looked surprised. Then she laughed. "Raul did ask me about hallucinating. I just shook my head and told him that when I run, I am in a different world. If he wants to call that hallucinating, then so be it."

"Were you lovers?"

"That is an inappropriate question," Xo said quietly, a look of unmistakable pain crossing her face. "Especially when you know we weren't."

"I'm sorry," Christian said. "I was wrong."

When Xo didn't say anything, Christian tried to explain himself further. "Xo, I was, I am jealous. I spoke without thinking. It's just I know nothing about you."

When Xo looked at him quizzically, Christian continued. "I mean about your past. I know you grew up here in Leticia. I know you spent some years at the missionary school. But you have never talked about how you arrived there. What went on all those years before you knocked on their door?"

Christian took a deep breath before continuing. "What happened before, Xo? Where did you come from? Who are your people? You were old enough to remember."

"In the article it just says that the nuns raised me. There is no time log. It doesn't say when I arrived. How do you know I was old enough to knock on the door?"

Christian laughed. "Jack, of course. That's why he was so suspicious of you. He said everyone has a past. The nuns couldn't tell him anything. In fact, they would put their fingers to their lips and say, 'A time to keep silent, and a time to speak.'"

"Did they?" Xo said laughing. "Ecclesiastes 3:7! That's what I would quote to them every time they asked me anything personal."

"I know about your love of running, of how you don't ever feel completely home unless you are here in what others would simply call jungle," Christian continued. "But I know nothing about how you came to feel this way. I've been waiting for you to tell me. I wanted you to feel free, to want to tell me. I wanted you to trust me."

"I do trust you."

"Good," Christian said, pulling Xo to him. "Then tell me about your childhood. Tell me about Koni."

Instead of answering, Xo asked her own question. "Does Jack trust me now?"

"Yes! But. . ." Christian's voice trailed off.

"But what?"

"He warned me that my mother would not be pleased. She would assume the worse. That you were some drug lord's bastard."

"That doesn't bother you?"

"Don't insult me," Christian said calmly. "I would never judge a person by their parents or their parentage."

Christian meant what he said. Xo could tell. Christian was a trained medical doctor, his knowledge founded on scientific research and fact. Christian would know that bloodlines had nothing to do with ethics. One's goodness was to be earned. It wasn't granted by a title.

"Rewe would agree," Xo said, meeting Christian's intent look with a warm one of her own.

"Rewe? Rewe would agree to what? Who is Rewe? How is he related to Koni?"

"Rewe would agree that one should not be judged by one's parents. What matters is how we treat the world and all of in it."

"You still haven't told me who Rewe is, but I already like him," Christian said. He didn't say anything more, waiting for Xo to reveal her past.

"I loved him," Xo said softly. "And Koni. I loved him, too." Then slowly, without any pity or complaint, Xo explained who Rewe, Koni, her mother Manuela, and everyone else who had been part of her tribe and family were.

But Xo didn't tell Christian everything. Although she had told him about her daily life, how the world went from dry to wet and back again in wonderful cycle, she didn't speak of what Rewe had revealed before dropping her off at the mission. Xo saw no cause to share with Christian that part of her history. There was no reason for Christian to know that she was only a substitute for Manuela's dead baby. That was still a wound, a wound so deep and open that even now years later, it had not healed. The hurt did not come from being a foundling. It came from being unable to tell Manuela that if Xo had had a choice, Manuela would have been the mother she would have chosen.

"But you were vaccinated. . ." Christian said. "You survived," he said. "Clearly somehow, somewhere, you have a connection outside of what you remember."

"I presume so. I have a small pox scar, and if I was given that vaccine, I assume I got diphtheria, tetanus, measles, and all the rest. Including, of course, whooping cough."

"You have no interest in finding out who your biological parents are?"

Xo shot him an angry look. "No."

"Are you sure?"

"Why wouldn't I be?"

Christian spoke slowly, but without hesitation. "I would. I think most people would."

"I'm not most people."

"No, you're not!" Christian said pulling Xo to him. "And it makes you all the more special." Christian held Xo, her back to his chest, his head resting on her head, his arms around her middle.

"You were fortunate," he said slowly. "You had a loving family. A loving village. You feel their loss. But maybe there are others who feel your loss. People you don't know about."

"Ah, the people your mother will suspect are drug dealers?" Xo asked, a mischievous tilt to her voice. Then turning so she could look Christian directly in the eye, she said, "Your mother may well be right. In fact, most probably. In this case, and by in this case, I mean in my case – everyone's story is their own with their own path to take – I think it is best not to delve into my beginnings. My past – the one that I know – is a good one. If only all could be so lucky."

"You could take a DNA test. You could find relatives. A little bit of detective work, and you might be able to find out exactly who you are."

Xo shook her head adamantly. "You're not paying attention to what I am saying," she said. "I know who I am. I know exactly who I am. And most important, I am content with who I am."

There was silence for a moment, and then Xo's expression became wary. "You haven't. . . Jack hasn't. . ."

"No!" Christian said. "I wouldn't without your permission."

"But would Jack?"

"I don't know," Christian said slowly. "Now that you mention it, it seems a possibility. I could ask him."

Christian expected Xo to be angry. He was ready to defend Jack by pointing out that however Xo felt, Jack was only performing the job he had been hired to do. If he delved into Xo's DNA, it wouldn't be to hurt her. It would only be to protect Christian. Much to Christian's surprise, he didn't have to explain anything. Instead, he needed Xo to start explaining why she had suddenly burst into amused laughter.

"Remember that creep Reginald Cooper?"

Christian felt a hot surge of anger. "He hasn't been bothering you again?" he demanded.

"No, no," Xo said. "I haven't seen hide nor hair. But he did a DNA search."

"What? When? Christ, Xo, why didn't you tell me? What aren't you telling me?"

"Relax, big guy," Xo said, once again patting Christian on the arm. Geronimo – do you remember him?"

"The ten-year old boy who helps Gustavo. The man with all the monkeys and all the other animals he has saved. Of course, I remember him. Why?"

"Reginald asked Geronimo to get some strands of my hair. Said he had to do it without me knowing, and he would pay him 100,000 pesos."

"How do you know this?"

"Because Geronimo told me."

"Geronimo told you?"

"Of course," Xo said. "We take care of each other here. Reginald is nothing but a stinky foreigner. Why would anyone trust him?" Her eyes twinkling mischievously, Xo continued. "I put some strands of hair in a plastic bag and told Geronimo to bargain hard with Reginald. Make him pay at least five times over the initial offer."

"It wasn't worth it, Xo. Why did you do that? You're going to have to have the same test done now. You can't have Reginald knowing something that you don't."

"Oh, he doesn't!"

"What do you mean? You had your DNA analyzed? Is that why you said you know who you are?"

"I told you before I'm not interested."

"But. . ." Christian looked at Xo, and then it was his turn to chuckle. "You put someone else's hair in the bag," he said. "So, tell me, how much did Geronimo get for it?"

Xo clapped her hands in delight. "Geronimo raised him from 100,000 pesos to 500,000!" "About 120 Euros," she said gleefully. "Not a bad price for some hair!"

"Whose hair?"

"A woman's of course. They can tell, I think. No one you know. She's about my age, a mix, like me, living in a village on the Brazilian side. I told her exactly what it was for. She wouldn't let me pay her for it, but I went ahead and paid for her kids' school fees. Geronimo didn't know it wasn't my hair, so Reginald wouldn't have suspected anything amiss by his behavior. It came out well for everyone. And you know what gets even better about all of this?"

Christian could only stare mutely.

"Her father was a drug runner."

Christian, visibly shocked, ran a hand through his hair. "This is all a bit unbelievable. I'm just surprised you didn't mention this before. After all, you asked Jack for help. He would have wanted to know about this."

"He did help, and I didn't need to tell him."

Christian said. "He probably found out. If he traced all of Reginald's actions, he would have tracked down the result of the DNA analysis."

"Right!" Xo said. "So, Jack, your parents, Reginald, and who was it that Reginald worked for – Lord Hampton, and let's not forget who Reginald is sleeping with – the lovely Princess Carolina, probably all know, too! They think they have proof of me being nothing more than a motley mix of poor, low caste, unremarkable and undistinguished genes. I'm okay with that."

"Don't forget Carolina's sister Princess Rose. I'm sure she's in on the rumor train," Christian said. Then he looked at Xo and said slowly, "We're assuming that they all know the results of the DNA analysis. You're assuming that they all have no reason to be suspicious. They all think it is yours. But what about Jack? Do you think Jack knows it wasn't your hair?"

For the first time a look of uncertainty passed over Xo's face. "I don't know," she said. Then shrugging, she said in a tone that booked no argument, "It doesn't matter."

"Unremarkable? Undistinguished?" Christian smiled lazily and nuzzled Xo's neck. "If I were describing you, I'd take off the uns. Then I'd add intelligent, beautiful, determined, gracious, intrepid, and audacious."

"Audacious?"

"Yes. Audacious."

"Is that meant as a compliment?"

Christian removed his shirt and began to unbutton Xo's. "Most definitely," he said. "And it makes you perfect. The most perfect mix ever."

"Good enough for royalty?" Xo asked as Christian threw her shirt on the floor.

"For the spare, at least," Christian said before he lifted Xo's hips so he could remove her skirt.

"Audacious," Xo said, her voice sultry, as she pulled off Christian's shorts. "In and out of bed."

Twenty-Seven

"I thought she would disappear by now."

"Not bloody likely." The baleful expression Rose gave to her little sister Carolina matched her angry tone and words. "Especially now that the *Nanny* has been identified. *Tarzana. Ballerina of the Amazon.* What rot. How do you think she pulled that off? What a conniving bitch. And all that running she does? You know she's on drugs. Probably some jungle dope they don't know to test for yet. No way could she do that on her own."

Carolina sat up and looked at Rose in surprise. "Do you already know what I'm about to tell you? I thought we were in on this together. What happened to Big S and Lil S being a team?"

"Of course, we're a team," Rose said quickly. "What do you know? Did you find out something from Reggie?"

"She might well be on drugs." Carolina couldn't hide the glee from her voice.

"What?" Rose jumped up from her chair and said, "Can you prove it?"

"No, but we have enough. Reggie, at Lord Uptight Hampton's request brought back some of her hair to get it analyzed for DNA tracing."

"And?"

"Ends up she's the spawn of some lowly drug dealer."

Rose wanted to believe it so badly that she felt a warm rush of adrenaline course through her body. Rose, though, was too calculating to give in just yet to her delight. "Did Reggie tell you that? Does he have proof?"

Carolina crowed, "Reggie kept a few strands of hair to himself. So, he knows what Lord Hampton knows. And of course, I know what Reggie knows. You know, I think he thinks I am going to marry him."

"You very well could," Rose said slowly, looking appraisingly at her sister. "After all, he is useful."

Carolina was so surprised that she couldn't speak for a moment. She stared at her older sister, absorbing the words that still seemed to be lingering in the air. "He's useful now, and I'm not married to him," Carolina said slowly. "And what about Christian? I'm better off with a prince. *We're* better off with a prince. You're the one who has said that all along."

"Yes, a prince would be really good for us; I'll marry Christian."

Rose had spoken softly, but Carolina knew her sister well enough to know the decibel belied the resolve behind the words. Rose, in this case, just like she had throughout all of Carolina's life, determined what and how Carolina was to behave. All because she had been born first. It wasn't fair. True, Rose always said she was doing what was best for the both of them, but now, to swoop in and take Christian and leave her with Reggie? Reggie who Carolina would have never slept with if Rose hadn't suggested it?

Suggested it she had – ever so gently, but Rose was the one that said it would be ever so helpful to have a spy in Lord Hampton's office. Rose was the one who said sex was a tool. Rose was the one who said so many times with a smirk that lust was always present, and if one didn't have enough wherewithal to use lust to one's advantage, then the loss was to the prig. Winning took means, and winners used every tool available. Tool using. That's what made winners. And isn't that what separated humans from all other animals? The higher-level use of tools?

All these years Carolina had never doubted that she and Rose were a team. Carolina knew full well the fate of being born second – the spare to the heir. In truth, she hadn't minded it. Carolina didn't want the burden of responsibility. Carolina liked sex. She liked that her sexual escapades were seen as frivolous rather than bringing down a kingdom.

But with Rose's nonchalant taking possession of Christian, something changed. Carolina had been the one to go to Norway. She had been the one to have to feign interest in that country which held zero interest for her. All everyone did was talk about the majestic scenery and other ridiculous topics like, for example, polar bears. Why would anyone care about polar bears, for God's sake? That's what zoos were for. Anyone who wanted to waste their time looking at a polar bear could go there, where wild creatures belonged, safely behind bars.

Rose hadn't had to put up with Oscar, either. Oscar who felt so entitled with his being the first born and heir to the Norwegian throne that he couldn't keep his hands to himself. Even in his own house! Well, palace, but still! Carolina had turned down his advances at first, brushing his hand off of her thigh with a coy smile but nary a word of protest. Did Oscar really think she would be foolish enough to immediately and thoughtlessly jump into bed with him in his own country, his own home, and with his wife and children present, without her knowing how to protect herself first?

So now that Carolina had done all the groundwork, obeisance to whom she thought was going to be her future mother-in-law and allowing herself to be humiliated by Xo who would not leave

Christian's side, Rose was going to swoop in and marry Christian? Where was the teamwork in that?

For the first time in her life Carolina saw clearly what it was. She had been used. And now she was being tossed aside. Even worse, she was being offered up to Reggie. Reggie, the epitome of a whore. He slept with anyone who would give him something. Reggie who didn't love anyone but himself. Reggie who only cared about pleasing himself.

"If I marry Christian," Rose said, interrupting Carolina's train of thought, "it will please mother, father, and even Lord Hampton. It will please them so well, in fact, that mother might step down. I've already talked about it with them. They were absolutely thrilled, and even stodgy old Lord Hampton didn't object. In fact, I'd say he quite admired my political savvy."

When Carolina didn't respond with excitement the way Rose expected her to, Rose continued. "Lil S, we're almost there! I've got it totally figured out. All this mess about Brexit. Everyone is angry and divided. I marry Christian, and it will be seen as healing."

"But Norway isn't/wasn't a member of the European Union," Carolina pointed out. "So how can tying yourself to Norway bring those who wanted to stay in the EU happy? I think you just want Christian to yourself. Why wouldn't you – Norway's sexiest man of the year yet again."

"Carolina," Rose said in patronizing voice, "You're forgetting that even though Norway wasn't part of the EU, it's associated with it through its membership of the EEA. You do know what the EEA is, don't you? The European Economic Area. It always comes down to money, Lil S. I've told you that a million times."

The truth was that Carolina hadn't known what the EEA was, but she resented the fact that Rose was treating her as if she was stupid. Rose always said they were on the same team, but Carolina didn't feel like it now. She sat silently, shoulders hunched, looking down at her clenched hands while Rose continued.

"Partner with Norway, and we keep the people who wanted out happy while strengthening our economic ties to the Union all at the same time. It's a win-win situation. Do you want me to explain it to you again?"

"It wouldn't have to be you."

Rose stared at her sister, perplexed. "What do you mean it doesn't have to be me? Were you even listening to me?"

Carolina flung her head back and stared at her older sister with barely veiled hatred. "It doesn't have to be you who marries Christian. It could be me. I could be the one that unites and heals."

"It could be me," Carolina repeated, and then she did something that she had never done before. Carolina walked away from her Rose. It took all the self-control Carolina could muster not to slam the door behind her, but she didn't slam it. Instead, she closed it quietly but firmly, making sure that it was securely latched before she made her way through the wide and lushly carpeted hall, down the ornate marble steps to the grand foyer, and out to where her favorite wheels, an Austin Martin DB6, was waiting.

Twenty-Eight

"What are you doing here?"

Carolina laughed delightedly. "You look so surprised! Shocked, in fact. I thought you were famous for your charm and poise. Among other things, of course," Carolina said, letting her gaze range appreciatively over the man in front of her. "Aren't you going to tell me you're glad to see me?"

"Yes, yes, of course," Christian said. With a small rueful smile he said, "I just never expected to see you here. I'm surprised, that's all. Are you running?"

Carolina laughed again. "And compete against Xo? You know as well as I do that I would only make a fool of myself. No, I'm here to cheer you both on. Hopefully pass some time together. It's a perfect place for us to get to all know each other better. In Perce, nothing more than a tiny village on the Gaspe Peninsula. The Canadians are such a polite people. I'm not even sure I've been recognized yet, but even if I am, no one is going to harass me. I can't believe I'm saying this, but in a way it's kind of nice to be incognito."

"I know what you mean," Christian said reservedly, masking the fact that he didn't believe her at all. Carolina thrived on publicity. Wasn't she the social media queen of all the royals?

"We're two of a kind," Carolina said, taking Christian's hand and looking at him earnestly. "No one else can understand what our lives are like. Second born. The spare. Always under the shadow of the heir. Still, born to privilege so we better not fuck it up. And we better be there because you know, what if."

"Oh, I understand, Christian said, "but I don't think I've ever heard it phrased with such. . . color," Christian concluded, breaking into a laugh. He was still laughing when he turned, Carolina having nudged his arm with seeming familiarity and nodded at someone coming up behind him. It was Xo.

Before Christian could say anything, Carolina took a step forward, spread her arms wide, and spoke emotively. "You're here! We've been waiting! I've got your tickets. If we leave now, we will get there just in time."

Xo looked at Christian, and though her expression remained neutral, Christian could tell by the stillness in her eyes she was on high alert. Christian wanted to tell Xo right then and there that he had no idea what Carolina was up to, and that her presence was just as much a surprise to him as it was to her. But Carolina had been clever in the way she had spread her arms and welcomed Xo. Just enough that people had turned and paid attention. And that just enough was enough that Xo could no longer fit seamlessly into the environ. The people who had come to participate in the race recognized her instantly, somewhat surprised and unsure of how they had missed her before.

As people began to gather, whipping out cell phones and taking photos, Carolina tossed her hair, smiled, and took both Christian's and Xo's arms so that she was standing between them. Carolina seemed oblivious to the audible gasps and whispers, but, in fact, she was well aware of what made for a better photo, and she missed no measure –

turning her torso just enough to make her waist seem smaller, angling her head so that the contours of her cheeks were enhanced, the size of her nose diminished.

"Oh my God, is it...? Could it be? Yes! It's Princess Carolina! And that man, that's Prince Christian of Norway! And Xo Bosque, did she know she's the Nanny? The Nanny, no? What Nanny? You didn't know? Oh my God..."

This time in a voice only loud enough for Christian and Xo to hear, Carolina said, "Smile, you two. Xo, don't waste this. You'll get more contributions for your reserve. Trust me. This is one thing I'm good at it. And Chris, *Doctors Without Borders* is going to get more notice than you ever got with all those free address labels your organization sends out. Who's the one who thought that up? Don't they know they're just landfill?"

Even though Xo detested the situation she found herself in, there was part of her that was fascinated by Carolina. Carolina's temerity of meeting them here and her brazen awareness of how publicity could be leveraged to one's advantage was astounding. Carolina was a product of her urban surroundings. She had learned to not only survive within its glitzy steel and concrete social strata but to thrive in it, just as Xo had survived and thrived in her world of leafy greens. Whatever personal dislike Xo felt for Carolina, Xo had to pay her grudging respect. Carolina had come at them with full force. She had successfully blindsided them. She had put herself in a situation where she had nothing to lose. Carolina had offered something, and if she or Christian turned it down, they were the ones to look imperious. Worse, ungrateful.

"What is it that there is just enough time to get to?" Xo asked, honestly curious.

"The ferry."

"To Bonaventure Island? The bird colony?" Xo asked, astonished. When Carolina nodded and said, "Of course," Xo told her to lead the way. One of the reasons Xo had decided to compete in the race the next day was because of its proximity to the island bird sanctuary. Miles of trails, unique flora, and over 200,000 nesting birds, 110,000 of which were Northern Gannets. Xo had tried to purchase tickets out to the island, but to her great disappointment she had been unsuccessful, as she had been told that they had all been sold in advance.

As they made their way down to the ferry, Carolina acted as if there was nothing unusual about the three of them meeting up together the day before a 100-mile ultramarathon so arduous that a survival blanket was required and bear bells recommended. "I knew you would want to see it. It's the most accessible Northern Gannet colony in the world. To tell you the truth I didn't even know there was such a thing as a Northern Gannet. I actually thought it was garnets, at first, and was I so confused. A colony of jewels? Now that would be a sight to see, but of course that wouldn't make sense, would it? Come to find out they are nothing but rather large sea birds."

"I knew it was the kind of thing you'd like, Xo," Carolina continued. "And I knew the tickets would be in high demand so I went ahead and got enough for everyone. My detective, of course, and your bodyguard, Christian. He's right behind us. Robinson, isn't it? Your mother told me I'd need a ticket for him, too. She's the one who told me you'd be here. My detective is the woman in the blue jacket, red hair tied back in a ponytail.

"A perfect thing to do the day before the race. We'll get back before dark, so you'll have plenty of time for dinner and an early bedtime. What's your start time? Five in the morning, isn't it? My God, what an ungodly hour. I don't think I've ever been up at five AM ever. Oh, wait, of course I have. All those times when I stayed up all night and hadn't gone to bed yet."

Carolina continued with her nonstop prattle even as they walked onto the wooden pier and toward the ferry. "It's quite small. No cabin. Let's just hope it doesn't. . ."

Carolina never finished her sentence. Instead, she stopped short and stared in shock. Xo followed her gaze and saw a woman sitting primly on a wooden bench. Her legs, draped in tailored slacks, were crossed at the ankles, and her hands were resting on her lap. A cashmere sweater was casually tied around her neck, and her oversize sunglasses only seemed to heighten the fullness of her brightly red painted lips. By her side was a large, lidded wicker picnic basket.

"Hello," the woman said, rising from her seat in a way that reminded Xo of a python unwrapping its coils. "I'm Rose, Carolina's older sister. Xo; Christian; a pleasure to finally meet you. I've been so looking forward to making your acquaintance."

"What are you doing here?" Carolina gasped, her face mottling red with anger.

"To bring lunch," Rose answered, acting as if her appearance was nothing out of the ordinary. Rose then nodded to a woman standing a few feet from her. "Looks like we're all aboard. Tell the captain he can leave now."

As Xo watched the woman walk away, her back rigid, Xo thought to herself, "Rose's bodyguard, or detective as they call them. Christian would never order Jack around like that. Not even a please. I doubt Rose even knows her name. What a horrible person to be ruled by. Or related to."

For the first time since she had made Carolina's acquaintance, Xo felt a little bit of sympathy for her. But all thoughts of Carolina and Rose evaporated the instant Xo saw a huge plume of spray bursting out of the water. "A whale!" she cried in delight. "A whale!"

"A humpback," Christian said.

Xo ran over to the side of the boat to get a better look, and Christian followed her. They were joined by a young man in a grey knit fisherman's cap. "It's a humpback," he said, confirming what Christian said. "We'll spot minke and fins, too. If we're really lucky, once we're further out and closer to the island, we might even see a blue."

"And the birds?" Xo asked, her face lit up with excitement.

"The gannets of course, and there – there are some razorbills. And that, that's a puffin. We'll also see common murres and black guillemots," the young man replied. Xo didn't seem to be aware of the effect she was having on the young man, who with Christian's familiarity to the developing body, had placed as fifteen or sixteen years old, but it was apparent to Christian. Christian grinned, thinking about his own teenage years. He forced himself to stop smiling though when he noticed the anger on Rose's face.

"She's jealous," Christian thought in amazement, "of a teenager!" Then, because he was his father's son, he hid his amusement and walked over to where Rose stood and initiated a conversation with such ease that no one would ever know – expect Jack of course who was watching all with his usual stony face – that to Christian, this was nothing more than practiced diplomacy.

When they arrived at the island, it was obvious that news of the ferry's royal passengers had already spread. It seemed that every tourist, food and service worker, and ranger was milling around the dock. The number allowed on the island at any one time was limited so it couldn't be more than a 100 people. Rose stepped to the side of the boat that was bumping against the pier. Ignoring the extended hand of the deckhand, she smiled at Christian and said, "I'll need your help getting up."

"Of course," Christian said. He stepped onto the pier and held out his hand for Rose. Rose grabbed it, and somehow, she lost her footing and fell into Christian's arms. Rose smiled up at him, knowing full well that cell phones were recording all. Xo, who was standing next to Carolina, heard Carolina snort in disgust. "You know she didn't lose her balance," Carolina said. "She's an excellent sailor."

"Maybe," Xo said, nudging Carolina, "A bird will drop something on her."

Carolina looked at Xo in sheer surprise. "What did you just say?" she demanded.

Xo said nothing, but she smiled and nodded her head ever so slightly while putting a finger to her lips. Carolina's eyes widened, and then she laughed. "Right on her head!" she said. "Right on her head!"

"Let's save her poor detective from that picnic basket," Xo said. As Xo walked over to the picnic basket and bent over to grab a handle, once again Carolina looked at Xo with sheer surprise. It had never occurred to Carolina that anyone would need help with a picnic basket. Picnic baskets just appeared when needed, just as clothes dropped on the floor appeared cleaned, mended, and pressed in one's closet. What would servants do if drinks weren't spilled and sheets didn't need daily changing?

Then without really knowing why, perhaps because for the slightest of moments, Xo had made her feel better about Rose, Carolina hurried over and grabbed the other handle of the basket. She was shocked at how heavy it was.

Twenty-Nine

"What do you mean we should drop out of the race?" Xo hadn't raised her voice, but the ferocity in her tone told Jack that her question was more than a question. It was a demand. Why should she and Christian drop out of the race? It was the Ultra Trail Gaspesia 100. It covered sandy and rocky shoreline running as well as extreme mountaineering. Not that well known, but Xo had been drawn to it because even though it was a coordinated event, it was more of a solo running experience due to scarcity of aid stations, rugged terrain, and fast flowing rivers to cross.

Christian had been the one who had talked it up to her. He had said they could both sign up, and of course run at their own pace (he knew full well he could not keep up with Xo), but the days preceding and following, could be a time just for the two of them. They could spend a few nights in the historic city of Quebec, picnic on deserted coastal beaches, and hike trails in parks they discovered while driving the Gaspe Peninsula.

All that was enticing, but it was the bird colony on Bonaventure Island that had convinced her. True, Carolina and Rose were a complete surprise, and not a pleasant one, but Xo had long learned how to compartmentalize her feelings during her years at the mission school. Nothing could take away her pleasure at something good even if something horrible was going on at the same time. So however acerbic Rose was with her comments and manipulative her maneuverings to separate Carolina and Xo from Christian, nothing could take away from the pleasure of having seen whales break the ocean surface and white fields of gannets sitting on the same nest from the year before protecting their single egg.

"You couldn't have told us that before we had to put with those two women all day?" Christian said angrily. "Jack, what is going on? Are they ruining the race for us, too?"

Xo looked at Christian in surprise. "You didn't like them?" she asked. "But you were so polite. You acted so interested."

"It's my duty," Christian said, the tiniest bit of bitterness in his voice. "I had no choice."

"You had a choice," Xo said, kissing Christian on the cheek. "You chose respect to the crown. To your family. It was the right choice."

"You didn't seem to mind," Christian said.

"No, you're wrong," Xo said. "There was part of me that was jealous. Not of Rose or Carolina, of course. But of your time. Your time spent with them because each second. . ."

"is an hour and each minute. . ." Christian said, taking over from Xo.

"is a day," Xo concluded.

There was silence. The two looked at each other with such a level of intimacy that Jack felt he was trespassing. He cleared his throat and said, "I failed in my job today. I did not know Princess Rose or Princess Carolina would be here. I was not prepared/ am not prepared for all the extra paparazzi that you know will descend on us. Perhaps even by race time. And of course, now that people know you are running, they may be anywhere on the course. I can't guarantee your safety."

"But, Jack, you'll be with me," Christian said. "I always run with you."

"And I can take care of myself," Xo said.

Jack didn't respond. It was Xo who broke the silence. "Is there some reason why you can't run tomorrow, Jack?"

Jack looked so startled at Xo's query that Christian started to laugh. "Jack," he said, "Xo thinks you're too old to do your job."

"I didn't say that," Xo said quickly. "But there's no shame in not being able to run the race."

"Would that be reason enough for you to drop out?" Jack asked Christian.

Christian looked at Jack intently. "Then you'd be lying," he said slowly, "if you said you weren't able to run the race."

"What is it then?" Xo asked.

Jack rubbed his cheek with one hand. "Something isn't right," he said slowly. "I don't know what it is yet, but there are pieces that don't fit together."

"Such as?" Christian had asked a question, but there was no doubt that it was an order to defend one's words.

"A number of things. One: it makes no sense that Princess Carolina and Princess Rose are here. Two: Princess Carolina didn't know Princess Rose was going to be here. Three: Princess Carolina said Queen Juliana told her you were going to be here, but Queen Juliana told me she did not tell them."

"Do you think my mother is telling you the truth?" Christian cut in before Jack could continue. "Speak freely."

"I believe she is telling me the truth. That fact adds to my discomfort."

"But you were concerned enough to ask her," Christian said. Why? True I had you enter us under a different name, but we always do that. Everyone understands. It just keeps my presence low-key, even though I'm always identified at some point during the run."

"I signed up with my own name," Xo reminded them.

"There is one other thing," Jack said. "Number four."

"Which is?"

"There is someone here who doesn't fit."

"Reggie. Is it Reggie? That man who works for Lord Hampton? The one who followed Xo home?" Christian asked. "He could have told Rose or Carolina or both that Xo was running. He's wily enough. Did you see him?"

"No."

"Then who?"

"I didn't notice anyone," Xo said.

Jack looked even more uncomfortable. He looked directly at Christian and said, "It's someone I didn't tell you about."

Jack grimaced when Christian said, "I trusted you. I thought we always told each other what was going on."

"I consider it an honor that you consider me a friend," Jack said, "but I am here to protect you. Your safety is always what comes first."

"Enough," Xo said impatiently. "Christian, you'd be angrier if Jack wasn't doing his job. Jack, just spit it out. Who doesn't belong here?"

Jack couldn't help but grin and shake his head at Xo in admiration. "I like you," he said. "Right to the point." Then Jack explained. It wasn't Reggie, but it was someone else who worked for Lord Hampton. Much higher up and much more secretive. "And that's what worried me," Jack said. "He's so good you never noticed him, Xo. You saw Reggie, but you missed this guy completely."

"Who is this man?" Christian demanded. "What does he want?"

"His name is Colin Smith. Ex MI-5, and I would guess current MI-6." "Military Intelligence," Jack added when he saw that Xo looked confused. Section 5 is the United Kingdom's domestic counter-intelligence and security agency, and Section 6 is part of the Secret Intelligence Service."

"So very secret I didn't notice him," Xo said. "You answered the who, but how about the what – what does he want?"

"It would have been almost impossible for you to notice him, Xo. Even Reggie didn't know he was there. I'm pretty sure he was in town the entire time Reggie was, but I'm not sure. It was sheer luck that I found out about him."

"How did you?" Christian said.

"I met him years ago," Jack said. "Your parents were attending a State Banquet at Buckingham Palace."

"I remember. I didn't go, but Oscar went."

"That's right. You were studying for your entrance exams to medical school and said you couldn't go. That precipitated a visit from this Mr. Smith."

Before Christian could ask why, Jack continued. "Ends up your turning down the invitation made the British Crown nervous."

"What?" Christian's outburst was an explosion of indignation.

"I was alerted that someone had tapped into your phone." Before Christian could interrupt again, Jack put up his hand to stop him. "He never got in. We have several levels of security. I was alerted as soon as the first level was broken. The first level is more of a red herring. A warning to us. But it was an alert. So, we tracked it down, and surprise, surprise, it was not coming from a common hacker."

"Don't tell me – MI-6?"

"I don't know if it ever got to MI-6. Before I could trace it further, Smith shows up. Says he works for a special detail whose sole purpose is to protect the Crown."

"But what does protecting the British Crown have to do with Christian?" asked Xo, her confusion apparent.

"Second son syndrome, was what he called it."

"Now I'm really lost," Xo said.

Christian remained mute, but he shook his head, a pained expression on his face.

Jack explained. "Terms of succession. The king of Norway and his heir at dinner with the Queen at her palace on British soil. The second son invited but refuses to come. A perfect time for something to happen to the first two in line. Not that they cared about Norwegian succession per se. They just didn't want anything to happen on their territory in the vicinity of their Queen."

"Smith was just doing his job. They were just doing their job," Jack said quietly. "It was nothing against you personally, Christian. I reassured Smith, and I never saw or heard from him again."

"Until now," Christian said.

"Until now."

It was Xo who broke the silence. "Jack, why are you so suspicious? Obviously, Colin Smith is here to protect the Crown. He works for Lord Hampton, you said. He's here to protect Rose and Carolina. Let him do his job. Let me go to sleep because I have a race tomorrow."

"He didn't tell me he was here." When Christian shot Jack a piercing glance, Jack explained his cryptic statement. "He should have told me he was here. We're on the same team – protection. If he knows or even thinks something is going down, he should warn me. It's more than curtesy. It's the way we do our jobs. Working together is what makes us so effective."

"Maybe nothing is going to happen," Christian said. "Maybe he's only here for damage control. Why alert you to his presence if he's only here for damage control?"

"Damage control?" Xo asked, trying to contain her amusement. "You really think there could be some kind of international incident at a bird colony? What, you think Rose and Carolina were going to try and steal a bird or something?" "No," she said continuing her musing out loud. "They're not going to fight over birds. They're going to fight over you, Christian! Wouldn't that make for great news!"

Her shoulders still shaking with mirth, Xo crawled into bed and pulled the blanket over her head so she was in complete darkness. She was asleep before Jack had left the room.

Thirty

The race was everything that Xo wanted it to be. Steep trails up and down majestic mountains, stretches on windblown beaches where feet sank deep into sand, and always a brisk nip to the air that instead of making Xo feel cold made her feel more alive. She ran with Christian and Jack the first thirty miles, and then she left them to take her usual spot twenty feet behind the leader.

When Xo crossed the finish line, she laughed with sheer joy. That expression, of pure happiness that come from earned exhaustion, was what was caught on the hundreds of photographs being taken. Noted, too, was the way she immediately turned to face the course so she could congratulate the man coming up a few feet behind her. "We did it! You did it!" she said, raising his hand in the air with her own.

Xo accepted verbal congratulations, and thanked those who made sure to tell her they would be sending money to her forest preservation project. Then, with cheese and a fresh baguette in hand, along with a cup of scalding hot coffee, Xo moved away from the crowd and perched herself on a rock where she could see the finish line. One had to finish in less than 30 hours. Xo, with her time of 21 hours, 35 minutes, and 24 seconds had set a course record. Now she was waiting for Christian. She expected to see him shortly. Just the idea of his coming closer, Jack a few feet behind, made her heart beat faster. "I like this being in love," she thought to herself. "I like it."

Xo waited. And waited. And waited some more.

As the hours passed and more and more runners began to trickle across the finish line, Xo went from surprised, to puzzled, and finally concerned. With a last look at the course, she climbed down from her perch and asked a race official what time Christian had crossed the last check point. Her heart skipped a beat when the official told her that there were no active runners with that name still in the race. Then, with a huge sense of relief, Xo remembered that Christian and Jack always signed up using an alias. She asked the official to look again, but this time for two males who crossed seconds or a few minutes apart.

"No, I've got nothing," the official said, looking at his phone screen. "This list is updated automatically, as soon as a chip is registered. Are you sure they're still in the race?"

It was an innocent question, but it jolted something in Xo's mind. She hadn't seen Rose or Carolina. No sign of them. Were they still here? Wouldn't they want to be here when Christian crossed the finish line? How could she have forgotten about them?

Xo tried texting both Christian and Jack, though she knew it was very unlikely they would get her message if they were still on the course. Her texts did not go through.

"This might be them," the official said. "I've got two males ages 28 and 36 who both dropped out at the same time."

"When?"

"Let me check. Sometime between mile 30 and 40. They checked in at mile 25, but they never got to 50."

"How do you know they dropped out?"

"Someone called it in. Too bad. They were going at a good clip. Probably a fall. Could happen to anyone."

Xo thanked the man and took off running to the hotel. As she ran, all she could think of were Jack's words: *Something isn't right.*

Their hotel was perched on a hill at the edge of town. They had chosen it for its view of the bay. Xo had thought it the perfect location, as it provided them privacy. They had sat on the back porch in the cheap plastic chairs that were part of the hotel furnishings and had feasted on the still hot croissants that Jack had brought from the bakery below. When Xo had licked the last of the crumbs on her fingers, she had sighed in contentment and said, "I feel like we're royalty, here."

"Yes. . ." Christian had drawled. And then Xo had realized what she had said and she started to laugh. Christian had joined in, and he had still been laughing when he pulled her from her chair and put her on his lap. "Royal, indeed," he said, as he had kissed her, long, leisurely, and deeply.

The parking space in front of their room where they had parked their rental car last night was empty. The three of them, Xo, Christian, and Jack had walked to the race start, as it was only half a mile. Was it a good sign or a bad sign that the car wasn't there now? Xo wasn't sure.

Xo's hand trembled as she fit the key in the lock. Jack hadn't liked that the hotel was so old that it still had the traditional doorknobs and keysets rather than electronic entry systems, but Christian had laughed at his concern. "We'll put a chair against the door," he had said.

"You better," Jack said.

Jack had also given them a steel rod to place in the track of the sliding glass door that opened onto their tiny porch. When he had come into the room carrying it, Xo has been astounded. "Just happen to have one of those lying around," Xo teased.

"In the trunk," Jack said tersely.

"Right," Xo said, "You just never know when a steel rod will come in handy. "I've always got one in my handbag."

"You don't carry a handbag," Christian had laughed.

There was no one to laugh with now. The hotel room was empty. Yet something seemed off. As soon as Xo stepped in and shut the door behind her, she knew what it was. To be certain, she surveyed the room, the closet, and the bathroom. Xo's possessions were still there, but all of Christian's were gone. When Xo went through the adjoining door to Jack's room, she found that his room, too, was empty. Unlike the bed that Xo and Christian had shared, Jack's bed was made up. Xo noted that fresh towels and soap had been placed in the bathroom, too.

With a face that hid all emotion, Xo walked across the parking lot to the office with the reception desk. The young woman behind the desk was playing a game of solitaire on her computer.

"A quiet day, then?" Xo asked pleasantly.

"Always," agreed the woman, returning her attention back to the computer screen. "Not much to see or do here," she said, tapping at a key. "Nothing ever really happens."

"Perhaps it's better that way," Xo said.

"Why is that?"

"I believe my heart has just been broken. My man has done a disappearing act on me."

"What?" Startled by Xo's confession, she stared at Xo directly for the first time. "Just now?" she asked. "He left you just now?"

"Gone from my room," Xo said. "Took everything he owned, and the car, too. His friend was in the other room, and he's gone, too. Can you tell me when they left? Did he at least pay my bill?"

"Wow!" the young woman said. "I had a boyfriend who once ghosted me. Never contacted me again. Deleted me from his contacts. Blocked my number. Before him, I thought that there was nothing worse than being broken up by a text message. That's what happened to my girlfriend Andrea. But being stuck with a hotel bill? I think this is a new low!"

Wanting to be helpful, the woman turned the screen so that Xo could see what information she was pulling up on the screen. Both rooms – Jack's and the one she shared with Christian had been paid for. "Well, that's something," the woman said. "He can't be all bad."

"Did he leave any message?" Xo asked. "Who paid?"

"Both rooms were paid for in cash. And no, there's no message for you."

"Did you see who paid for them? When?"

"They were paid for when the keys were picked up. The day you arrived. One set has already been turned in. Do you have a set?"

Xo wasn't surprised that the rooms had been paid for in cash. Jack and Christian both preferred it. Jack always said paying cash meant more anonymity. Credit cards were a trail for paparazzi or other unwanted elements.

"Do you have a set?" the young woman repeated. "I'm afraid I'll have to charge you if you don't. I'm so sorry."

"No, no," Xo reassured. "I still have mine."

"What are you going to do?" the woman asked. "Do you need a place to stay? I could put you up for a night or two."

Xo was so surprised at the woman's serendipitous kindness that she felt overwhelmed. Impulsively, Xo reached over the counter with her hand and gently squeezed the woman's hand. "Thank you," she said. "You don't know how much your offer means to me. I thank you, but I think I'll be okay. I've got a few hours until check out, and by then I'm sure I'll find a car or some way out of this town."

"We girls have to stick together," the young woman said. "I'm going to put my phone number in your phone, just in case."

As Xo crossed the parking lot heading in the direction of her hotel room, she thought about what steps she would take next. By the time she was back in the room, she knew immediately where to start. First, she tried once again phoning and sending text messages to both Christian and Jack. Next, she looked at her news feed to see if there was any breaking news coming out of Norway. Xo knew that Jack would have given her contact information on file or to others who worked with him in security. The fact that no one from the palace had contacted Xo told her that it was unlikely that Christian's whereabouts were unknown or that he was in danger. If he had gone missing, surely someone would want to question her. Even if it was to check that she somehow wasn't involved!

Finding nothing about Norway, Xo began to check for stories about Princess Rose and Carolina. One photograph seemed to have been picked up by every celebrity site imaginable, as well as other more general news publications. Looking at the image repeated in story after story on her phone, Xo, for a brief moment, was able to set aside her fear, worry, and growing anger over Christian's disappearance. "Someone's going to be very angry," she thought as she studied the photograph closely. "Very. Very. Angry."

Thirty-One

"You did this on purpose!"

"Your face is so red! It's all splotchy you're so angry! Oh, you don't look so good. Shall I . . ."

"Don't you dare!" shrieked Rose. With one powerful blow she knocked the phone out of Carolina's hand. "Don't you dare take a picture! Don't you dare!"

Carolina watched her phone skid across the floor. Perhaps quite wisely, she did not try and retrieve it. Instead, she sat down, put her hands up in a placating position and said, "You can't blame this on me."

Rose sat down heavily on the chair next to her little sister. Rose held up the paper so that the large color photograph was visible to the both of them. It was an amazing shot of Carolina taken when they were on the boat on the way to the gannet colony on Bonaventure Island. Carolina was laughing, her hair caught in the wind, swirling in a cloud around her, as she struggled to hold up her end of the picnic basket. The rail of the boat just a black line against the azure blue of the ocean made for a background of vivid contrast. A princess, vibrant and royal, taking delight in the world as all people, no matter their class, should be.

There was no artifice. It could not have been staged. And Rose was nowhere to be seen.

The caption underneath the photograph read: Princess Picnic for . . .?

And under that question was another photograph. It was of Christian. There was no question that he was on the same boat, and it was clear that he was looking in Carolina's direction because of the exact same background rail and water. The look of tenderness on his face was unmistakable. Rose was not in that picture either, but neither was Xo.

There was no caption under the photograph of Christian. There was only the first line of a news report in much larger print than the rest of the story that seamlessly followed. **First Comes Lunch, then comes**. . . could it be marriage for the long single dashing Prince of Norway?

Carolina silently studied the photographs. The one of just herself is what interested her the most. When she spoke, her voice held a trace of wonder. "I look happy," she said.

"What do I care about that?" hissed Rose. "I'm the one going to marry him. In fact, I'm going to tell that to mum at the meeting this afternoon. She'll be pleased. Then I'll work on getting her to abdicate. It's long past time. The old bat."

Carolina remained silent, and Rose, thinking the matter settled, dropped the paper on the floor. "This might work out to our advantage," she said thoughtfully, her lightening quick mood swing nothing out of the ordinary. "When my nuptials are announced, everyone will talk about how the press got it so wrong. They couldn't even get the right princess. It will help clean up both our reputations, as this is proof of how they just want to make up sordid stories about us."

"Good on you, Lil Sis!" Rose laughed. "Now why do you think mum called us back home? I swear, I spent more hours flying in a plane that I did on that God forsaken peninsula!"

"It's part of our Commonwealth, that peninsula," Carolina said softly. "It's not god forsaken."

"What's gotten into you?" Rose said. "All of a sudden you're some kind of diplomat? Next, you're going to be telling me that all those abandoned buildings aren't just rotting. Rather, they're the last standing witness of the cod-fishing industry."

"What?" Rose demanded, as looking at Carolina with the same mischievous expression on her face that she had when she and Carolina were staying up past their bedtime, reading fan magazines underneath the blankets with a flashlight. "I can play the diplomat, too, you know. When I want. Call anything rich architectural heritage, and you've got it covered. I'll be a good queen. Do you know why?"

"Why?"

"Because Lil' Sis, I'll have you there at my side. You're my secret weapon. Any peninsula, any decrepit shack, it's yours for the asking."

Carolina was going to ask Rose what would happen if she asked for more than a decrepit shack. Would that be freely given? But before she could, Rose made a strange gurgling sound and covered her mouth with a hand.

"Rose! Are you okay? You face, its gone white!"

"Sodding scones," Rose said. "The stupid cook must have used something rotten. I think I'm going to throw up. Probably did it on purpose. When I'm queen, I'll fire the lot. A whole new staff, that's what I want. No one with loyalties to Mum or talking about how it was done before."

Carolina was about to say that the scone that she had eaten from the tray that had been brought to them tasted fine, but she didn't have time to comment, as Rose suddenly took off for the bathroom, just in time to sink to her knees and empty the contents of her stomach.

"Just close the sodding door and leave me alone," Rose snapped, when Carolina asked if she could do anything to help.

Carolina obeyed, standing for a moment behind the door she had just closed and listening to her sister's distress. She started to walk over to the tea tray with all of its accoutrements when she heard something rustle under her feet. It was the newspaper with a photograph of her lifting the picnic basket on the boat. Rose, in her fit of anger, had crumped it and thrown it on the floor. Carolina bent down and picked it up. Sitting down on a chair, she smoothed it out and studied it again. It was without question a beautiful photograph. And, indeed, Carolina did look happy.

Carolina hadn't wanted to leave the peninsula, even if Rose considered it God-forsaken. She had liked being with Christian and Xo. She couldn't put her finger on exactly why, but she felt comfortable around the two of them. Less artifice, perhaps, but whatever it was, she felt lighter, as if the air she breathed was freshened, allowing her greater clarity.

Hearing the water in the sink begin to run, Carolina quickly slid the paper under the bed. She would put it in a safe place later, where there was little chance of Rose finding it.

As she stood, ready to do her sister's bidding once Rose opened the door, Carolina had a confusing thought. Rose said she didn't know why they had been called back to the palace. But Carolina knew that it was a phone call Rose made to their mother that had precipitated the order to immediately return home. Rose had made the phone call when they returned from the island. Rose had asked Christian what his dinner plans were. Christian had said that he and Xo had to return to the hotel for an early night, as they had to get up at such an early hour. It was then, as Rose watched with narrowed eyes the diminishing backs of Christian and Xo as they departed, that Rose took a step away and called their mother. She stepped away before

Carolina could hear what was said, and Carolina had never gotten a chance to ask about what was said because of what had happened immediately after.

Rose had come running back to her and breathlessly said, "Mum wants us home. Oh, the biddy's raging at something."

But why had Rose called home in the first place?

Thirty-Two

One by one, King Haakkon made eye contact with those he had called to the table: first, his wife Queen Juliana; second his eldest Oscar who was trying not to yawn; finally, Christian, offspring conceived and born as succession insurance. Christian's face was without expression, but Haakkon could tell that his youngest was seething. Haakkon knew that he would have to tread carefully. The king knew that after this meeting, the family would never be the same. Relationships would be broken. Haakkon just needed to make sure they were not irreparable.

"Thank-you, Christian for coming home."

"He gets a thank you for coming home?" Oscar asked peevishly. "We all bow down in gratitude for his gracing us with his presence? Meanwhile, we're all working while he's out playing tag. Second son gets all the perks and never puts in the time."

"I would advise you not to speak," King Haakkon said. His voice was quiet, but it held force. Oscar opened his mouth to say something, and then he quickly shut it. "Christian's contribution to the good standing of this family is immeasurable," Haakkon continued. "He never spends his royal allowance, always putting it back into social causes. He is always here when needed."

"Why am I needed now?" Christian's voice was steady.

Once again King Haakon had only admiration for his second born. Christian did not show or express feeling. Instead, without fanfare, complaint, or hysteria, he directed the conversation to the problem at hand.

"The Queen of England called me. It was a personal call. She told me something in complete confidence. Her daughter is pregnant."

Oscar sneered. "It was bound to happen. What did she expect?"

Christian, well ahead of Oscar, knew now why he had been called home. He looked at his father and said, "I will not marry either one of them."

Juliana could not contain her gasp of surprise. "Pregnant?" she asked weakly. "Which one?" And then it registered what Christian had said. "Haakkon, what did she want? Why did she tell you?"

"Because she claims that our son is the father."

There was a stunned silence, and then Christian spoke. He looked hard at Oscar. "Is she lying?"

"Is who lying?" Juliana shrieked. "Why are you asking Oscar?"

"Is she lying?" Christian asked again, his glare relentless, as he stared at his older brother.

"Answer him," King Haakon said. "Oscar, answer your brother now."

Oscar seemed to melt in the chair. His face twitched. "I only slept with her once."

"Oh, dear God," Juliana said, her hands raised to her face in horror. "How is this possible?"

"You're the one who had her stay with us," Oscar said, making sure that his mother was partly to blame. "She came on to me."

"But you're married! A father! Your wife is pregnant..."

"Do you really want the details? What good is that going to do?" Oscar replied angrily to his mother. "Brigitta had gone to bed. She's tired all the time now, and she refuses me. I had drunk too much, but Carolina kept filling my glass. When she took my hand and led me to her room, I just couldn't. . . I just couldn't not. I felt terrible about it after. We both did."

"I won't marry her," Christian repeated.

"You slept with Carolina when she was guest in our home?" King Haakon demanded.

Oscar visibly shrunk under his father's ice tome. "I wouldn't say your home exactly.

"All castles are my home. When we had her stay with you at the summer castle we did it because. . ."

"Because you were looking out for Christian," Oscar said bitterly. "Always Christian."

"I won't marry Carolina," Christian said.

"It's not Carolina," King Haakon said wearily. "It's Rose."

"Princess Rose, the Crown Royal?" Juliana said. "But I don't understand."

Oscar seemed to regain some of the air that he has lost when he confessed to sleeping with Carolina. "I didn't sleep with her!" he said, as if he should be applauded for only sleeping with one sister instead of both. Avoiding the disappointed faces of his parents, Oscar looked at Christian with bitterness. "No one knew. I should have never said anything. It would have never come out if everyone wasn't so concerned about who you're going to marry. No one cares who you sleep with. You can run off and sleep with some drug-runner's bastard, but me, no, I always have to think about what's best for the crown."

"I'd be careful about what you say next."

Christian had addressed Oscar calmly. Christian hadn't raised his voice. Yet there was something so lethal in his tone that no one moved. There was complete silence. If a pin had been dropped, it would have been heard.

It was King Haakkon who broke the silence. Clearing his throat, he said, "We should all be careful about we say. What has been said and is said in this room remains confidential. We will be telling no one else."

Oscar's sigh of relief was audible. "Well, then," he said almost smirking.

"Be warned," King Haakon said. "Know, too, son, that if your wife Brigitte ever asks me a direct question, I will answer her honestly."

King Haakkon started to say something else, but Juliana broke in before he could finish. "But why did she call you to tell you Rose was pregnant? Surely Christian. . ." her voice fell off because she didn't know what to think. She couldn't believe Christian would be so careless as to get anyone pregnant. He was a doctor, for goodness' sake, and he knew all about birth control. In fact, he argued for free access to birth control for women all around the world. Whatever faults Juliana felt her second son had, his stance on women's rights wasn't one of them. Truth be told, Juliana was incredibly proud of the way Christian advocated for women's health and control of their bodies.

"What did she want?"

Juliana's thoughts were interrupted by Christian's question. King Haakkon looked at his younger son and once again thought what a fine young man he had grown up to be. Anyone else would have been whining about being pulled out of a race and asked to return home without telling anyone. Instead, he had come immediately. He had asked if Jack could remain behind to care for that woman he was seeing, but when he was told Jack needed to remain with him, Christian had obeyed. Even when his older brother taunted him and tried to pick a fight, Christian had remained stoically focused. King Haakkon gave an internal sigh. If it hadn't been for Oscar's unexpected confession – and oh, what a shocking surprise that was – Christian's question would have already been answered. Christian had waited long enough. It was time to tell him.

"The Queen of England called to apologize. And to warn me."

Juliana sat up in concern, while Oscar just looked relieved that he wasn't the subject. Christian just sat, but he nodded at his father, showing that he was carefully listening.

King Haakkon continued. "Rose is pregnant, as I said before. She says that you, Christian are the father. She says that she will marry you."

Oscar let out a chortle of amusement. "Not so innocent are you, little brother, as you want us all to think!"

Before Christian could respond, Juliana said in a fierce tone. "She warned you, Haakkon? Is she threatening Christian? How dare she!"

For the first time, King Haakon's expression relaxed. Looking at his wife with tenderness, he said, "You sound like a mother tiger protecting her young."

"Of course! No one but no one accuses my son of something he did not do and then tries to foist her ugly daughter on him."

"How do you know he's innocent?" Oscar huffed.

Christian leaned over and gave his mother's hand a squeeze. "You think Carolina is the pretty daughter, then?"

Juliana looked abashed, as she knew what Christian was referring to. She, after all, had tried to set Christian up with Carolina! But then she saw that Christian's eyes were twinkling. "A mother sometimes isn't perfect," she said. "But the love is always there. Always." "Always," she said again, this time reaching her hand out to hold Oscar's.

It was a light hearted moment that brought them all back together. King Haakkon was well aware that it was Christian who had managed it. Christian had known exactly when and how to show forgiveness with lightness of being. It was Christian, again, who brought them back to the matter at hand.

"The warning, Father?"

King Haakon nodded. "The Queen is well aware that Christian could not be the father. She did not tell me how she knew but I would guess that Lord Hampton with all his minions has apprised her of the situation."

"I don't understand. The apology is because of her daughter's lie, but why the warning?" Juliana asked.

"Rose's life has been threatened."

"But what does that have to do with us?"

"Rose's life has been threatened," King Haakkon continued as if there had been no interruption, "as well as the man believed to have impregnated her."

Christian laughed. "Seriously, you brought me back for this?"

King Haakkon said, "Yes, this is serious. Rose said you are the father."

"But royals are threatened all the time," Oscar said. "There's always crazy people out there. Anarchists, mentally ill, you name it."

Christian nodded in agreement. He had never felt threated by the ilk that Oscar had mentioned, but Christian had at times extracted shrapnel and performed other surgeries with machines guns pointed at him. Christian had trained himself not to pay attention. All that mattered was the life of the patient on the table. Focusing on anything else did no good at all.

Christian stood up. "Tell Rose to tell the truth. Since you've taken my phone, I'm going to get a burner."

"You're not to call Xo."

Christian had already started to walk away, but he stopped midstride so he could look at his father. "Why not?"

"This man feels you have wronged him. He wants you dead. He wants to hurt you. Killing someone close to you would be a means. What better revenge that raping and impregnating one's . . ."

"Enough!" Christian said. "Who is it? Or is our supposed British ally not telling all?"

"Prince Anak."

There was a silence so profound and shocking that it was as if sound had never existed. It was several seconds before anyone could speak. It was Christian who broke the stillness.

"Prince Anak of Muta?"

"Yes, Prince Anak of Muta, first born and favored son of King Brei or as he is more familiarly known, the Sultan of Brei. Richest leader in the world. Owner of vast fields of petroleum and natural gas. His son Anak, made Rose's acquaintance while studying in England. Oxford, graduate degrees in engineering. A brilliant scholar."

"But he wants to kill my brother," Oscar said, dryly.

"Passion is a powerful force," Christian said. "Do I talk to him? Has Rose spoken to him? You know I'm not going to go into hiding, Father. And I need to make sure Xo is safe. Because you are right – he would kill her. Make her disappear, but we would know. Perhaps sent a body part. What steps are we planning to resolve this?"

Juliana said thoughtfully, "Whatever we do, we do it united and with great diplomacy. Think about it – a wedding between the British Crown Royal and the favored son of the King of Muta. Do the Brits want a wedding? If Prince Anak becomes King, what an empire! This is a far cry from some prince marrying a commoner and then deciding he is no longer a working royal. This is, why this is momentous. Maps will be redrawn!"

"We know only one thing for certain," Christian said. When everyone looked at him, he said, "If there is a wedding, I won't be on the invite list."

Thirty-Three

Xo stepped off the plane in Leticia and was instantly enveloped by hot humid air. The familiarity of its weight felt like an embrace, and though others may have found it suffocating, Xo found it reassuring. She was home.

Xo had thought about flying to Norway, but after considering all her options, she had decided against it. There was no one in Norway she knew, except of course the elderly widow Rigitza. Although Rigitza would gladly provide a room for Xo, Rigitza would not be able to provide any information about Christian or access to the palace. If the palace had any use for Xo or would have been willing to provide her with any information, Xo knew she would have been contacted.

Xo had to be patient. If Christian ever surfaced, she would find a way to contact him, even if it was only to tell him how he had hurt her, but also how she had recovered from his disappearance. If, however, Christian was victim to circumstance beyond his control, he would know that she would go home. He would know where to find her.

Grabbing her soft pack from the pile of luggage heaped on the tarmac, Xo put it on and made her way to the road. She hadn't taken more than a few steps when she saw someone she knew waiting on his motorcycle. He offered Xo a ride, as long as she was willing to pile on with his girlfriend who was about to get off her shift at one of the airport shops. Xo nodded acquiescence, and soon the three of them, along with Xo's pack and a basket of bananas, were on their way down the single road into town.

Xo said good-by to them at the town's single grocery store. Before entering, she called her main helper Rafael to come and pick her up with her own motorcycle. When Xo had begun to travel and be away for days at a time, she always left the vehicle with him. The agreement was that he could use it as long as he maintained it. The tropical climate was hard on any kind of machinery, and if it had sat unused, there was a good chance that it would not have started again. Wires would have rotted or been eaten, rust would have built up, and snakes, spiders, insects, or lizards could have and would have tried to nest in any pipe or hollow.

Once Xo had made a few purchases, she left the store and moved to a bench in the shade across the street. Even as she began to unshoulder her pack so she could sit down, she knew something was wrong. She had spotted some tanagers in the tree – a mixed flock of yellow bellied and turquoise – and that was where they remained. They weren't flying down and eating the pieces of fruit that someone had put on a home-made and rustic feeder of a board on a pole.

"You, behind the tree," Xo said in a conversational tone but loud enough to be heard, "you're frightening the birds."

There was no response. Minutes passed, but the pieces of fruit on the wooden platform remained untouched. Xo saw Rafael making his way down the lane on her motorcycle, and she stood up. Once again, she spoke in the direction of the tree.

"Those flies buzzing around that tree – they're not houseflies. They're botflies. Perhaps to you they look and sound the same, but one familiar with them can recognize the difference. Judging by how still you stood and how long you waited, quite a few have landed on you or bitten you. Perhaps all depositing eggs. The lumps soon to be appearing on your skin? Some will grow to be as big as grapes. Hard, sometimes painful. Sure signs of the larvae underneath feasting on your flesh."

Xo had no sooner finished talking when Rafael came up to her on her motorcycle. She swung her leg over and found her seat even before he came to a complete stop. She didn't bother to turn her head as they continued on their way past the tree, but only because she knew she had little chance of seeing who had been lying in wait.

Xo remained cautious, but nothing was out of the ordinary when she returned to her little home. All seemed right, with all animal activity and noise as it should be. It was only Xo who didn't feel truly balanced. Try as she might, she could not stop thinking about Christian. Why didn't he contact her? Had he decided they were through? The longer the silence, the more she began to feel like she had been tossed aside. Had she been played with? Was she naught but a toy outgrown and now disposed?

Uneasy and restless with this train of thought, Xo did something out of character. Usually, upon returning to her jungle sanctuary, she remained for some days, sometimes weeks, before going back into town. This time, it was only hours after her return that she found herself making her way back to Leticia. Now that she was unencumbered with luggage and time was at her leisure, she could more easily investigate the shadowy figure behind the tree.

Her first stop was at the mission school where she dropped off bananas, cassava, and a bottle of topical skin ointment that she had mixed up for one of the nuns – Sister Martha – who suffered from psoriasis. "Bless you, child," Sister Martha said, as Xo rubbed some of the ointment on the worst of nun's scaly patches. "I've tried everything, but nothing takes away the rash or eases the pain except what you bring me. I was praying for you to bring me more. I ran out because I shared it with Sister Teresa and some other congregants."

"Shared?" laughed Xo. "I'm betting you gave it all away because you saw others in need. No worries. I'll bring you more. Just let me know when you begin to run low."

"Did that man find you?"

"What man is that?"

"I didn't like him. When I told Mother Maria, she made me say five extra rosaries. If I was younger, I'm sure she would have had me scrub the kitchen floor. There are times, my darling girl, where age and losing one's senility can be a blessing."

Xo looked carefully at the wrinkled face in front of her. Sister Martha gazed back at her with a benign countenance. "Do you remember his name?" Xo asked. "Or what he wanted?"

"He wanted to know about your reserve. But I don't think he cared about it. I think he wanted your land."

"Was he a gold miner? A logger?"

"Oh, that feels good, child," Sister Martha said, smiling at Xo as Xo rubbed some of the ointment on the nun's forearm. "If I were a cat, I would be purring."

"The man, Sister Martha, who was asking for me," Xo gently prodded gently, "Can you tell me anymore about him?"

"I didn't like him," the nun said, repeating herself. "I had to say five extra rosaries. Be quiet, now, or I'll have to scrub the floor."

Xo knew it was useless to press the aged nun for more information. Her moments of clarity were becoming shorter and less frequent, and if Xo continued to ask questions, facts would be mixed with fantasy, the past blended pell-mell with the present.

Xo said her good-byes soon after, and as she walked back toward the center to town, she found herself impatient. Something was amiss, and she was tired of waiting for it. Xo thought of the small frogs that abounded in the dark foliage. Despite their lack of claws or mighty body armor, they boldly advertised what advantage they did have – lethal poison – with their brightly colored skins. It was time for Xo to be as bold.

Xo walked to the town plaza. Once there, she stood on a bench for several minutes so that she could be easily seen. Only after she had turned a few times in full circles, ensuring that there was no mistaking who she was, did she sit down. She would wait. She had time.

It was only a matter of minutes. Xo spotted the man looking at her from across the plaza. He had dark hair, swarthy skin, but more important than the physical features was the way he held himself. He had the same controlled sense of power and command that Jack, Christian's bodyguard, had. He was no typical tourist.

Xo made a motion with her hand for him to come close. It was only when she extended her arm and patted the bench seat with her hand that he made a faint nod with his head and walked toward her. Keeping his eyes on Xo, he sat exactly where she had signaled him to – close enough that they could talk quietly, far enough away that there was space between them. Far enough away that no sharp knife or shiv could be slid into flesh without a warning movement and time to escape.

Xo was expecting some connection to Christian. Ever patient, she began on a completely different topic. "Let's start with the botflies," she said amiably. "Antibiotics aren't going to help. What you're going to have to do is suffocate the larvae. Just smear petroleum jelly over the air hole. It takes about a day or two, but the larva will begin to emerge. Time it right, and sometimes you can see the little worm heads poking out. Give it a good squeeze, and out they pop. Of course, if you don't get all of it, what's left behind rots. Nasty, nasty. That's why people less familiar and a little more squeamish have them surgically removed."

"You're being paid enough, I hope," Xo continued in the same conversational tone, "to compensate for this kind of thing. Will you file it under health insurance or is it part of your hazard pay?"

"I'll remove them myself."

Xo felt a cold chill at the man's stoic response. There was something unnerving about his unflappable composure. Feigning nonchalance, she asked, "Who are you? Why are you here? Am I in danger?"

"I'm buying land."

Xo nodded. "I heard that. For whom?"

"How do you know it isn't for me?"

"Don't play with me," Xo said sharply. "You're a hard man. There is nothing soft about you. You're the type of man who is hired to get things done. Clear the way. No questions asked. You'd slip a knife under your own skin to rid yourself of a parasite as easily as you would slide that same knife across a jugular in some poor tortured soul's neck. Are you working for a mining company? A drug cartel? What?"

"I've purchased 5,000 acres. I have been ceded sole mining rights to 40,000 acres more."

Xo's intake of breath was audible. She knew what roads would do. They would open up the land not only to the large-scale mining operations but also those on a smaller scale. Forests would be stripped, erosion would be rampart, and bodies of water would become polluted cesspools. All those close by and within the same water shed would be unable to escape the effects of mercury and other toxins that mining released into the environment. People would suffer brain and organ damage and memory loss. The harm would not only be to humans. Animals and plants would suffer, too. In addition, roads were a way for illegal loggers and poachers to enter the forest. Once the forest was destroyed, there would be no bringing it back. It was a path with only one direction.

Xo's face was ashen. "To cede those right, someone was bribed. Whomever you work for – they have deep pockets."

"Be careful with your words. Bribery is for nefarious hooligans. It does not speak well of leaders who want money for building and improving infrastructure as well as the national education and health care system."

"Clever words have always been used to mask evil. What do you really want? If you have that much sway, why are you here? With me?"

"It could be held in trust, those mining rights. In perpetuity. Never to be used. Never to be used unless. . ."

Xo looked at the man with narrowed eyes. "Unless what," she said bitterly.

Whatever Xo expected as an answer, it wasn't what was given. She sat there, paralyzed by shock, even as the man took out a sealed envelope and placed in the space between them on the bench.

"Proof of mining rights," he said, as he slid the envelope over to her side. Xo didn't look down, maintaining contact with the man as he stood. The man's own unwavering gaze met her own. "Never to be used, those mining rights," he said, "unless. . ."

It took all of Xo's youthful training in jungle survival to maintain eye contact and keep her body still while the sentence was finished. It wasn't until the man had turned and began to walk away that Xo remembered that she needed to breath. She waited until the man had turned the corner and completely disappeared before she picked up the envelope. Even then, she was so unsettled that her hands were trembling. She didn't open the envelope. Instead, she clutched it to her chest as she began to walk to where she had parked her motorcycle. She would read the papers later, carefully perusing them for hidden details, when she could think more clearly. For now, all she could think of was what might happen to her land and the sanctuary she had dedicated her life to.

"Unless," the man had said. "Never to be used, those mining rights, unless you marry Christian of the House of Haakkon, Prince of Norway. Marry him, and any hope you have of saving that measly piece of forest you call your own will be gone. Completely. There will be nothing but bare soil so poisoned that not even an invasive weed will grow."

Thirty-Four

"She's not answering."

Jack watched silently as Christian threw down the phone in frustration. Jack wasn't surprised at Christian's outburst. Anyone else would have fallen apart long before, but Christian had kept his cool as he had gone through a series of machinations in an attempt to get hold of Xo.

He had tried several burner phones, Jack's personal phone, email, texting, a telegram, and even a hand written letter. Xo had never responded, even when Christian had tried to contact her with the emergency code he had set up. Xo had laughed when he made her memorize the secret password and steps to follow, but Christian had insisted.

All his attempts had been to no avail. It had been days, almost a week, since he had abandoned her on the Perce Peninsula. He couldn't bear to think of what she must think of him. Finishing a race and then coming back to an empty hotel room. What kind of person would do such a heinous thing? He had! He had done it! He was the male beast who hadn't even left her a note. No wonder she was ignoring him. What he had done was unforgiveable.

He knew that. He had to explain. He wanted to tell her that he had no choice. He wanted to tell her that the circumstances were beyond his control. He needed to apologize. He needed to ask for her forgiveness. He would beg, if need be, but how could he right what he had done wrong if there was no one there? It was as if she had erased him.

"There's something wrong," Christian said, pounding the table with his fist. "She wouldn't do this to me! She wouldn't ghost me. I know her too well for that."

Christian stood and said, "I'm going to Colombia. I can't stand this any longer."

"I can't allow that," Jack said quietly. "Don't make me do something I'll never be able to forgive myself for."

Christian felt his rage course through him. In a blind fury, he picked up a chair and hurled it against the wall. It was thrown with such force that it splintered, and it fell in pieces to the floor. The clatter of it falling was enough to bring Christian to his senses.

"Well, that wasn't made to last," he said, shaking his head at the splintered pieces.

"Oh, it lasted for quite a while," Jack said. "I'd say a good 1,800 years. It's an antique. Was, rather. Was an antique."

Christian looked at Jack. "You're serious?" he asked.

"Yes."

"It couldn't be a replica? A good imitation?"

"No," Jack said shaking his head. "I'm pretty sure that what you just destroyed was a medieval box chair. I'd put it a bit before the 13th century. Amazing the carving. So intricate and detailed. Priceless."

"Priceless?"

"Yes, priceless. Absolutely."

"I'd say beyond gluing." Christian couldn't help himself. The tiniest bit of a smile began to form at the side of his mouth.

Jack couldn't help but begin to notice the change on Christian's face. With a sense of great relief, he said, "You were always a clever one."

Christian cocked an eye at Jack, and then he couldn't help himself. He started to laugh. "I can't believe I just did that," he said. "What a mess. What a waste."

"You're being dealt a hard hand."

"Yes, yes, I am," Christian said wearily rubbing his head. "But that's no excuse. And regret won't bring back that chair. Or Xo."

Christian began to clean up the mess, but he hadn't picked up more than a piece of two when he suddenly stopped. "Jack," he said, with great excitement. "You go. You go to Colombia. Tell me she's okay. Tell her I'm on my way."

Jack narrowed his eyes. "You know," he said slowly, "I might be able to arrange that."

"Do it," Christian said. "Tell her I'll come as soon as I can."

"If she's there," Jack said slowly, "I will tell her."

"Thank you, Jack," Christian said. "I thank you not as a prince but as a man."

Jack could not speak. Jack had always felt a sense of pride at having been chosen to protect Christian. Over the years the prince had only garnered his respect, in how he treated people, who hard he worked, and how deeply he cared for his family and country. But the simple words "as a man" resonated with Jack. Christian was asking Jack as an equal. And that sense of equality is what made Christian a great leader. It was why any soldier, and Jack especially, would follow his command.

His jaw tight with determination, Jack didn't trust himself to speak. He gave a single nod of acquiescence, but that was enough.

"Yes!" Christian said, waving a clenched fist in the air. "Yes!" For the first time since abandoning Xo midrace, Christian felt his sense of malaise begin to lift. Jack would tell Xo to ignore the headlines and frenzied reactions on social media. His impending meeting with the Queen of England was nothing more than a discussion about her desire to set up a royal patronage of *Doctors Without Borders*. She had invited him. Christian could not decline. Despite what pundits and royal watchers were suggesting, it was not to finalize nuptials or discuss dynasties. Christian would try his best to make sure of it.

Jack went straight from the plane to the Mission School. He was greeted warmly. When told there was things that needed to be fixed, he laughed good naturedly. "I'll give you a day," he said, "but first I need to see Xo. Can you find someone to take me to her? Or let her know that I'm here."

"Isn't she the popular lady these days," one of the nuns laughed. "It seems everyone wants to find her."

Jack felt a prickling of unease, but he didn't let it show. Instead, all he said was, "Oh?" and laughed.

"All men," another nun commented, gently patting Jack on his upper arm. "Your prince better be careful. He's got a lot of competition."

"But we like him best," the first nun said, "Some of those men, well. . . confession is a private matter."

"Are they still in town?"

"How would we know that? Do you think all we do is sit around and gossip about people's goings and comings?"

"Never!" Jack said with a broad smile. "But I'll just wander about for a while."

"That's the only thing you can do, dearie," said yet another nun, speaking for the first time. "Because you will never find Xo. She will have to find you."

"Which is why I came to you dear sisters first," Jack said, bowing.

Christian didn't bother with salutations. "How is she?"

"She isn't here."

There was dead silence on the other end, but Jack knew Christian wasn't ignoring him. Jack knew that Christian's mind was methodically going through scenarios of what action to take next. That's why, when Christian said tersely, "Tell me what you know," Jack was ready.

"She was here. She met with Raul van Maartin as well as a woman named Lara Tran. Lara is married to Tom Winters. Tom is …"

"I know who Tom is, though I've never met him. He's the one that got her into running races. Why did she meet with them? Is Raul writing another article about her? Do they know where she is?"

"No, but what I do know is that both Raul and Lara came at her request. Xo asked for their help. Ends up someone has been given mining concessions to a huge tract of land. Thousands of acres, with her little sanctuary smack dab in the middle."

"Who?"

"That's what she wanted Raul and Lara to find out. Raul because he's an investigative journalist and has done things like this before. Bribery and government kickback schemes are common ground for him. Lara because she was trained as a lawyer. That's how she met Tom – when she was consultant to some of his initial start-ups. She has a sharp mind, and she loves playing the detective. She's good at it. She can follow a trail through front companies and financial records like a bloodhound."

"Two questions, then," Christian said slowly. "Where did she go?"

"I'm working on that. But there is something else you should know."

"What?"

"There was at least one other person looking for her. A stranger. No one recognized him. He met with her on a bench in the plaza. No reports of anything untoward."

"She's being careful," Christian said. "Broad daylight. Public view. She's well known. Find out what you can."

"Done," Jack said with assurance. "The second?"

"The second?"

"You said, 'Two questions, then.' The first was where she went. What's the second?"

The pause went on for so long that Jack wasn't sure Christina would answer. When Christian finally spoke, his voice was flat, devoid of all emotion except pain. "Why didn't she come to me or to you for help?"

Jack didn't answer. He knew why, and he knew Christian did, too. There was nothing Jack could bring to the conversation that would assuage Christian's guilt. Better to be silent. Jack was not one to provide false reassurance.

To start with, Christian had abandoned Xo. He had left her with nothing but an empty hotel room and nary a word of good-bye. It was true that Christian had wanted to talk to Xo before leaving, but he would have had to battle Jack. Jack had been told that Christian was in possible danger, and the safety protocol he was told to commence did not allow time to wait for someone to finish a race, especially a race where for most of it, there was no cell service. The protocol also dictated Jack taking Christian's phone. There could be no messages sent, as the act of tracing movements or contacts had to be null. Christian knew he had to comply, for he did not know if he was the one at the risk or another member of the family. The protocol had been established to protect the family, and any misstep might cause yet unseen but great harm.

The great harm had been to Xo. The Crown had come first. Xo had been treated as something disposable. That alone was more than ample reason for her not to seek Christian out.

And from that seemingly inexcusable act, it only got worse. While Jack had made his way to Colombia, Christian had met with the Queen of England. It was supposed to have been a secret meeting of diplomacy, but somehow the fact that the reigning head of Great Kingdom had met with a sexy Norwegian prince had leaked out. The media world, print and social, had gone wild. Speculation was heavy that Christian was there only to ask permission, a mandatory prerequisite, to asking a princess's hand in marriage.

The news world loved it – what princess? Rose or Carolina? Bets were being taken for one of the other. Odds went first for Rose and then for Carolina and then back again, undulating like the roar of a crowd watching their team in overtime as they continued to lose and then regain control of the ball. Tea towels, cups, and souvenir plates were already being manufactured, as entrepreneurs were betting on all outcomes. Possible and auspicious dates for Christian's nuptials were headlining news stories.

It was not possible for Xo to be unaware of the frenzy. Xo was an intensely private woman. No matter how desperately she was in need of help, Xo would never go to Christian for succor now that his image was plastered over every form of social, print, and televised media throughout the world. Never.

Thirty-Five

"Scoot over. I'm cold."

"No," Carolina said, groggily trying to keep a grip on the blankets so she could remain curled up in them. "It's too early. Leave me alone. I want to sleep."

"You're going to share those blankets, or I'll take them all."

Carolina appeared motionless, but there was a slight rustle as her hand appeared outside of the covers.

"Don't press the panic button. It would only make more trouble. Be still, and I'll turn on the light."

"Holy shit!" Carolina said, leaping from the bed, just as the light was turned on. "You scared the bejesus out of me! How the hell did you get in here?"

"Do all princesses swear? Or is it just you?"

Carolina stared openmouthed at Xo who was making herself comfortable on Carolina's bed. "Crawl in," Xo said, lifting up the covers. "We can share. You don't want to get cold. I must say, this room is freezing. In fact, the entire castle is freezing. Is it always this cold?"

"I almost wet myself!" Carolina said, her voice shaking. "Look, I'm still trembling."

Xo didn't respond verbally. She just continued to hold up the blankets and pat the bed next to her. Carolina continued to stare incredulously at her very unexpected visitor. Then, shaking her head and because she was cold, she crawled back into bed.

"I never really thought about how much I swear," Carolina said slowly.

"It's hard to have to be an example," Xo said matter-of-factly, "but you are."

Carolina braced herself. She was expecting Xo to now tell her what a poor example she was. In fact, she was so sure that she was going to be lectured that Xo had to repeat herself before she understood what Xo was saying.

"I really like the way this room is decorated. I like the colors. Much better than the bedroom next to this one. Those ghastly pinks. So bright. It was like some disturbed baby doll on acid went at it with a sledge hammer."

"That's Rose's room," Carolina said. "She chose the colors."

"And you chose these," Xo said, looking around again. "They're restful. More you."

No one had ever paired Carolina or anything she had ever done with the word restful. "That's a compliment?" she asked slowly.

"Yes."

Carolina remained silent, mewing over Xo's directness, and then she asked, "How did you get in here? You'd be considered an intruder. How did you get past all the security?"

"Oh," Xo said breezily, as nonchalant as if she had knocked at the castle gate and been escorted up, "I climbed in the window. From the left side of course."

"My bedroom is on the third floor! And why the left side?" Carolina asked, curiosity overtaking her astonishment.

"The security camera has a blind spot on the left."

"Of course. Everyone just happens to know that. I didn't know that! How did you know that? How did you get past all the other security spots?"

"I'll show you if you want."

"No, that's okay!" Carolina said quickly. "I'll take your word for it."

Carolina laid down on her side, her head on the pillow, facing the middle of the bed. Xo did the same, and the two young women looked at each other – Xo companionably, Carolina with a sense of surrealism.

"That was a good photo of you on the boat," Xo said. "I'm glad they printed it."

Carolina thought about how Xo's reaction was so different from Rose's. "I liked it, too," was all she said.

Xo smiled and said, "You're wanting to know why I'm here."

"Well, I am guessing you came to do more than describe Rose's room to me." Carolina suddenly giggled. "Quite vivid and somewhat disturbing, your choice of words. I'm never going to look at that room in the same way again."

Xo didn't say anything, but her eyes twinkled, and Carolina could tell by the movement of the corners of her mouth that Xo was trying not to burst out laughing. Years ago, when Carolina was much younger and before Rose had made fun of her for enjoying them, Carolina had read some books from a series where two young girls wanted to be detectives. They were the best of friends, and they often had sleepovers where they talked and giggled throughout the night. Carolina would read those passages over several times. Carolina had envied the closeness of the two friends. When she had mentioned this to Rose, Rose had mocked her.

"There's a reason that rot is called fiction," Rose had said contemptuously. There is no such thing as friendship. No one helps anyone else unless there is something else in it for them. That's why we have to stick together."

"But all of Mum's friends are her ladies in waiting, and everyone lines the street to see her," Carolina had objected.

"Only because she's queen. If she wasn't, do you think they would walk behind her and pick up after her? Mum doesn't have any friends."

"Being Queen must be lonely, then," Carolina had observed.

"I won't be lonely," Rose had said stolidly. "I won't be lonely because I have you."

It was the thought that Rose needed her that gave Carolina a sense of worth. It made her feel important. It was why Carolina did not object when Rose had tossed the book Carolina had been reading out the window.

Now, so many years later, years of doing Rose's bidding so that Rose would feel she had a friend and not be lonely, Carolina realized with a jolt that Rose didn't care about having a friend. Carolina had never been Rose's friend. Rose viewed Carolina as no one special. Carolina was only one to be ruled over. Carolina was there to be used, to obey, and to show loyalty to the one who one day would be given the crown.

Carolina was 25 years old, but it wasn't until this very moment, right now, that she had ever felt such companionship with another woman. This is what the two budding detectives in her childhood reads had experienced during all their adventures and sleep overs. Rose was wrong. It wasn't fiction! Friendships were real!

"I'm sorry I flirted with Christian," Carolina blurted out. "And it's not me you need to be worried about. It's Rose you have to worry about. She wants to marry him."

"What do you want?"

"Aren't you worried about Rose?"

"No."

Carolina was silent for a moment. Then she said slowly, "You should be. Rose has a way of making people do what she wants."

"If Christian decides to be with Rose, then he was never for me," Xo said. "I'll get over it."

"But you two seemed so perfect for each other. That's partly why I was so jealous. Rose, too. You both seemed so happy together. And Christian. It was as if there was no other person in the world that mattered except you.

"I've never had that feeling about anyone before. I thought Rose and I were close, but not in the way Christian felt for you. The way he looked at you. It was as if you were his world."

"What do you mean? Rose and you are family. You are sisters."

"He puts you first," Carolina said softly. "Rose has never put me first."

"Everyone deserves to be first sometimes," Xo said.

"Only sometimes?"

"Only sometimes," Xo laughed. "And only because there is joy in helping others be first."

Carolina shook her head in disbelief. "Who says things like that? Who believes things like that?"

"My family. They were good people."

"How can drug dealers be good people?" Carolina asked.

The words had sprung from Carolina's mouth without thought of consequence. It wasn't until she had actually heard them being spoken that she realized what she had revealed. She had known about Lord Hampton sending Reggie to investigate Xo. She had known that Reggie came back with hair he believed to be Xo's. Reggie had given some of the hair to Lord Hampton, but he had kept some for himself. Reggie had revealed this all to Carolina, as they lay in bed together amidst tangled sheets, Carolina making murmurs about how the man she was going to marry would never keep secrets from her.

Carolina grimaced and made a distressful sound, but Xo only laughed. "Ah, yes, Reggie and my hair."

"You know? You're not angry?" Carolina asked in a worried tone.

"No. He paid good money for what he got."

"Well, I'd be angry. It's also a little creepy, if you think about it. That someone could know so much about you. Rose couldn't figure out why Lord Hampton was going to such trouble to investigate you, but then there is nothing on that man's mind except keeping the monarchy squeaky clean. He'd whitewash anything just to make the Queen look more Godlike. All he does is lecture us about our behavior. His eyes. He just stares at us in a way that sends shivers down my back. He never sees us."

"What do you mean he never sees you? You just said he stares at you."

"It's the way he looks at us. As if Rose and I aren't really people. Not flesh and blood. Not with personalities and hopes and dreams. We're just temporary shells that the whole Monarchy/God/Royal thing passes through. We're just vessels."

"Now that sounds more than a little creepy!" laughed Xo. "Your description of Lord Hampton is, in fact, quite vivid and somewhat disturbing."

As Carolina looked at the merriment on Xo's face, it struck her once again that this woman who was lying in bed across from her had listened to her. In fact, she had paid such close attention that she remembered Carolina's own words and could say them back to her in a way that united them. Rose only listened when Carolina was giving her the information she had demanded. It was never a fair interchange. It was always a one-sided give and take. And take some more.

It was at that moment that Carolina came to a decision. She sat up. "Let me tell you all I know," she said. "And then you can decide what you want to do or not to do about Rose."

"Before or after I tell you why I'm here?"

Thirty-Six

"I'm not Philippides."

"I know who you are." Prince Anak, favored son of the Sultan of Brei, stared at Xo with eyes so cold they appeared reptilian.

"Right," Xo said. "Of course, you do."

Prince Anak didn't say anything further. He simply continued to stare at Xo with an expression devoid of all emotion. Xo felt a wave of revulsion pass through her. It wasn't natural that a man could look so dead when Xo knew what violent thoughts he was harboring. Taking a deep breath, she spoke quickly, but without faltering.

"Carolina got your contact information from Rose's phone. Carolina gave it to me. Rose does not know I'm here, nor does she know that Carolina asked me to meet with you."

Xo took a deep breathe before continuing. "I have a message for you from Carolina, but before I tell you Carolina's message, I need to say something of my own."

Xo looked directly at Anak, and despite her fear, she moved her chair a bit closer. Xo felt her skin ripple in unease with the closer presence, but she needed to show that she was not afraid. As Rewe had taught her so long ago when it was just the two of them and her people had died of the monkey sickness, *One cannot hide from Evil. One can only face it. And that is a good thing,* Rewe had said, *because then one can be prepared.*

"I'm not Philippides because although I'm a runner and a messenger, I don't plan on dying. At least for a while. Not now, at least."

For the first time Prince Anak's granite exterior showed a crack, albeit a very small one. More akin to a sharp sliver. A small bitter smile crossed his face, and he said, "Do you think he died happy? Full of joy?"

Xo sat back, appraising Anak anew.

"Yes, I know the story," Anak continued. "490BC. Philippides was a messenger. A dispatch-runner. Back and forth, about 350 miles in four days. He died on his last leg, when he ran from the battlefield near Marathon to Athens to announce the Greek victory over the Persians. One legend has it that he cried, 'Joy to you, we've won,' before collapsing and dying. Do you think it was a good death? Do you think Philippides felt joy?"

Xo said calmly, "I told you at the very beginning that I was not Philippides. Precisely because I don't plan on dying."

"You didn't answer my question."

Xo pushed back her chair, rested her chin on her hands and looked directly at Anak. "It was a wasted death," she said. "They won. He could have walked from Marathon to Athens, and it would not have changed the outcome. But then again, he did gain immortality. He is legend. To think that all over the world people are still running marathons – the same distance of his last run. For many, perhaps Philippides himself, that is/was cause for great joy."

"Why is Carolina using you as a messenger?" Anak askes harshly.

Xo grinned. "Actually, I'm using her."

"What do you mean?"

"You're the man with all the mining rights. I don't care about immortality. I do care about. . ."

"Saving the planet and all that," Anak said, dismissing the notion with a disdainful hand flick. Xo didn't argue with him. Instead, she saw quietly, waiting for him to want her to speak. It took several moments.

"I am surprised you know that it was I."

A mischievous grin crossed Xo's face. She wasn't going to reveal that it was Raul and Lara, but she did say, "I have some really smart friends. They had the right skill sets. To be honest, I wouldn't have had the patience. But they loved it. Said it was the best puzzle they had solved in years. Said, too, that it was the hardest puzzle they had ever solved. All your shell companies. It was described to me, and I quote my source, as 'one of the most complicated conundrums they had ever come across.'"

"How much do they know, these sources of yours?"

"I certainly didn't mention marriage to the Prince of Norway to any of them," Xo said. "I only told them I wanted to know who was behind the mining rights. They'll stay quiet for now."

"Is that a threat?"

"You're too powerful to threaten."

Whatever Anak was expecting Xo to answer, it wasn't what she had said. Visibly surprised, Anak exhaled audibly. For the first time he looked like he wasn't ready to explode in anger. "You went to Carolina to get to me. Why didn't you just come to me?"

"I'm nothing to you. But Rose, she means something to you."

"How do you know that?"

"You think Rose wants to marry Christian."

"She does."

"You want her to get what she wants, even if that means she can't be with you. That is true love. It's also not right."

Anak spoke bitterly. "You're just saying that because you want to marry the Prince of Norway yourself. You want to be a princess. You think you're in some magic fairy tale where you run around in your little forest, and then the prince marries you and carries you off to his palace where you live happily ever after. You know nothing of reality. And, you know nothing of stewardship. You think you're noble because you're trying to protect a little piece of land. I have a country, a population, I will be responsible for."

"And a child on the way."

Anak stopped breathing. Perhaps someone else would not have noticed, but Xo did. She stared at Anak intently. "Is everything all right?"

Anak remained as stone for several more seconds, and then his hand clamped down on Xo's arm, holding her so tightly that she knew that if he ever let her go, five bruises, imprints of his fingers, would remain. Through gritted teeth, Anak asked, "Whose child?"

"Yours."

Anak's grip didn't lesson. His eyes malevolently glittering as he stared at Xo. "You're making that up."

"No," Xo said, shaking her head. "Carolina told me. She says it's yours. That's why Rose wants to marry Christian. The baby will come early of course, but if they marry right away, they can laugh about how they couldn't wait. With the right media spin, it can increase their popularity. That they are more relevant, more attuned to the social changes happening with the younger generations, but still wanting to do what is best for their child."

"You just said it was my child."

"Yes, but you're not in line to marry her."

Anak finally released Xo's arm from his grip. She could feel a painful tingling as the blood flowed back through the expanding capillaries, but she forced herself not to show discomfort. "Now," she said, leaning forward and speaking with careful diction so Anak would be sure to take in everything she was saying, "we come to why Carolina sent me to you. What she wants you to hear."

Anak didn't say a word, but he nodded. Xo took a deep breath and said, "Rose doesn't think you have interest in marrying her. She won't risk rejection. She thinks it will make her weak. Carolina says that Rose is only marrying Prince Christian so as to give the child a name. Rose does not love Christian. Carolina says that Rose will get her way and marry Christian because you know how she is if you do not do something."

"There," Xo said, sitting back. "I've played the part of messenger."

Anak didn't say a word. Xo knew that once again Anak had stopped breathing. He sat upright, his face drained of color, his hands resting on the table. Without thought of how presumptuous one might think her, she put her own hand over one of Anak's. "Breathe," she said quietly. "Breathe."

"Now," she said, "I'm going to talk to you as a plain girl. Not as someone wanting to protect her home. Not as a messenger. But as a plain girl. A girl who believes in love. Love because when you lose someone who should still be alive and with you, the pain never goes away."

There was no artifice in Xo's words. She spoke from the heart, surrounded with the memories of Koni, Rewe, and the rest of her people. "You don't want that pain. You love Rose. Don't lose her. Tell her how you feel."

"You're," and here Xo smiled wryly, "two of a kind. You belong together. Go to her. Don't let your pride stop you. Matched, you're formidable. Show your strength by being the one to ask of the other."

Thirty-Seven

The door burst open without the usual quiet knock beforehand. Lord Hampton did not show surprise only because he had trained himself never to show emotion. It wasn't until he had finished perusing the paper he was holding that he looked up. "Yes?" he said, as if there was nothing untoward or unusual with his very unexpected visitor.

"First time in the inner sanctum without being summoned." The speaker's tone was impudent.

Lord Hampton looked over his reading glasses at the woman standing in front of him. Without being asked, she sat down and made herself comfortable. Lord Hampton's first impulse was to reprimand her with an acerbic reply, but then he stopped himself. The woman had taken a chair without being invited, true, but she was not sitting sprawled all over as if she were limp rag doll. Instead, she sat poised, knees together, one ankle demurely crossed over the other.

"To whom do I thank for your visit," he said gravely.

"You are a cool cucumber," Princess Carolina said, shaking her head in bemusement. "Do you ever lighten up?"

"Are you giving me a reason to . . . lighten up?"

Carolina laughed. "Those words – lighten up – sound so wrong coming out of your sour mouth, but kudos for trying."

"Thank you."

Carolina opened her mouth to say something, but she stopped. Lord Hampton looked at her silently, and then he tilted his head just a bit to indicate to her that she was free to speak.

"First time you've ever thanked me," Carolina said, shaking her head in wonderment. "I was all ready to say something else, but I had to bite it back."

"Perhaps you could be a tad more decorous," Lord Hampton said, "and still work on filtering what you say." But then Carolina saw Lord Hampton's face change. He did something that she had never been witness too. He smiled. Albeit, a very small one, but it was directed to her. She had caused it!

It disappeared, quickly, the smile, but Carolina still felt its lingering warmth as Lord Hampton continued. "You are making good effort."

"I'm trying not to swear," Carolina said, immediately wishing she hadn't. Putting a hand over her mouth in mock dismay she said, "I sound like a toddler showing off that I'm out of nappies. Oh sorry. Oh bollocks, oh f. . . I'm doing it again. Spouting off without thinking. I'm. . ."

"Becoming a true Royal," Lord Hampton said in a fatherly tone.

This time Carolina words did not gush from Carolina's mouth. She sat more upright in her chair, her hands lightly clasped on her lap, and she said, "I thank you for taking note. I am trying, but that is not the reason why I am here today."

"And your reason is?"

"I think I've put someone in danger. I'd like your help. I need to make sure they're safe. I've gone over and over in my head about what I've done – or may have done – and what has happened – or may have happened – and who could help, and you're the only person I can think of."

"I see," Lord Hampton said. "May I ask how many other people you've gone to before coming to me?"

Carolina could not help but look a little abashed. "Well, that is why I'm here. You're not thick. You don't miss a trick. Everyone else would have thought they were top of my list."

"Exactly how many people have you discussed your problem with?"

"Right," Carolina said. "You don't care that you aren't first. You just want to know how much I've talked. How many fires I've started that you'll need to put out. No need to worry. I tried to talk to someone else, but they wouldn't talk to me. You're the first person who is listening. Or will listen, I hope. That's why I didn't request a meeting. I couldn't have you turn me down. Safer to barge in. It helps when people expect you to behave badly because when I do, no one thinks it's odd."

"Hmmm."

"Reggie doesn't know."

"You've done one thing right."

Carolina shot Lord Hampton an impish glance. "He has his uses." Taking Lord Hampton's silence as agreement, Carolina continued. "Rose doesn't know either."

"Stop circumventing. Out with it."

"Well, I tried to contact him, but he won't respond."

"He?"

"Christian. Prince Christian of Norway. To be honest, I don't blame him. If I were him, I wouldn't want anything to do with Rose or I, and he's so stuck on Xo Bosque that there's nothing we can do to get him to notice us. Get her to disappear, and things might change. You

195

know who I mean, don't you? That lady who everyone's calling Tarzana of the Amazon. I guess they met at some race, and well, you're not going to get me running a race. Or Rose. Well, I would run a race before Rose, but that's not saying much because. . ."

"Anyway," Carolina said, stopping to breathe, "I can't get hold of him. I need you to."

Lord Hampton's brow furrowed, and Carolina said quickly, "It's not what you think. I don't care about him. Or his disgusting brother. Just the thought of that cad makes my skin shiver in revulsion. But hey, good times. The past is over with. Every morning is a new day. But I do need you to get Prince Christian to listen to me."

It was a rare occasion for Lord Hampton to be confused. Words spoken to him were like a move in chess. Immediately, his brain saw possibilities of the interlocutor's intent, just as the chess master sees moves ahead. Now, in a rare instant, he realized he had no idea what game Carolina was playing. Why would Carolina need to speak to Christian so urgently?

The practiced diplomat, Lord Hampton didn't reveal his confusion. Instead, he relied on his demeanor and silence. Silence, he had learned, often was the key to appearing wise. It was a means of keeping secret what one did not know.

"I think I've put her in danger. Do you think he killed her?"

For the first time in his working life, Lord Hampton had no idea what the conversation was about or where it was going. He felt himself losing his temper. If he had been playing chess, he would have lifted up the board, pieces and all, and hurled it onto the floor. With no game board to vent his frustration on, he instead slammed his fist on his desk. "Enough! You have five seconds to convince me not to have you removed from my office."

Anyone else would have turned ashen in fear, but Carolina continued on as if Lord Hampton had simply taken a sip of tea. "It's Tarzana. I gave her Anak's – you know Anak, the Prince of Muta – the one who Rose has been secretly seeing. I gave Tarzana his phone number. To meet up. To tell him Rose was pregnant."

As Lord Hampton looked at Carolina, it occurred to him that perhaps Carolina wasn't as simple minded as he had always supposed. Was her babbling a front? Was she capable of the same machinations that he had built his career upon? As Lord Hampton's mind raced with possibilities of both trajectories, Carolina continued.

"I did it because Rose doesn't really want to marry Christian. Well, not exactly. She wants to marry Christian only if Anak doesn't want to marry her. Christian is her back up. For her reputation."

"But Tarzana – Xo – has not returned."

"Yes!" Carolina said, clapping her hands. "She hasn't come back. And I know she would tell me what is happening if she could. At least I think she would. I keep telling myself nothing may be wrong. And the only way to know if there is really really something wrong is if Christian can't get a hold of her. He knows more about her than anyone.

"Of course, I understand the palace blocking my trying to get hold of Christian. And Christian blocking my phone, but what if Xo's been kidnapped? You hear about that happening to all those princesses in the Middle East. Of course, Xo isn't a princess, but still, what if she's imprisoned in some dark palace room? And they only feed her once a day, sliding the food on a tray underneath the door? That would be horrible for her. Horrible for anyone, but worse for Xo. She needs the jungle. She needs to be outside more than any of us. You have to make sure she's safe. You have to."

Lord Hampton noted how Carolina had carefully shifted the responsibility to him. "Well done," he thought. "Well done."

"I'll see what I can do," he said.

"I thank you," Carolina said, flashing a dimple at him. Lord Hampton said nothing further as Carolina got up, demurely tucked her handbag over her arm, and walked out. As the door shut behind her, Lord Hampton thought, "She's a clever lass. She knows what she's doing. I know what she wants. She wants to marry Prince Christian. She's clearing the field of competition. Rose is now out of the running. By showing concern for Xo, Carolina gets Christian to see her in a new, benevolent light. She'll charm him with her concern for Xo, all while she makes sure Xo stays happy in the forest. Carolina will leave no one standing. She'll marry Prince Christian before the year is out.

As Lord Hampton thought about how a conjugal bond could unite and strengthen a monarchial dynasty, he raised a hand in toast to the God he followed. Speaking out loud, but softly so that no one else could hear, he said, "Carolina, my girl, I like you. I'm going to help you get what you want. Prince Christian, we'll be meeting you in the chapel!"

Thirty-Eight

King Haakkon stared down at the bed. He tried to mask his incredulousness, but he couldn't. He had been woken from a sound sleep. He had been told it was urgent. He wasn't sure what he expected to see, but it wasn't this. "What does this mean?" he asked, lifting up the blanket and looking at the pillows underneath it.

"It means I didn't do my job."

"You are doing your job. You came to me. Mr. Robinson, what is our next step?"

"I need to find him."

"Yes, Mr. Robinson, that would be a good start." King Haakkon pulled the blanket back up over the pillows. "Last time he did this he was eleven years old. No one knew he was missing for hours. It was what precipitated your hiring."

King Haakkon looked at Christian' bodyguard assessing him anew. Despite the objections of his security team, King Haakkon had been the one who had insisted on the hiring of Jack Robinson. Although Jack was only 20, just eight years older than Christian, the king had thought Jack's youth a plus rather than a detriment. Jack could keep up with Christian, and if what the king sensed in Jack to be correct, Christian would come to like and respect his bodyguard. Loyalty would begat loyalty.

The naysayers had said that Jack would grow bored. He would leave for perceived greater glory on a battle field, or he would become tired of the constant following and soon desire a more stable domestic setting. Instead, the king had been proved right. An affinity between the young prince and the young soldier had grown so strong that at times words were not needed. They subconsciously anticipated what the other would do or how they would react, and the two of them would adjust their behavior accordingly. In addition, Jack had shown his mettle more than a hundred times over. When Christian had become involved with *Doctors Without Borders* and insisted on working on front lines, the king knew that if anyone could keep Christian alive it would be Jack. So it was that when he asked if Christian left on his own or if there could be something more sinister to his missing, he knew he could trust Jack's answer.

"No, he was not kidnapped."

"Then, why?"

"He was upset yesterday. He wouldn't tell me why."

"Do you usually check on him this early, Mr. Robinson?"

Jack shot the king a startled look. "No," he said. He started to say something, but then he hesitated because he didn't want to sound unprofessional.

"Speak freely," King Haakkon said, acutely aware of Jack's sudden reticence.

"I can't explain it. I just woke up and knew something was wrong. I immediately came in to check. At first glance, all was well, but even though he appeared to be under the covers, I still felt a sense of malaise. So, I came closer and that's when I knew."

"Is he in danger?" King Haakkon kept his voice calm, all emotion tamped down, but he could feel his heart beating with extra adrenaline.

"I think" Jack said slowly, "he's racing to it."

There was a measured silence. "Then find him," King Haakon said. "Find him before it's too late."

Thirty-Nine

"It's been two days. How long are you going to keep me here?"

Prince Anak studied Xo appraisingly before he answered. She was not like any other woman he had ever met. She exuded confidence, but not brazenly. Earlier, when he had told her he wasn't going to let her leave, she hadn't shown any fear, at least outwardly. Not even a tremble. Instead, she had nodded, and said, "If that helps you, then. I'll explore the city during the day."

It had never been Prince Anak's intent to let her out of the palace walls, but there was something in Xo's manner that made him reconsider. Her words tipped the scale. "I won't run off; you know full well. Not when you own the mining rights."

Anak had expected Xo to object when told she could only leave the palace with a guard, but she had merely shrugged and said, "As you wish."

"The reason I'm asking," Xo said, "is because I've decided what we are going to do."

Anak sat back. "Okay. You've got my attention. What are we going to do?"

"We're going to have a race. Well, several races. A 5k, 10k, 30k, 50k, and 100k. All on the same day. Men and women. Lots of prizes. A water bottle of some kind of apparel that you approve of for everyone who signs up."

"Women?" Anak was visibly stunned.

"Of course, women," Xo said. "One wears a hijab on one's head, not one's feet. There's no reason why a woman can't run. Everyone feels better after a good run. Think about it, this race can help unite people. Help your country. Open it up to outsiders, if you want. Make it something people plan ahead to come for."

"It might just work," Anak said slowly. "Women," he said again, shaking his head, "women." Then he looked at Xo and said, "My people will organize it. You won't be needed."

"But you're going to include women? You have an opportunity here that you shouldn't waste." Xo started to list all the merits that came from women running, but Anak stopped her.

"Enough," he said. "Women will be included. I'm not allowing you to be involved with the set up because you are going to run. You'll be a draw. I can't have you knowing anymore about the course than any other participant. You can't be seen as being given an edge."

"You're not as horrible as I was led to believe."

Anak stared at Xo. In his entire life, no one had ever spoken to him so bluntly. "I can't believe you just said that," he said.

With eyes twinkling, Xo said, "I can't believe I said it, either. It just slipped out."

"Compliments don't and won't work with me."

"I know that," Xo said. "And threats don't and won't work with me."

"My threats aren't idle."

There was a brief silence while the two looked at each other. Xo felt like saying that she didn't waste her time giving idle compliments, but she didn't. "Noted," was all she said quietly. "Noted."

"I'm waiting," Anak said.

Xo looked at Anak with a quizzical expression. Anak couldn't help but smirk, unable to hide the pleasure he felt at seeing, for once, Xo not in charge of the conversation or sure of where it was heading.

"I'm waiting," he repeated, and then seeing that Xo was not going to ask again, he explained what he was waiting for. "For someone to react."

Xo felt an unsettling in her stomach. "Why a reaction?" she asked. "Why not someone to answer?"

"Words aren't always truthful."

"It's a hard world to live in if you have no trust in what you hear," Xo said thoughtfully. Then she added, "A lonely world, too."

"It's a curious thing," Anak said, studying Xo anew, "but you resemble them a bit."

"That's a change of topic!" Xo grinned. "Whom do I resemble?"

"Princess Rose and Princess Carolina. Not in the way you act, of course, but there are some faint similarities."

Xo shrugged. "If you say so." Then she said, "I took a leap of faith. I trusted Princess Carolina. That's why I came. Are you going to just wait for this someone to react? Why would you do that? What are you afraid of? Why don't you just talk to them? Are you afraid of rejection?"

"Be careful."

The ice-cold chill in Anak's voice would have inhibited anyone else from continuing on the same line of topic, but Xo wasn't daunted in the least. "What is it with all you royals and keeping secrets?" she snapped. "Stop playing games. Just out with it."

"Out with what?"

Xo threw up her hands. "What to do with the baby! Tell Princess Rose how you feel! Do you love her? Do you want to marry her? Let her know your intentions. Woo her or walk away. If you want a future together, it is going to have to be you to make the first move. You know that because Rose has already set her safety plan in motion. She's not going to ask you to marry her because she's afraid of being told no."

"Do you think the baby's mine?"

Xo took a deep breath. "You'd have a better idea than me," she said. "But if it means anything, I believed Carolina. That's why I'm here."

"Or are you here because I have the power to destroy everything that is of value to you?"

Xo grinned mischievously. "Why bother to say – you're the one that said words can't be trusted."

Anak leaned his head back and laughed. His phone buzzed, and still chuckling, he bent down and looked at it. He stopped laughing immediately. His face became so rigid that if Xo had not seen the transformation spread over his face and body, she would not have believed Anak capable of showing anything but menace.

"What is it?" she said, forcing herself not to shiver. "What is it?"

"What we've been waiting for," he said coldly. "The reaction."

Forty

Years ago, at a time before the Monkey Sickness, Koni had been attacked by a Harpy Eagle. The encounter was so terrifying that it was indelibly etched on Xo's brain.

Harpy Eagles are colossal raptors, and there are no other eagles in the world with bigger, stronger talons. Monkeys are easy prey for these apex predators, and Rewe had told stories of seeing one eagle carry away a deer that was larger than the eagle itself.

The dry season had set in, and the waters was beginning to recede and give the land back to the People. The main river was still full and fast, but the smaller tributaries were beginning to disappear, leaving pools that grew black and stagnant as they became smaller and smaller until finally disappearing. The caimans that inhabited them grew fat on the trapped fish, but as the pools evaporated and the fish became scare, the caimans became more dangerous. The black ani birds that warned of their presence called more often, and the monkeys and capybaras grew warier, ever more nervous about what could suddenly grab hold and drown them.

Xo and Koni had run along the main river just a short while before deciding to turn off and follow one of the small streams feeding into it. They had run along that rivulet, following it even as it grew narrower and shallower and more of a trickle. They stopped when they came to its source – an unsavory, dark puddle of water.

"There's a snake – an anaconda!" Koni said, pointing to a dark slithering mass. "It's too large to fit in the water!" In great excitement, Koni stepped closer to the water's edge. He squatted, his back bent over, and that was when Xo saw a medium sized caiman dart out on the opposite side of the water from where Koni was.

"I see it," Koni said. "It's running from the anaconda!"

No sooner had the words left Koni's mouth, when the anaconda shot out of the water and grabbed the tail of the caiman with its sharp, curved teeth. The caiman thrashed and spun, but it could not escape the great snake's hold. Koni and Xo watched mesmerized as the snake began to wrap its muscular body around its victim to asphyxiate it before swallowing it whole.

The danger didn't come from the caiman or the anaconda. Those two animals were too intent on their own fight for survival to take notice of two small humans. No, the danger came from a direction that Xo and Koni were oblivious to – above.

The Harpy seemed to appear out of nowhere. Its massive wingspan covered Koni in shadow, and then, still on the wing, the eagle had driven its talons into Koni's back. Koni looked at Xo in shock, the pain so great and the ambush so unexpected that he didn't know yet what was happening.

As Koni was being lifted off the ground, Xo acted without thinking. She threw herself onto the back of the Harpy and began to pound with her fists at its head. Startled at the unexpected assault, the bird turned its head to look at what brazen being or thing was attempting to interfere with the natural order of the jungle.

It could not have been more than a split second, but it seemed time immortal as Xo and the huge bird looked directly into the eye of the other. Xo saw the bird's pupil dilate, but she met the unblinking stare with one just as hard and long. She did not think about how the bird could easily rip off her nose or tear off a cheek with one swipe of its powerful beak. Her mind was dark. She had no thoughts. She could only stare into the endless black tunnel of the raptor's eye.

Then the magnificent bird slowly blinked, and somehow, Xo knew it was over. She rolled off the animal's back at the same time that the predator opened its talons and released Koni. As the bird took off in search of an easier meal, Xo and Koni lay in a mingled heap on the muddy ground.

It was Koni who acted first. "The snake," he said, separating himself from Xo and standing, "the caiman." He kept his eye on the water as he gave a hand to Xo and helped her stand.

"It's as if they were never there," Xo said, wonderingly. Then looking at Koni's back, she said, "You're really bleeding."

"And you look a little battered, yourself," Koni said.

"Yes," Xo said. There was nothing she could do about their bruises, but she made sure to clean Koni's puncture wounds as well as cover them with a poultice made from special leaves before they started back home.

"You did well," Rewe said approvingly to Xo as he examined Koni's back. "You were right not to seal the holes."

"You taught me that," Xo said. "With that kind of wound, you don't want to trap the bad inside. It has to heal from the inside out."

It was a lifetime ago that the Harpy had come out of nowhere. It was a different person who had stared into the black tunnel of its dilated pupil. Circumstances had put Xo in a different world, forcing her to adapt in ways she could not even begin to imagine. She was no longer a young girl balancing on fetid mud that edged a pool of dark stagnant water. Now she was a grown woman, standing on a hand knotted rug worth tens of thousands of dollars draped over a marble castle floor.

Different times, different environs, but Xo had an eerie sense that she had lived it before. They were all there – the anaconda, the caiman, and the Harpy. Just in human form.

Forty-One

Anak was the snake. He was surrounded by wealth, but his castle, instead of being filled with light, was nothing but a walled pool of darkness and unhappiness. Anak had made it that way with his misery and meanness. He went after all he felt were blocking his way with razor teeth and crushing muscle.

Xo was the caiman. Not because she was cold-blooded or reptilian but because she was trapped in Anak's grasp. Her fate was unknown. Anak could make her disappear. He could wipe her existence from the planet as easily as one could swipe one's finger across a phone screen to delete a message. Her reserve would follow. It would be swallowed by his mining operation before anyone was aware that it was gone. It would be as if she and the reserve were never there.

Christian was the Harpy. Xo knew this because of the look he gave her. His dilated pupils were the same endless black tunnel of the eagle, and just as before, she could not look away.

"Are you all right?"

Christian's appearance was so unexpected and so shocking that it took a moment for Xo to realize he was talking to her. "Are you all right?" he said again, his hard stare still unbroken by a blink.

It was Christian who was speaking. Xo knew it had to be Christian who was speaking. But Xo had the strangest feeling that the Harpy Eagle was there, too, as it overlaid on top of Christian, ready to disappear with one sweep of its powerful wings.

"Do you think I slept with her?" Anak taunted.

Anak's words were enough to shake Xo from her hypnotic stupor. She turned her head from Christian so she could look at Anak. "Grow up," she said.

No obscenities. No threats. No asking. Just two simple words. Words one would say to a child who knew better.

It was possible that nothing else could have been said that could have altered the situation so immediately. The anger that filled the room, the aggression bristling from both Anak and Christian just seemed to disappear. It lifted so quickly that it was as if the air had become lighter. One could breathe more freely.

"What did you just say to me?" Anak said, shaking his head in disbelief.

Christian answered, and as he spoke, it was obvious that he was trying not to laugh. "She told you to grow up."

Anak turned and spoke to Christian, but in a tone loud enough for Xo to know that he clearly meant for her to hear. "Is she always like this?"

"Worse," Christian replied. Christian spoke so amiably that it was as if he had just met up with a best buddy, and the two of them were catching up on what they had been up to. "And not only that, she's a better runner than I am."

Anak made a choking sound. "I'll be glad when she's gone," Anak said.

"I'm hoping to take her with me," Christian said, nodding agreeably.

Xo had listened to the two men with increasing disbelief. It was as if she wasn't even the room! They were speaking about her as if she had no right or reason of her own! Her indignation rising, she opened her mouth to say something. The words never came out. For at the very moment that she was going to protest, she saw something out of the corner of her eye. It was a slight motion of Christian's hand. It didn't last more than a fraction of a second, but Xo knew it was a warning. She should stay silent.

Xo met Christian's eyes, and once again she saw the Harpy Eagle's black dilated pupils, transparent like a clear film, but there. Was it part of Christian? Was it a warning? Was it a sign that just as the Harpy so long ago had disappeared, so would Christian? Disappear yet again as he had in Canada on the rugged peninsula, leaving her without notice or sign?

"I'm here for Rose." Christian had spoken quietly, but there was power in his voice. He didn't look at Xo. Instead, he moved toward Anak, but he stopped after several steps. Perhaps another person might not have noticed it, but Xo was aware of it. Whether by conscious choice or just by happenstance, Christian had separated Anak from Xo. Christian had placed himself so that if something came at them, he would be in the first in the line of assault.

As for Anak, he had undergone the same transformation that Xo had been witness to before. No longer was there any sign of amusement in his being, nor any banter in his voice. Rigid, a throbbing tic pulsing down his cheek, Anak stood so abruptly from the chair he had been sitting in that it tipped over and went crashing to the floor.

Christian didn't flinch. "It's your child," he said. "I'm not going to raise your child."

Anak's eyes narrowed, and his entire body tensed like an iron spring. He clenched his fists so tightly that Xo was sure he was going to pierce his own flesh.

"The child needs you," Christian said. "You," he repeated the word with emphasis. "The father."

Whatever Anak has expected Christian to say, it wasn't what was said. The look of confusion that spread across Anak's voice was so in contrast and incongruous to the tautness and anger in his body that it was almost comical. If it had been Koni or any of her People, Xo would have burst out laughing. They all would have. They would have turned it into a dramatic story – the snake who only shed part of his skin.

"Why don't you marry her?" Xo asked, deciding to break the silence as it seemed the two men were waiting for the other to speak first.

"She's going to marry him," Anak said, staring at Christian with malevolence. His voice rasped, but Xo felt, more than heard, an undertone of agony.

"It doesn't mean you can't be part of the baby's life," Xo said. "Children aren't all or nothing." Xo thought of the way every child was cared for with her People. There was a special bond between mother and child, father and child, but the child knew that care and love came from every member of the family. A family that was not just kin, but a family that extended to the entire community. Every cooking pot had food for every child.

Xo couldn't help herself. She felt an overwhelming sense of nostalgia. She ached for all the people and the love who had once surrounded her. Now here was this yet to be born child, and everyone was already fighting over who was going to claim it. What about the child's well-being? Who was fighting for its best interest?

Xo clapped her hands just once, but very loudly. It was enough that the all attention was drawn to her. "I'll take it," she said.

The two men stared at her. "Take what?" Christian asked.

"The baby. Someone has to care for it who doesn't give a fig about whose it is and who is going to claim it. What's wrong with all of you people?"

Anak started to say something. He opened his mouth, but then he closed it. Xo's eyes flashed, and she shook a finger at him. "Don't you start with me," she said. "I'm sick of royalty. You all have money and riches and houses of ridiculous sizes. And what do you do with all your privilege? You worry about your title! You worry about getting even more money! You worry about nothing that matters! Nothing."

"What a waste of privilege," Xo said, shaking her head. "What a waste of good."

Xo was quiet for a second, and then she walked toward Anak. She didn't stop until she was close enough to touch him. She looked him directly in the eyes.

"Enough," she said softly. "Enough."

Xo put a hand up and gently placed it on his cheek. "I'm going home," she said. "I'll raise the child with love."

Xo began to lower her arm, but Anak seized her wrist. He held it tightly, his fingers grasping so firmly that Xo knew her release would only be at his will.

"It's not as simple as you make it sound," he said. "You have no idea."

Xo put her free hand on top of Anak's hand, the hand gripping her own. "You need to let me go," she said. "I don't belong here."

"You're right," Anak said, releasing her. "You don't belong here."

"She can go, then." It was Christian who spoke, the force and tone of his voice changing the words phrased as a question into a statement.

"You will stay." Anak said, addressing Christian.

"She goes," Christian said.

Once again Xo felt like she was being left out of a conversation that was bordering on absurd. "Why don't we all go?" she said. "Let's go see Rose and Carolina. Have a real party."

Xo meant to be sarcastic, but somehow, by the time she finished talking, she didn't want to be sarcastic. She meant what she said. Although, of course, her use of party was intended as a formal noun – a social gathering of invited guests. But its use could just as easily be an informal verb. All those princes and princesses in the same room together? Wouldn't that be a wild time!

"If you give me back my phone," Xo said to Anak, "I can ask Carolina."

No one spoke for a moment, but then Anak looked over at Christian. With a bemused expression on his face, Christian made a shrugging gesture. "I won't say no," he said.

Anak stared long at hard at Christian. But when he spoke, he looked at Xo. "Yes," he said, very slowly. "Yes, we should all meet."

Forty-Two

"I'm going to be rich. Richer than Mum. Richer than you'll ever be."

Princess Carolina looked over at her sister who stood before the mirror assessing her figure. "You barely show," Carolina assured her. "And yes, you'll be so soddin' rich that you'll never want for anything."

"Wouldn't it be something if Mum or Parliament had to come and ask me for a loan?" Rose sighed contentedly at the thought as she pressed a hand over her belly.

"Would you give it?" Carolina asked, curiously.

"It depends," Rose said, turning so she could see herself at a different angle in the mirror. "I'd make them crawl first, that's for sure." Satisfied with her appearance, Rose came over and sat next to Carolina who was on the window seat in Rose's sitting room. "You know," she said with a smirk, "I'm probably the most famous person in the world right now."

"Without a doubt," Carolina said. "You're a princess. You're pregnant. And you are heir to a throne you may very well turn down."

"And nothing," Carolina continued, nudging Rose in the side, "and nobody is going to take your place. At least not till Mum dies. The bookies already have odds on whether you'll abdicate or not."

Rose smiled smugly. "I know," she said happily. "Even Anak wants to know, but I told him that's a decision we can wait on. For now, we have to focus on our child."

"Would you?" Carolina asked.

"Would I what?"

"Abdicate?"

"That depends," Rose said.

"You don't want me to be Queen?" Carolina asked.

Rose looked at Carolina dismissively. "That wouldn't matter. I'd still be a queen, just of a different country. And I'd have more money than you. You'd always be the one who was second choice. Only queen because of me. Sorry, Lil S, but that's what comes with being born second. Any photo of the two of us, and I'll always be the headliner."

"I do want to thank you, though," Rose said to Carolina, as if her words were a present, "for telling me that we should include Lord Hampton in all the negotiations. I never thought I would never say a good word about him, but he's been instrumental. A sharp cookie. Nothing gets by him."

"Yes," Carolina said, nodding. "He's the one who insisted Anak has to be made King before you even think of renouncing your standing, and he's the one who said you needed to go public with the pregnancy. It's thanks to him in part that you and Anak are now the world's most romantic couple.

"Your wedding is not huge. It's more than that. It's the wedding of the century. It's the initial rite of a modern all-encompassing monarchy. People are already fighting over invitations. So many tea-towels have been printed up that they could stretch around the world several times over if laid end to end. And the fact that it is happening so soon – in six weeks rather than in a year – only makes it bigger news and the invitations more coveted."

Rose smiled happily. "I know," she said. "I know!" "And did I tell you," Rose continued, "that Anak says his father wants to know if the child is a boy. If it is, and it's healthy, he will step down and let Anak take the throne. So that means Anak might be king in less than a year. Hardly any time at all as Prince Consort. No wasted 70 years like that poor Prince Philip. King and a kingdom so wealthy that no one but no one in the world will have more money than me sooner than you can blink an eye!"

"Is it a boy?"

Rose nodded smugly. "Yes! Though I haven't told anyone yet."

"Not even Anak?"

Rose laughed. "Why would I? Right now, I have the upper hand. I'll tell Anak when I need some leverage. Now's the time to focus on the wedding. Then we'll see if Anak really becomes King. Then we see how long mum lasts."

"You'll have options, that's for sure," Carolina said. "To think that being Queen of Great Britain and Head of the Common Wealth is your back up plan!" Carolina couldn't help but repeat herself. "Your back up plan!" she said, in amazement. "Your back-up plan!"

Rose put her hand under Carolina's chin, lifting it so Carolina had to look at her. "Don't worry, Lil S," Rose said softly. "I'll always look after you. I always have."

Forty-Three

Even the running didn't help. Xo had been running since early morning, and the sun was now at its apex. She hadn't gone at a leisurely pace, either. She had pushed herself hard. A run of that length and clip should have gotten the endorphins flowing. It should have triggered a positive feeling. It should have made her feel better. Instead, she still felt the sense of malaise that she had woken up with.

Realizing that the running was to no avail, Xo slowed her pace until she got to the riverbank. There, she cooled herself in the water before making her way back home. She walked slowly, following the river, but staying a bit back from the edge so as to remain in the shade.

I'm here for Rose.

Those were the words that Xo couldn't get out of her mind. They kept repeating themselves on an endless loop. *I'm here for Rose. I'm here for Rose.*

That's what Christian had said. Anak had refused to let Xo leave, treating her as some kind of bait. Yet Xo hadn't been needed.

Christian would have come anyway. He told Anak that, and Xo was there to hear it. *I'm here for Rose.*

Yes, Christian clearly wanted her out of the picture. He had asked if she was all right, true, but after that there was nothing. Just a *she can go then* before an argument about not being willing to raise another man's child.

She can go then! Well, she had. Anak had given her phone, and while he watched, she had texted Carolina. "Call me."

Carolina had responded immediately, and to show that there were no hidden machinations going on, Xo had put her phone on speaker without being asked. She also told Carolina as soon as she answered what she had done and that both Anak and Christian were present.

Carolina was the one that made it all happen. She told Anak how relieved her sister would be. That Rose needed to talk to him but was afraid of what she might lose if she asked. She thanked Christian for showing such responsibility to the monarchy. She said that all would be resolved when they sat down together, and the sooner the better. In fact, she had already met with a certain somebody – a diplomat from the Queen's Court – who had a meeting place already set up.

Anak's face had darkened when Carolina had mentioned a diplomat, but he didn't say anything to fill the silence when Carolina stopped talking. Xo, sensing that a meeting might not happen, stepped in. She chose her words carefully because she knew Anak was the weak link. He would not participate in anything he viewed as harmful to his image. A diplomat unschooled in negotiation could easily ruin any chance of reconciliation. To Anak, everything was about keeping face.

"Carolina," Xo said, "I'm worried about privacy. Where are we meeting exactly, and who is this diplomat? How do you know he can be trusted?"

"Quite honestly," Carolina said, "I'm not sure I like him. In fact, I don't like him. But that's not what's important. You don't pick a surgeon because you like their looks. You pick a surgeon who you trust with a scalpel. Hampton's a cold fish, but he's no fool. He keeps secrets. He doesn't reveal them."

"Hampton?" Christian asked. "Lord Hampton?"

"Yes," Carolina said. "Lord Hampton. He's old. Been around forever, but. . ."

"If he wasn't there, he would know what was going on anyway, Christian said. Christian turned to Anak and said, "He is not our friend. But he will do what is best for your child. Not because he likes children, but because he believes only in the monarchy. Your child is the future king or queen of all that Lord Hampton holds dear. He'll do the child right."

Anak nodded assent. "Everyone will be there," Xo said, but before she could end the call, Carolina said one more thing.

"Okay then, it's all set. And Xo, thanks for everything. You can go home now. You must be so relieved to be going home. Anak give her the mining rights! You don't want Xo showing up and upsetting Rose."

Christian had come for Rose, and Xo had been told not to marry Christian if she wanted her land kept safe. So, Xo should feel relief, just as Carolina suggested, that she could go home. There was nothing for her here, with any of these people. Christian had made his choice clear when he and Jack had left her in Canada. She couldn't fault him for it. Or hate him for it. He had done what was needed to protect his family and the dynasty that fate – for want of a better word – had chosen to lead their country. He had honored his heritage.

Xo had no doubts that what Christian had felt for her had been real. He had loved her. He might still, but that was of no matter. Xo could not judge him for his decision. Wasn't she doing the same? She was choosing her land over Christian. She would not/ could not touch him or let him touch her, or even meet his eye because she might succumb.

There was no winning. If she followed her heart, her land and all her people she felt responsible for, would be destroyed. If she kept her land safe, her people's ancestral land with all its flora and fauna intact, she broke her heart. How could her one heart be enough to risk all that?

Perhaps it was the same for Christian. Perhaps he, too, was as torn as she was.

She would never know. Xo knew that in many marriages, not just royal ones, no one looked askance at paramours. Affairs were expected. Some even considered it a perk or even worse a right of hierarchy. Xo would never consent to anything of the sort. She would never abase herself in such a manner.

And that is why, when Anak had said that he could arrange to fly her anywhere, riding with he and he and Christian to England and from there to Colombia or flying directly back to Leticia, as Anak had more than one plane at his disposal, she did not hesitate when she replied, "I'm going back to Leticia, but I'll make my own way, thank-you."

Christian had tried to catch her eye, but Xo had shaken her head and turned away. Her turn was fluid, but she made sure to make it fast enough that she could not see his expression. She didn't know what would make her feel worse – a look of yearning, mourning, or pity. She didn't need to know because whatever had been between them was over. It had to be. It had to.

Forty-Four

You can't go home again.

It was great clarity that Xo remembered the first time one of the nuns had said those words to her. Xo had been at the mission school a little over five months. She still had not gotten used to sleeping within four closed walls and on a bed. Xo was used to sleeping in a hammock strung on poles helping to support a thatched roof. Windows didn't help. They were no substitute for the endless depths of green that graced one's eyes in all directions.

When the nun – it was Sister Martha – had done her nightly rounds, she wasn't surprised when she found Xo's cot empty. Sighing, she walked outside to the dusty courtyard where she knew that Xo would be standing at the iron gate looking out. Sister Martha hadn't reported Xo's nightly wanderings before, and she wouldn't do so this night, either.

Sister Martha knew that some of the more dogmatic nuns when it came to obedience would see Xo's nightly peregrinations as flaunting the rules. Sister Martha was young enough to know that there was no disrespect intended. It was a manifestation of unhappiness – an unhappiness that came from, despite all the other orphans present, being all alone.

"There is a saying child," Sister Martha said, as she gently laid a hand on Xo's head, "that goes like this: *You can't go home again.* Do you understand what it means?"

Although Xo didn't answer, Sister Martha continued to talk, her voice soft as a cooling night breeze. "I know you understand. You're quick with words though you don't speak often. No reason to change that.

"I don't know what brought you here, but you have changed for being here. Whether you like it or not. This means that it will not be the same if you ever go back to where you were before. It can't be. It can't be because you are not the same. You have different eyes."

Sister Martha moved to Xo's side and looked out from behind the gate's bars with her. "When I was a little girl, I lived in Belgium. I became a nun because I wanted to go to Africa, to the Congo, a country in the middle of that vast continent. I wanted to go to atone. Long ago my country had a king – King Leopold – who had done terrible things there. Atrocities. It was before I was born, but still, I wanted to make it right. At least a little bit better.

"Yet here I am. As far away from Africa as one can imagine. At first, when I saw that it was here the Church had ordered me, I was angry. Disappointed. So upset in fact that I thought of leaving the church.

"I didn't, of course, as I am here. Perhaps because I was too fearful of standing on my own. I will never know. But now, with years gone by, I see that God has done well for me. I am grateful. He did send me to a jungle – what I had prayed for – just a different one than what I was expecting.

"This is my home now. Not Belgium, and certainly not anywhere on the great African continent. You can't go home again child because you can't go back to the past. You can only live in the present because it leads to the future."

Although Xo had not fully understood everything Sister Martha had said that night, she had comprehended enough. Sister Martha wasn't saying that Xo couldn't go home because everyone had died. Sister Martha was saying that Xo couldn't go home because Xo *hadn't* died. If Xo was to ever have a home again, it had to be one of her own making.

All these years later, and still Sister Martha's words held prescience. Xo was back in Colombia. On her treasured piece of land. The flora, fauna, and trail dwarfed in shadow to it familiar, as was the clearing that housed her cozy thatch. But it wasn't the same. Not just because of the modern accoutrements that provided comfort and ease she had allowed herself.

It was because Xo herself had changed. She had fallen in love. Not with a family member, as that is a different kind of love, but with a being that one had to allow in. She had opened her heart, and now it was empty. Again.

"And what's worse," thought Xo angrily as she fileted the fish she had caught for dinner, "is that I let him come here. And now everywhere I look I see him. Oh, Sister Martha, you are so right. You can't go home again."

With a wry smile, Xo thought of how her people would move their village every few years. Xo knew that was no longer an option. It wasn't, she thought, that she needed civilization (for want of a better word), but now that she knew there was a very different world outside of her piece of the Earth, she couldn't ignore it. She was part of something bigger, and she knew that isolating herself – hiding Rewe would say – wouldn't do her any good. She needed more. Not yachts or crystal chandeliers or any trappings of what others measured a good life by, but other human beings. Companionship.

And just at that very moment, as the word companionship went through Xo's mind, Xo heard voices. Instantly alert, she stood, tensed, just as ready to disappear into the underbrush as she was to greet the intruder. As the sounds became more audible, Xo relaxed. "Why, they're children" she thought.

"This way," she called out. "You're just in time to eat."

Xo continued to prepare her meal, making sure to make more than usual, as she waited for her two guests – a boy and girl – Xo was fairly sure from what she had heard, to show themselves.

It wasn't until Xo had set three plates and began to dish out the food that the children showed themselves.

"Three plates," the little girl, Xo guessed her to be about eight years old, said, her eyes round. "Did you know we were coming?"

"I heard you."

"I told you to be quiet!" the boy said to the girl. Xo guessed the boy to be about ten.

"And whom do I owe the pleasure?" Xo asked as she sat down at the table and made a motion for the children to join her.

"I'm Juan," the boy said, once he was seated. "And this is Mariyella."

"A pleasure to make your acquaintance," Xo said, as she introduced herself.

Xo didn't ask the children any questions. She simply watched them eat. Their hunger wasn't voracious, and although they were thin, it looked to Xo that they were naturally so. They wore little clothing, but in a tropical climate, little clothing was the norm. Their shirts and shorts were well-worn, the color faded from many washings, but they were clean.

When the children were finished, Juan said, "Aren't you going to ask what we're doing here?"

"I'm waiting for you to tell me."

"Oh," Juan said. He looked at pensively. "What if we don't say?"

Xo didn't answer Juan's question. Instead, she said in a mildly inquisitive voice, "You don't think someone is worried about you?"

"No," Juan said, shaking his head. "They just spend all their time praying."

"Ah, yes," Xo said, understanding instantly. "You live at the Mission. I used to live there."

"We know," Mariyella said. "They talk about you a lot. Well, Sister Martha does. She likes you."

"You don't think Sister Martha misses you? You don't think she's worried about where you are right now?"

Juan looked at Xo, weighing his words before he spoke. "You know Sister Martha talks to people who aren't there. She might not even know we're gone."

"She's getting old," Xo agreed. "And often old people talk to people in a different world. A world we can't see. But that doesn't mean that she can't miss you. Or she can't be worried about you."

When Juan and Mariyella didn't say anything, Xo didn't immediately try and fill the silence. Instead, she let the children think about what she had said. Then, when she did speak, she didn't speak to them as if there was a great age difference. She spoke to the two children as if they were equals.

"It's hard. I felt tears inside me all time the first years I was there. You can't live with me. I travel too often, but I can promise you this. You can come visit me again. And I'll come visit you."

Xo looked at the two youngsters in front of her. She recognized all the emotions running across their faces – sadness, doubt, and acceptance. Standing, she shared what gave her comfort. "Come," she said. "We can run together. To the river, and then back to the mission."

"All the way back to the mission?" Mariyella asked, her sweet voice trembling.

"No," laughed Xo, aware of exactly what Mariyella was afraid of. "That's too far for you. I have a scooter hidden in the bushes. We'll ride for part of the way."

The relief on Juan's face matched Mariyella's. Never the less, he turned to Mariyella and said, "I'll carry you on my back when I get tired."

His gesture, so spontaneous, so caring, gave Xo's heart a lurch. Xo's people had many sayings. They didn't have one about not being able to go home again. Or anything close to it, in fact. Rather, they had one about newly birthed children being nothing but goodness. That adage could stand alone, but it was often coupled with a second saying. "The village keeps the goodness on earth."

"Juan," Xo said, "you are a good man."

Juan knew from Xo's manner that she was not making fun of him. She meant what she said. Her words had the ring of truth despite the fact that he was only ten years old and no one in his short life had ever called him a man.

His eyes shining, he smiled shyly. "I'll run every day after we get back to the mission. I promise. One day I'll run farther than you!"

"Yes, you will," Xo said. "Sooner than you think."

Forty-Five

It was well past dark when Xo dismounted from her scooter and pushed it into the undergrowth where she had erected a small thatch shelter to keep it dry. Taking the children back to the mission had taken longer than expected. Despite her protestations that she could go the distance all by herself, Mariyella was exhausted. She had turned down Juan's offer of a piggy back ride, but she did consent to being carried by Xo. Their pace had increased after that, but the fact remained that Juan was only ten and did not have the longer limbs of an adult. He never complained though, and Xo, recognizing his effort and not wanting to shake his confidence, made sure to keep a pace he would not fail at.

Their travel went much faster once they reached her scooter, but with two children clinging to the back, Xo had driven slower than usual as she didn't want any mishaps. When they finally arrived at the mission, the children were reluctant to get off, as they were worried they would be punished for running away. Xo had to promise that she would talk to the nuns and make sure there were not repercussions before they were willing to slide off the seat. All that took time, and now that Xo was finally by herself, she felt a wave of loneliness creeping over her.

"No," she said to herself sternly as she made her way down the narrow dirt path, "You are not to feel sorry for yourself. You are not."

Perhaps, if Xo had been walking a hard city street or had taken up the invitation of the nuns and spent the night at the mission, her mental state would have continued in a downward spiral. Something else happened instead. Something so very different that all thoughts of loneliness disappeared in a flash of light. Literally.

Even in the years before, when Xo had run with Koni, it was not often that she saw leaves glowing bright with light. This was because at night, always it was safer to be at home with others and fires burning. It wasn't until after the Monkey Sickness, when it was only she and Rewe, that she had seen what one would think impossible. Leaves that glowed bright green, lighting up the dark night with a bioluminescent glow.

As Xo had stood in wonder, Rewe had picked up some of the glowing leaves and showed her how it wasn't the leaf that was shining, but instead the fungus growing on it. When Xo had asked why and how it was possible, Rewe's eyes had twinkled. "I might never know," he had answered. "It doesn't happen all the time. For that, child, relish this night."

Rewe had then shown Xo what leaves were best for harvesting. "We want to take the ones that will make good medicine, and we have to make sure as to leave enough for there to be even more."

Over the years, Xo had seen the occasional shining leaf, but what she was seeing now – it was as eerily bright as when she and Rewe had found that amazing patch so many years before. Xo stood for a moment, her eyes shining, and then she twirled, her arms outspread. "Oh, Rewe," she said out loud but soft enough for it to melt in the dark, "You're telling me that I'm thinking in the wrong direction, aren't you?"

Then, as she carefully began to gather some of the leaves, she thought to herself, "Who am I to worry about loneliness? I am most fortunate." Xo knew it was true, for she had experienced love. She had taken it. She had given it. Not only had her mother Manuela treasured her, but so had an entire community. She had brothers, sisters, aunties, uncles, and babies to hold and help take care. She had a family. She had been gifted. All because of Rewe being in the right place at the right time. All because Rewe had found a baby who had dropped from the sky and landed in a soft nest of moss.

Filled with a sense of well-being, Xo picked a supply of leaves. After packing them carefully in her bag, she slung the bag over her shoulder, the strap crossing her chest. Her step was light as she made her way back home.

Xo reached her clearing in less than thirty minutes. She started across the bare ground, her little house so near, but suddenly she stopped short. Something was amiss. Oddly, she didn't feel a sense of danger. Her skin didn't prickle with unease, and the roots of her hair on the back of her neck didn't tingle. Yet something was different. Something had changed.

The dishes! She and the children had dined at her little wooden table that sat outside on the ground under her thatch. Wanting to get Mariyella and Juan down the trail and home before dark, she had not washed the used plates and utensils immediately after eating the way she usually did. Instead, she had left them sitting on the table. The dishes were no longer there. The table was bare.

Xo took a step closer. She stood silent and puzzled. What had happened to the dishes? Her eyes swept ground around the vicinity of the table, but she didn't see anything. If the birds had come to feast on crumbs or a monkey come to make mayhem with scraps, one would expect at least to see over turned plates or spoons scattered about. Yet there was nothing. The ground was a bare as the table.

"I washed them."

Xo froze. Rigid with paralysis, her mind racing so wildly, she could not speak. Instead, she stood as if rooted to the ground only breathing out of primitive instinct. She remained silent, heart pounding, eyes wide, waiting.

Or was she poised to flee? In the dim light, the man intently observing her wasn't so sure. Slowly, with measured tread, he moved out of the shadowed interior of her home. He moved closer, his eyes on hers, and he didn't stop until Xo took a step back and put up her hand to stop his advance.

Xo's retreat tore at him, and his jaw clenched, but the man had not come all this way to be dismissed so easily. He stopped moving immediately. He had not traveled all this way to have Xo disappear into the jungle. He had so much he needed to say to her, but first, it seemed, he would need to convince her to listen.

"Xo," he said, trying anew. This time he was stopped not by her withdrawal but by her words.

"You washed the dishes."

It wasn't a question. Xo had spoken declaratively. It seemed then, that the most expedient thing to do was offer an explanation.

"They were dirty."

"They were dirty." Xo said, slowly repeating the words that had just been uttered. Her face slightly askance, a strange expression on her face, she made a slight nod, as it agreeing that such an act made sense. "Did you," she asked curiously, "come all this way to wash my dishes? Is that why you came, Christian?"

"Xo!" Christian said, repeating her name again, this time in exasperation. "You know I didn't!" Once again, Christian made a move to come closer, but once again Xo held out an arm to stop him.

"Fair enough," Christian said, "I can understand why you don't want to have anything to do with me. Detest me, in truth, but you won't get rid of me that easily." He spoke quietly, but his voice was strong and firm. "I won't leave until you hear what I have to say. And after you listen, I have something to give to you. Actually, two things but the second isn't from me."

"Maybe I don't want to listen to you."

"But you're going to," Christian said, a hint of laughter in his voice. "You know I'm not going to leave until you do. You know how stubborn I can be. Might as well get it over with."

Christian stood, as still as Xo, calmly meeting her gaze. He looks so confident, Xo thought. And here my heart is jumping so strangely. Taking a deep breath in an attempt to calm herself, Xo moved to her little table. She didn't speak until she put her basket with its glowing contents on its top. Then, looking up at him, her face lit softly by the bioluminescent glow, she said, "For an uninvited guest, you're very bossy."

For the first time in a long time, Christian felt he could breathe properly. He had been so afraid that at the sight of him, Xo would not listen to him. That she would call him despicable and insist that he leave at once. Even worse had been the fear that she could not abide his presence long enough to castigate him. Instead, once spotted, she would turn and melt into the jungle as no one but she was capable of.

When Christian had arrived and found the unwashed dished on the table, he was sure that that was what she had done. Knowing he would never be able to follow her or find her unless she wanted to be found, he had decided he would wait her out. He had washed the dishes, knowing she would notice immediately, hoping she would see it as a sign of good will. As the hours had passed, he had thought about what more he could do, for he was determined not to leave before saying what he had come to say.

Now was his chance. Moving without haste but with no hesitation, Christian took the few steps necessary to where Xo was sitting. He sat down across from her so that he could face her.

"Xo," he said, his voice tender, "I. . ."

But before he could finish, Xo cut in. "I don't want anything from you."

"They're already yours."

Xo and Christian stared at each other, the bioluminescence bathing them in a pale aura. It was Christian who broke the silence. Despite the turmoil he was feeling inside, he smiled. His worst fear had not materialized. She had not fled from him. "Xo," he said again, "I. . ." but once more she cut him off.

"What's mine?" she asked. "I don't need anything from you."

"Who is the bossy one now?" Christian asked, shaking his head good naturedly and speaking in jest as he got up and walked over to his backpack so that he could bring a small flat package to the table. Sitting back down, he opened it up and took out a folder that was protected in a plastic zip bag. "You want this," he said. "Trust me. You do."

Xo cocked her head inquisitively, but Christian didn't say anything more. Instead, he smiled broadly and pointed to the bag.

"I swear his eyes are twinkling," Xo thought bitterly. "How can he be enjoying this?" Forcing herself not to sigh or to show any sign of hurt, she slowly picked up what Christian had placed on the table. Carefully, she unzipped the bag and pulled out the folder. She opened it, and then she looked up at Christina in shock.

"It's all yours Xo," he said. "All of it."

"But how. . ." Xo said weakly, putting her hands to her head. "Anak wouldn't have. . ."

"The land is yours. And you've got all the rights to the mining concessions. Not that you'll ever use them."

Xo traced her fingers over the papers. She perused the signatures on the pages, and then she looked up at Christian. "You did this," she said quietly. "Anak would never have been this munificent. He would have held something back. He's too calculating. If I get all this, then Anak has nothing to leverage."

Christian shrugged. "I wanted you to have what you wanted. I wanted you to be safe."

"What did you have to do to get this?" Xo asked.

Christian shook his head. "It's yours. That's all that matters."

Before Xo could query further, Christian said, "There's one more thing I have to give you." Once again reaching into his bag, he pulled out a creamy envelope. "It's your wedding invitation," he said, as he slid it across the table.

Christian watched with narrowed eyes as Xo fingered the thick, luxurious paper. Her fingers traced the exquisite calligraphy that lettered her name, but she didn't open it. What did this mean? Was she actually thinking of not attending?

"Xo," he said, his voice louder than he had intended, "You have to go."

Xo bowed her head. She knew why Christian had made sure to protect her land and grant her the mining rights. It was a grand gesture, magnanimous in its largess, and done for a very specific reason. It was atonement. Just as Sister Martha had wanted to atone for King Leopold's sins, Christian wanted to do the same. This was his way of making it right, or using Sister Martha's words, "at least a little bit better." After taking her heart, he had abandoned her. Left her in pain that would wound her to the end of her days. The gift of land and the mining rights were nothing but a way of making amends of his decision to do obeisance to the crown and his heritage. It was his way of saying sorry, I made you fall in love with me, but you're not the woman I'm going to marry. No, I'm not going to marry you. I'm going to marry a princess. A real princess. Not some jungle waif social media jokingly calls Tarzana.

"It doesn't stop the hurt," Xo said at last. Her voice cracking in pain.

In an instant, Christian was by her side. Gently, he placed a hand under her chin and lifted upward so that she had to look at him. "What hurt? I don't understand."

He was surprised to see a tear beginning to make its way down Xo's cheek, and he tenderly wiped it away. "Okay, we don't have to go to the wedding. We can make up some story about I don't know, food poisoning. Eating the wrong mushrooms or something."

Xo's intake of breath was so sharp that it was audible. "We. . ." she asked. "You have to go to the wedding. You can't have a wedding without a groom."

It was Christian's turn for his intake of air to become audible. "What are you talking about?" he asked, his face perplexed. "Anak is going to be there."

"Anak is the groom?"

Christian almost threw up his hands. "Xo," he said, his teeth clenched, "Of course he's going to be there. Rose would never settle for anything but the most public and grandest exchange of vows. He'll be there, the Archbishop of Canterbury, a revered Inman, probably one able to trace his heritage back to Mohammed, and anybody else Rose can think to add to the spectacle."

"Of course, though," Christian said shaking his head, unable to keep the amused glee from his voice, "Carolina won't be there. Rose isn't allowing Carolina there. Close to the altar, I mean. Carolina isn't even being allowed to hold Rose's train and follow her down the aisle. Rose isn't going to let anyone – not even their backside – take away from her glory."

Shaking his head Christian continued. "It's going to be a circus. A huge one. But that's what Rose wants. And as Carolina says, best to give Rose what she wants. That's why she'll be sitting in a regular pew, right next to me and you."

"This is Anak and Rose's wedding?" Xo asked, her voice a mixture of surprise, doubt, and confusion.

"Who else's would it be?"

"I thought it was yours."

Christian stared at Xo in stupefied amazement. "You thought I was going to marry Rose?" he sputtered when he could finally speak. "How could you think that? She's a horrible woman. A fiend."

Xo's mind was a flurry of confused thoughts. Then it became clear. "How could you?" she asked, her voice filled with sadness.

"How could I what?" Christian demanded.

"Ask me to go with you. And then to have to sit next to Carolina. Haven't you put me through enough? You broke my heart."

Xo didn't know how Christian would react to her truth. She hadn't meant to voice it. It was in the past. She had to make her future. But it had just come out. Without thought or guise. Spoken with no expectation. But even so, if Xo had thought about what how it might be taken, she never expected, not even a hint if she had searched the farthest reaches of her mind, was Christian's mirth.

"I broke your heart? I broke your heart! I broke your heart! Do you know what this means?"

Before Xo could answer, Christian swept her up in his arms. "You love me!" he said, "You love me!" He began to shower Xo's face, arms, head, shoulders with kisses. "You love me, you love me, you love me," he said again and again with great jollity.

Christian didn't release her, but he stopped his kissing only so he could look down at her. His eyes shining in happiness he said, "You made me wonder! Anyone else, I could tell. But you, so strong, so incredible, so different. I adore you, I want you, I desire you, and I knew you felt something, but still. . . Xo, you've made me the happiest man alive."

"It doesn't matter," Xo said sadly. "You did the right thing."

"Don't know what you're talking about," Christian said cheerfully as he released her. "All this confusion would have never happened," Christian said as he moved a stool closer to Xo and sat down directly in front of her, so close that their knees were touching, "if you had let me talk first. Or bothered to open the invitation." Without asking permission, he reached out and clasped each of Xo's hands in one of his own. "I told you," he said cheerfully, "that I had things to say, but no, bossy you had to take things first. Bossy, bossy, bossy."

Despite her inner turmoil, Xo couldn't help but be amused by Christian's antics. "Don't put this on me," Xo said. She tried to pull her hands away from Christian grasp, but he would not release her.

"No," he said shaking his head, "I can't lose you. I'm not letting go. Ever."

"Christian," Xo said softly, "You can't keep what you can't have."

For a moment Christian didn't react. But there was something in Xo's tone that he had not heard before. It was sad and poignant, and it had a finality to it that struck him to his bones. His heart that just seconds before had been filled with elation he literally felt turned to stone. "What don't I have?" he asked quietly.

"You were born a prince," Xo said. "You're a good one. You will always do what is best for your country. I know that's why you left me at the race."

"And that will never happen again, Xo, I promise you! I never wanted to, but. . ."

"Shh," Xo said. "I know. You had no choice. That's why there is nothing to forgive."

"I had a choice," Christian said with fervor. "And if my returning back to Norway as my father demanded and I've lost you I made the wrong choice."

"There were no choices," Xo said sadly. "You had to do what was right for your people. And you did it. It's one of the reasons I love you so." Tears began to flow from Xo's eyes and she said, "I hope. . ." and then she stopped unable to continue.

"Those tears need to go," Christian said, "and since I'm not going to let go of your hands until I know what you hope, I'm going to have to kiss them away."

"Oh, yes, there's a little smile," Christian said as he dried her cheeks gently with his kisses. "What do you hope?"

"I hope," Xo said, looking down, unable to meet his gaze, "that Carolina loves you."

Astounded by Xo's words, Christian dropped her hands and leaned back in surprise. "Why would you wish that?" he asked, his bafflement apparent in his face and tone. "What does Carolina have to do with us?"

"You're going to marry her."

"Marry her?" Christian started to laugh. "Oh, Xo," he said, still chuckling as he pulled her into his arms and on his lap. "I can't marry her."

"Why not?" The words were muffled, spoken softly.

"Because I'm going to marry you."

Forty-Six

"You wear it well. You look fab. Relax."

Xo made a wry smile. "I'm afraid to move," she said. "How do you do it? You look like you could spear and bone a fish and still not worry about that thing falling off your head."

"It's called a hat," laughed Carolina, taking Xo by the hand. "And don't worry. Trust me; yours won't fall off. I used enough hat pins to keep it on even if you. . . what did you say I looked as if I could do. . . spear and bone a fish! Ah, Xo, you and what you come up with. I've never had such a compliment. At least I think it is a compliment. I'll take it as one.

"Oh, Xo, those Norwegians are going to love you. Well, of course, you'll have some haters, but that just goes with the territory. Any time you need a pick me up because of some gaff you've made, you can give me a call, and I'll tell you a time when I did worse."

Xo smoothed down the front of her dress. "I want to thank you," she said. "The truth is that I'm a little nervous. I've never gone to anything like this before. It's a bit intimidating."

"Most watched wedding in the world," Carolina said breezily. "The entire world will be viewing. Millions and millions of eyes on you."

"Are you trying to make me feel better?" Xo asked, her eyes twinkling despite her nervousness.

"Showing you how easy it is," laughed Carolina. "Now, let me check one more time that we're presentable. "We don't want anyone looking at the videos years from now talking about uncut threads or undergarment lines."

Carolina stepped back and looked at Xo appraisingly. Xo stood patiently as Carolina walked around her. Xo's dress was colored a single creamy shade of green. It had a fitted bodice but flared out in graceful folds due to wide pleats sewn in at the waist. It had a simple round neck, cap sleeves embellished with darts, and a concealed back zipper. With its jacquard material and clean lines, perfectly fitted to Xo's torso, it was stunning in its elegant simplicity.

When Carolina had asked Xo what she was wearing, Xo confessed that she had no idea. She would leave it up to Rigitza. Xo then had to explain to Carolina who Rigitza was.

"Ah," Carolina had said. "The woman who helped put me in my place on Constitution Day. That dress – red, with all the state emblems – very clever. I need to meet this woman."

"You'll like her," Xo said. "She doesn't bite."

Carolina had started, staring with a shocked expression on her face, remembering clearly what had happened on the castle balcony with Prince Oscar's son Alexander and what precipitated Xo's comment. Then, seeing that Xo was trying not to smile, Carolina couldn't help herself. She started to giggle, and when Xo joined in, the merriment engulfed them.

"If I only knew then what I know now," Carolina said, wiping tears from her cheeks. "I really underestimated you."

"And now?" Xo queried.

"I understand why women have friends," Carolina replied.

Despite Rigitza's initial diffidence, Carolina and she got along famously. Carolina had put Rigitza at ease by admiring Rigitza's sketches and asking her how she got her ideas. When Carolina had made comments that showed her knowledge of fashion and what precision was needed for cutting and design, any shyness that Rigitza had once felt disappeared. With bent heads, the two of them discussed material choice, seam finishes, and detailed embellishments with the enthusiasm of true fashionistas. Xo had watched the two of them, feeling a sense of warmth that these two women, of such disparate ages and upbringing, could be united in what they found of such great import.

"Don't think I'm being disrespectful," Carolina had said to Rigitza after Xo's dress had been chosen, "but I'm going to need to go with a British designer. Or at least one from the Commonwealth."

"Of course," Rigitza agreed. "I understand. One in your position always has to be thinking of how one is perceived. It must be exhausting at times."

"Carolina has stamina," Xo said. "And she's expert at being politic when she wants to be."

Carolina couldn't help but laugh. "Xo," she said amiably, "That, I believe, is a backhanded compliment."

"Take it as you like," Xo said, seriously, "but you underestimate yourself. You're a people's princess when you want to be. Rose doesn't have that ability. She's too cold."

It took a moment for Carolina to respond. She was so used to Rose always being the star, always being the one complimented. After all, it was Rose who everyone expected to be queen. Carolina was just the one people liked to see get into trouble. They liked feeling superior when she messed up.

"I suppose because I was second born," Carolina said slowly. "I had a freedom that she didn't."

"No," Xo said shaking her head. "Rose is just cold. And driven. You're going to have to help her."

"Help her?" Carolina looked at Xo inquisitively.

"To make the child feel loved," Xo said. "You're going to have to be a good aunt."

A strange expression passed over Carolina's face, one that Xo thought looked almost sad. Before Xo could ask if she had said anything wrong, Carolina spoke. "I will be the best aunt ever," she said fiercely. "You don't have to worry. That child will be loved. I'll make sure of it. I know how important the next generation is."

Carolina then abruptly changed the subject. "Shoes," she said, clapping her hands. "Xo, Rigitza's already informed me about your resistance to heels and hats. Sorry, my lady, but you're wearing both. I won't let you attend my sister's wedding not looking your best. I'll take care of it all. And when you put them on, no complaints. You're going to tough it out."

"One more thing," Carolina had said. "No sneaking into my room like the last time you were there. I've already told Christian he is to drop you off at eight o'clock sharp. We can breakfast together. Christian can meet us here when we're ready, and we can call walk in together. You're both going to sit by me."

Xo didn't know much of royal etiquette, but she wondered about Carolina's breeziness with the seating. "Are you sure?" Xo asked. "Aren't you going to be in the front?"

"Second row," Carolina said. Right behind my mum."

"The queen," Xo said. "Right behind her. Don't you think. . ."

Carolina never let Xo finish. "You'll have a good view of the back of her hat," Carolina said with finality. "And she will assuredly be wearing one."

When Xo had told Christian about where they would be sitting, Christian hadn't been fazed at all. "Carolina has a better sense of how to manipulate social perception than anyone I know. She's a master of public relations. She needs someone at her side who won't steal her thunder. Our both being there is going to make people really wonder about how the three of us get along. Keep your enemies close, I suppose."

It was rare for Xo to disagree with Christian, but she never hesitated to speak her mind when she did. This was one of those times.

"I think you're wrong," she said slowly. "I think Carolina just wants a friend. It's going to be a huge day. Her sister is, right now, probably the most famous woman in the world. Carolina is going to need someone to hold her hand. Someone to let her know that her feelings count, too. I'm willing. I like her."

Christian, perhaps wisely, had not bothered to share with Xo his mother's reaction when she heard that Christian and Xo would be entering the cathedral with Carolina. "You might marry her yet!" Queen Juliana had said, clapping her hands in delight.

Christian had stared at his mother, trying to mask the revulsion he felt with her sentiments. Did she really think that he should and would marry a woman who had so casually slept with his married brother – with pregnant wife and child in the same castle at the time? And then for the first time in his life, Christian fully realized how lucky he had been to have been born second. He didn't have to worry about dynasties. He could marry for love.

"Are you all right, son?" King Haakkon had asked, as he had noticed Christian's tightening of the jaw. Haakkon was almost afraid to ask, but they were in private quarters, and he knew that some unspoken things if not spoken do not go away. Instead, they fester, and as time goes on, the stench of rot cannot be contained.

"Yes, I am," Christian had said. "There is no need to worry. The past is over and people change."

Haakkon looked at his son silently. He nodded in understanding. Christian held no malice. All was forgiven. Christian had moved on.

"You're a good son," he said quietly. "It will be a lucky woman, the one you wed."

Christian didn't bother to ask his father whether he meant Princess Carolina or Xo. His succinct reply was only one word. "Perhaps."

King Haakon wasn't sure what Christian meant. He looked at his son, waiting for him to speak elucidate, but without further word, Christian had simply kissed his mother and walked out of the room.

"Whatever you think of me," Xo said, as Carolina walked around her for a final check, "you should know that you look amazing. Truly, Carolina, you're beautiful."

Carolina laughed, "I had to promise Rose I'd wear something high necked." Carolina stopped walking only so she could grab Xo's arm and turn her so they were both facing the mirror. "Look at us," Carolina said, studying their reflection. "We look fabulous."

"All because of you," Xo said, comfortably.

"Almost like sisters," Carolina said. "We really do look alike." Carolina was silent for a moment and then she looked at Xo with an intent expression. "You don't think we could be "

"What?"

"Sisters. Or related in anyway?"

Xo laughed. "Not at all. Impossible."

"But we look. . ."

"Looks are of no import," Xo said. "I never saw a mirror until I was, I don't know, in my early teens. I thought I was the ugliest being ever put on this earth."

"Every teenager thinks no one is uglier than they are," Carolina said, laughing. "You might be able to outrun anyone, but not even you, my jungle princess, were able to escape teenage angst!"

"All I know is that I like you better than mirrors," Xo said, playfully nudging Carolina with her shoulder. "I don't know who first thought of them, but they are horrible inventions. Most unnecessary."

"I beg to differ," Carolina said as she picked up their purses and handed Xo the small clutch she had chosen for her. "Think of how they are used in telescopes and all kinds of things. Hold it right, and one can even use it to start a fire."

"All this knowledge you've kept to yourself," laughed Xo amiably. "What else don't I know about you?"

"I'll let you know in time," Carolina said. "There's a time to keep silent, and a time to speak."

Xo froze, just for a moment.

"What is it?" Carolina asked, curiously. You look like you've seen a ghost."

"It's nothing," Xo said, shaking her head. "It's just what you said – 'There's a time to keep silent, and a time to speak.' It's something I used to say quite often. When I was younger. Living with the nuns."

"Ecclesiastes 3:7," Carolina said. "Probably the only part of the Bible I can quote verbatim. "I, on the other hand, wasn't the one who said it quite often. In fact, it was often said to me. Every time I was reprimanded for making the monarchy look bad. Which as you know well, was quite often. Lord Hampton – he will be at the wedding. I'll point him out to you. He would stare at me with his black holes for eyes and recite it to me in a very very stern and disapproving voice."

"Lord Hampton," Xo said, slowly. "You've talked about him. Christian has mentioned him. Even Jack Christian's detective knows all about him. A cold man who wields great power. You weren't, you aren't, intimidated by him?"

"Not at all," Carolina said breezily. "He made it easy because I knew exactly what he thought of me, where I stood with him. It was a battle of wills, and I won."

Xo looked at Carolina curiously. Xo was remembering how both Jack and Christian had spoken of Lord Hampton zeal and fanaticism when it came to protecting the bailiwick of the monarchy. Yet here was Carolina sounding supremely confident that she had bested him.

"How did you?" Xo finally asked. "How did you win?"

"Before he could go on about how I was a disgrace to the throne, I'd look straight into his black soulless eyes and say, *There's a time to keep silent.*" Then I'd close my eyes and sit, motionless."

"You're not kidding me?" Xo asked.

"No, not at all. There I'd sit, focusing on relaxing my breathing, all while he railed away."

Xo laughed. "You're a worthy adversary! Noted. I feel much better knowing that you're my friend."

"That's why I'm keeping you at my side," Carolina said. "Now let's go watch my sister get married."

Forty-Seven

The wedding was everything that Rose wanted it to be. It seemed that the entire world had stopped to watch. Festivities by the populace had started well before the guests began their promenade to the cathedral. Streets were lined with flags, balconies draped with banners, and children and adults alike waved brightly colored pennants. It was one wild party, and the collective roar that thundered through the air as Rose's carriage made its way to the steps of the cathedral only heightened people's feelings that they were part of something wonderful, joyous, and earth shattering.

Carolina had been completely relaxed and at ease as she made her way past the crowds held back by the temporary barricades and police in splendid uniform. She smiled and waved at people, in between chatting with Xo and Christian. Carolina walked between the two of them. Before they had gotten out of their vehicle, Carolina had laid a hand on Christian's arm.

"I know you want to hold Xo's arm," she said, "but it is best if I'm in the middle. We have to look like the three of us are best of friends. Or, at least as if I don't have a favorite."

Christian understood immediately. Carolina was, as usual and he had come to expect, being nothing but strategic. After the wedding, even during, everyone would be going over video footage and photographs with a fine-tooth comb – what was the true relationship between the three of them? Which one of them was going to marry Christian? What raw emotions were they hiding? Carolina was making sure that in all captured images of her, she would look, not only enchanting, but happy. No one expected her to be with both Christian and Xo. That she had so prominently chosen to be with them added an enigmatic aura to her allure. A touch of mystery intertwined with high couture. Whatever Christian truly thought of Carolina, he had to respect, even if it galled him, her brazenness. She was a clever woman; yes, she was.

"Keep smiling," Carolina had instructed Xo. "You're doing great."

"I don't know how you can be so relaxed," Xo had said while following Carolina's lead. "I feel like I'm bait for a Harpy."

"Ah, the eagle. The colossal one," Carolina said, tilting her head while placing a hand on her heart in a show of endearment as she looked at a young mother holding up her baby – an act which the crowd loved.

"Ah ha, you didn't think I knew about those birds," laughed Carolina as she nudged Christian's shoulder. "Tell him, Xo. Tell him that I'm smarter than I look."

Xo never had a chance because Carolina spoke again before she could say anything. "And we have nothing to worry about, Xo. You're in green. To any bird of prey you're just a tree."

"And you're a. . ."

"Not a. The. The target," Carolina said cheerfully. "I look like a bright red parrot. Harpy's eat parrots, right? The big ones. The macaws. That's what I look like. Nothing but a big ripe luscious macaw."

It was at that moment that a photographer with a very powerful lens got his lucky shot – the two women and a man, regal and merry, reveling in the company of each other. It was a photo to be bought, shared, and spread around the world for all posterity. It was a photo that even if one could not explain why, made people enlarge it on their screens so they could stare at it more intently, or if holding a print copy, gently brush a finger over the image. It made one yearn to be inside their joyous circle. Regal, yes, but there was magic.

Carolina was familiar with the inside of the cathedral, and although Christian had not been in this particular one, he had been in buildings equally as sacrosanct and magnificent. It was all new to Xo, and she was in awe. The stained-glass windows were ablaze with light, the wooden pews shone bright with polish, and the frescoes on the ceiling were filled with radiant bucolic scenes. The stone floor, the arches, and the huge columns providing structural support gave subtle note to the age of the edifice as well as the years of toil that went into its building.

"It's a marvel," Xo whispered when she could finally speak. "I've never seen anything like this before."

"And here everyone else is looking at who is who, what they are wearing, and where they are sitting. All while you, Xo, look at the ceiling," Carolina said with teasing delight.

"Your eyes are sparkling," Christian said to Xo.

"They really are," Carolina agreed affably. "She's going to make this wedding less tedious for you, isn't she Christian? Anytime you're bored, you're just going to look at Xo. Enjoy her wonder."

"You know," Xo said, "I'm beginning to think that the two of you are treating me like some kind of pet right now. Just here for your entertainment."

"Never!" Carolina and Christian said, in good-natured unison.

Once the three of them had reached their pew, Xo cocked an eyebrow at Carolina. "Okay Princess Bossy, how do we slide in?"

Carolina clapped her hands in delight and laughed delightedly, well aware that they were the center of attention. "I can't deprive Christian," she said. "He so clearly wants to be with you. So, he's in first, you'll be in the middle, and I'll take the aisle."

It was not what Christian expected. He had resigned himself to alleviating his boredom with surreptitious sideways glances at Xo, but now, not only could he gaze down on her, but he could hold her hand. He spoke without thinking. "Thank you, Carolina."

"Xo will tell you," Carolina said, giving Christian a playful pat to start him moving down the row, "I'm not as bad as you think I am. Now scoot!"

Once the three of them were seated, Carolina leaned forward and said loud enough to take them into her confidence but soft enough that no one else could hear, "In truth, I'm selfish. I wanted the best seat for a clear look when my sister walked down the aisle, and I wanted Xo by my side so I could tell her gossipy details."

"Such as," Xo said, cocking her head in amusement.

"My sister's dress will make it into the Guinness Book of World Records as most expensive wedding dress in the world. It cost – I'll give it to you in Euros and dollars. Over 12 and a half million euros; over 12 and a half million dollars."

Xo was visibly stunned. "That's not possible," she said when she could finally speak.

"Oh, it's possible all right," Carolina said. "Hand sewn lace, thousands of minute beaded pearls, all having to be threaded on individually, and, of course, don't let us forget the over 150 carats of diamonds that bedeck the bodice and the hem. I haven't even started in on the veil. Not the longest train in the world, but then, that would just be tacky, wouldn't it?"

There was something in Carolina's voice that alerted Xo. It is doubtful that anyone else could have or what have picked up on it. Xo took one of Carolina's hand – the one closed to her – and gently squeezed it. "You haven't seen it, yet, have you?"

When Carolina didn't answer, Xo didn't say she was sorry or try to make Carolina feel better by saying how selfish and cruel Rose was. Instead, she simply raised Carolina's hand up her mouth, gave it a little kiss, and then said, "It must really hurt."

"I haven't seen the one for the wedding/celebration that happens in Muta, either. Though of course I've heard all the details. It weighs a ton. And whatever you think of this party, it's nothing compared to what will go on in Muta. The entire country gets a three-day holiday, and every person in the country gets a gift."

"It can't be much of a party," Christian said jokingly. "I wasn't invited."

"I wasn't either," Xo said. "But I can't help but be curious. What kind of gift?"

"Every household gets a food basket – made up of a variety of English biscuits, some scone mixes, and tea. Then everyone gets a voucher."

"For what?" It was Christian who asked. "Should I feel bad that I wasn't invited?"

"For running shoes."

Carolina started to laugh. "If you could see your faces," she said. "You both look shocked to the core."

"I just never expected. . ." Xo's voice trailed off.

"Expected or not, it's happening. And there's going to be some big race. Not as part of the wedding, of course. To celebrate their one-year anniversary. It will all be announced at some point during the celebration," Carolina explained.

Whatever you feel about your sister," Xo said, "This could be a really good thing. For everyone."

"I know; I know, although it's hard to admit. Everyone has a year to get fit. Muta's health score will edge up on the world chart.

Rose is all fired up about it. Says there will be ways for everyone to participate. Even women.

"Do you want to know what Rose's favorite thing about all this is?"

"I'm sure it's something I just never expected," Xo said.

"Rose says that every time people put on the shoes and walk or jog or whatever they do, they will be thinking of Rose. They won't be able to think of their country without thinking of her. An entire year to become part of their consciousness."

"I don't know whether to call her diabolically devious or very clever," Christian said.

"One can be both," Xo said. "It will be interesting to see if I'm invited to run now that Rose seems to be the one who is in charge."

"Oh, she's in charge, all right," Carolina said. "No doubt about it."

"But still," Xo said, "If Anak becomes king, which it seems he will, she's got an agonizing choice in front of her. She can't be Queen of two countries. She'll have to choose. Or will she?"

Christian, being well versed when it came to monarchial history said, "Modern Spain got its beginning when the king of Aragon Fernando, married Isabella, the heir to the throne of Castilla. And that's not the only time something like that has happened in history. Usually when a king and queen get married the result is a personal union between the two countries. And should they have children, with time, the countries often merge into a federal state."

"I don't like this," Xo said, a worried look crossing her face. "It's too much power in one place. Rose shouldn't – no one – should be in control of so much."

"Geopolitics," Christian said. "Superpowers. Everyone wants to be the Harpy. Just over a larger domain."

Even as Xo was chilled by Christian's comment, a scene from the faraway past flashed through her mind: *The massive wingspan of the Harpy Eagle covering Koni in shadow, the avian beast driving its talons deep into*

Koni's back, Koni being lifted off the ground, and Xo throwing herself onto the bird's back, poundings its head with her fists.

"But Koni got away," Xo said, unaware that she was speaking out loud. "The Harpy didn't win. I didn't let it."

"And it won't win this time," Carolina said with confidence.

There was something in Carolina's tone that made Christian scrutinize Carolina's countenance with care. Was she gleeful? Smug? Self-satisfied?

"What do you know that we don't know?" he asked quietly.

Carolina didn't answer. She just stared back at Christian with a glint to her eye and that strange little smile on her face.

"You should," Christian said, his tone the same as he would use with a recalcitrant patient, "share with us." He stared at Carolina unflinchingly, and she met his hard gaze with one just as unflinchingly.

Xo looked from one to the other. "I feel like I'm in the middle of something that isn't worth battling over it. And quite honestly, I don't completely understand. Come on, bend a little," she said. "Compromise."

Xo's words had no effect, and once again the chilling memory of that long ago day when the Harpy attacked Koni flashed before her. The Harpy had only been able to attack because they had not been paying attention to all of their surroundings. She and Koni were focused solely on the gladiatorial battle between caiman and anaconda. They never did find out what was the victor, if there was one.

Just minutes ago, she, Carolina, and Christian were engaged in friendly conversation. How could their good-natured banter turn so quickly to icy silence? "I'm not going to be in the middle of this," Xo said suddenly. "You two can sit together and stare at each other all you want." She started to get up, but before she could rise more than a few inches, Carolina grabbed her upper arm and said, "You can't! It's starting! Be still!"

"Impeccable timing!" Carolina said with a sly smile, "Rose always seems to have it," and then with a finger to her lips, Carolina turned her head so she could see the start of the procession. Xo could only follow Carolina's lead. She would have created a scene if she hadn't. But then, as she sat quietly, head turned to Rose walking down the aisle, she could not have moved if she had wanted to.

Rose was riveting. No one could look away. There were murmurs of awe, and it was no wonder. Rose was stunning. Whatever the cost of the dress, it fit her perfectly. It was an elegant vision of white glory, and Rose's face glowed with love and youthful hope. She carried a simple bouquet of red roses mixed with delicate white flowers of jasmine, the national flower of Muta. Rose was breathtaking. No one, not even a misanthrope or the hardest, staunchest antimonarchist could deny it.

The ceremony that followed measured up to the sartorial height of Rose's dress. It was filled with pomp and grandeur, and although their vows contained all the required declarations to make the marriage of Princess Rose of Great Britain and Prince Anak of Muta legal, it was the personal lines the two had written to say to each other while standing at the alter that gave heartfelt promise to the grandiose ceremony. Poignantly voiced, with soft intensity, the phrases made all in attendance and viewing feel a wash of love, unity, and hope. It was indeed a royal wedding.

Forty-Eight

It wasn't until Carolina was called to the Throne Room for official photographs that Xo and Christian had a moment to themselves.

"How are you holding up?" Christian asked.

"I'd love to take a run," Xo said, "but first I'd take off these shoes."

"I'd prefer it," Christian said. "We have to stay for the meal, but we can leave as soon as the dancing starts."

"All these people that keep coming up to us and introducing themselves. They all seem to know who I am. I'm afraid I'm not going to remember half of them."

"Don't discount yourself. Whatever you're feeling inside, you're coming across as wonderfully poised and kind. A little bit reserved, but that only adds to the mystery."

"Mystery?"

Christian grinned. "Of where you're going to end up. Very sensual. Very intriguing."

Xo bubbled up with laughter. "Okay, now you're making fun of me. There's no mystery about where I'm ending up. I know exactly where I'm going."

"Where is that?" The question was voiced gravely, and at first Xo didn't know it was meant for her, as it came from someone who had come up behind her. As Christian moved a bit to the side so he could extend his hand, Xo turned around to view her unknown acquaintance.

The man facing her had neatly trimmed white hair, and the chest of his uniform he was wearing was bedecked with honors. He had an aura of austerity, and despite the levity of the surrounding guests, he stood ramrod straight, as if on military duty.

"Excuse me?" Xo asked. "What are you asking?"

"You said you knew exactly where you were going. I'd like to know where that is."

"Is that any of your business?" Xo asked with equanimity.

"It might be."

"That," Xo said, meeting the piercing stare of the man in front of her, "is not reason enough for me to share."

Christian made a strangling sound, as if he was trying not to laugh. "Allow me to make introductions," he said. "Xo, may I present Lord Hampton. He was instrumental in the union of Prince Anak and Princess Rose. Lord Hampton, this is my girlfriend Xo Bosque, of Colombia. Lord Hampton, I believe you know who I am. I am Christian of the House of Haakkon, Prince of Norway."

Xo took a step forward, but she did not extend her hand. "Lord Hampton," she said, her voice matter of fact and without a tremor, "I believe you are the one who sent Reggie to investigate me."

Lord Hampton didn't move a muscle, and his gaze remained locked on Xo's. "I don't know what you are talking about."

Seeming completely unperturbed, Xo said, "Of course," and then she smiled slightly and extended her hand. As Lord Hampton clasped it in his own, Xo said, "Next time just ask. It will save you time and money."

Lord Hampton's grip tightened momentarily, and still holding Xo's hand, he made a slight bow. Then as he stood to his full height, he asked, "And where is it exactly that you are going?"

Xo couldn't help herself. She clapped her hands and laughed. "You are crafty," she said, her voice merry, "And determined. I'll give you that."

"I'm not being coy," she continued, her eyes sparkling, "but there are others to be informed first."

Lord Hampton leaned his head. "A certain prince of Norway?"

Christian who had been raptly following the conversation decided it was time to intercede. He opened his mouth to speak, but he never had a chance.

"Which prince of Norway are we talking about? Not the one I slept with; I hope."

All three – Xo, Christian, and Lord Hampton turned in shock to look at Carolina who had come up to their little circle. It was Lord Hampton who gained his composure first. "I would advise discreteness," he said, his tone dry.

"Relax," Carolina said. "I just wanted to get your attention. It worked."

"It did at that," Xo said. Then, not sure if Carolina was teasing or speaking in all seriousness, she asked, "What Prince of Norway did you sleep with?"

"Xo! You don't think that I. . ." Christian said, his voice almost angry.

Before he could finish, Carolina patted his arm. "Calm down Big Boy. Your brother of course. You've seen the photos."

"No."

"But you knew," Carolina said, appearing for the first time, a little unsure and taken aback as she looked at Christian.

"I had no interest," Christian, said, "but yes, I know of their existence. My family considers it a private matter."

Carolina looked at Christian pensively. "You should have been born first," she said slowly.

Christian's response was immediate. His words, though few, silenced them all.

"If I had been, I would have never met Xo."

Forty-Nine

"That went well."

"Did it?" Lord Hampton looked at Carolina who, with a little smile on her face, was watching the retreating figures of Xo and Cristian.

"Yes, because now I know."

Lord Hampton came as close to making a public sigh as he had ever had. "An explanation would be incumbent."

"Oh, ho," laughed Carolina. "Is this a first? Asking the why before the excoriation? Usually you just dress me down! Tell me what a disgrace I am to the crown!"

"Does this mean," Carolina continued, her voice playful, "that the kid gloves have been put on? That I am to be treated with extra care, as one day I may reign as queen?"

This time Lord Hampton did sigh. Audibly. The first time in public, ever.

The sound seemed to trigger something in Carolina's psyche. "I've gone too far," she said. "But don't worry. I have something to make you feel better."

Carolina opened up her clutch and took out a white envelope that had been folded in half. "It's the results of the . . ."

"Sonogram," Lord Hampton finished for her. "Rose is having a boy. I know. We've had discussions with King Muta. We've been informed that he will be stepping down when the baby is born. Rose has already agreed to step down once Anak becomes king. She will still be queen, but not of England."

"Old knowledge," Carolina said. "You aren't the only sly fox in the forest."

"Then what do you now know?" Lord Hampton asked irritably.

"That I'm doing the right thing for country and honor by destroying all evidence of my night with Christian's brother. An odious man, if I do say so myself. Not even a good lover. And cheating on his pregnant wife while she was in the castle. Same floor, no less! His children just down the hall!"

Lord Hampton looked at Carolina tactfully. "Will the Norwegians be informed of this?"

Carolina laughed. "You're a fox, old man, but I'm more of a chess player. Of course, I'll tell them, but you don't think they'll believe me, do you? You wouldn't."

"Will you? Will you actually do it?"

"Yes."

Lord Hampton said slowly, "Because of what you now know."

"Yes."

"And that is?"

"The thing about chess is that everyone worries about the king. They're all afraid of being checkmated. What people don't realize is they need to be afraid of the queen. She controls the board. There's no checkmate unless the queen is taken."

"Your point being?"

"Christian doesn't want to be king. He'd rather be with Xo. That's what I now know. That's why I'm going to destroy the photos. I'm the only one with evidence, and I'll be the one to erase it. Completely."

Lord Hampton looked at Carolina carefully. "What else is on the board?"

"Oh, I've thoughts moves ahead," Carolina said cheerfully. "I play to win. Now, take your present. You're going to get a real charge."

Lord Hampton took the envelope that once more was being offered. He took it, fingering it between his fingers, as if weighing the merits of revealing its contents.

"Open it, for God's sake," Carolina said. "It's going to knock your socks off. You're the one always talking about how knowledge is power."

Lord Hampton nodded, and very carefully, he slowly began to open the envelope. As he slid the paper out and began to unfold it, Carolina moved closer so they could both look down at the single sheet of paper. It took a mere fraction of a second for Lord Hampton to understand what he was looking at. "Dear God," he said softly. "Dear God."

"We're the only two who know. Even she doesn't."

"I'd like to know how. . ."

"How I know, how I got the information, yes, yes. I'll be succinct. I found Xo in my bed one night. In the castle no less. Climbed through a window, past all the security cameras. Out the same way.

"Scared me so I almost wet myself, but she was under the covers because she was so cold. The jungle is a lot warmer, and that's what she's used to, as you well know."

Carolina suddenly stopped short. "How does that saying go? Politics makes strange bedfellows. We were certainly in bed, but. . ."

"Please," Lord Hampton said. "Explain to me as if this was a game of timed chess. The clock is ticking."

"Very clever," Carolina said, her eyes twinkling. "You're already working on new ways to manipulate me, but you have a point. I said I'd be succinct. Okay, here goes. In very few words. At least for me!

As you well know, I sent Xo off to tell Anak that Rose was pregnant with his child and that Rose didn't want to marry Christian because she didn't love him but she felt she had to."

"But why was Xo in your bed? Why did she come to see you?"

"Now who is the one who is interrupting?" Carolina said, shaking her head in mock frustration. "She came because – she has resources, too – a smart cookie. A journalist. Name of Raul van Maarten and then some hot female lawyer. Her name is Lara Tran, and she's married to the man who got Xo into running ultramarathons. Xo went to them first because her land was being threatened. Told if she married Christian, the rain forest would essentially disappear. Because of who she is but mostly because of the way she was raised, Xo doesn't back down. And she knows when to ask for help, and to whom. Once she knew who was behind the threat, she came to me.

"What's frigging unbelievable is that Anak loves my sister. Strange bedfellows, that! I don't think Rose is capable of loving anyone, but being with Anak is the closest she will ever come. Rose wants power and money, and no one will best her at that, not if she's with Anak. But wow, those vows we just heard them say to each other. Two of a kind who belong together. Made me feel a lightness of being."

"But this. . ." Lord Hampton said, pointing to a particular section on the paper."

"Shows that both Rose, mum, and I are related to Xo. Rose and I are Xo's cousins. Mum's her aunt. I got Xo's hair sample when she was in my room. From her head. Not from some illegitimate drug dealer's daughter. Not that Reggie knows what an ass he made of himself. He thinks he got the right sample. You thought he got the right sample."

"You said we're the only two who know?" Lord Hampton asked quietly.

"Yes. Lab work done anonymously. Premier labs. Triple checked. Xo is the daughter of Prince David and Princess Phillipa. Rightful present queen of our great empire."

"Am I being checkmated?" Lord Hampton asked slowly.

"Never! I need you. Will need you," Carolina said, her eyes twinkling. "When I'm queen."

"You're going to be Queen?"

"Rose will be otherwise occupied, and Xo doesn't want to be queen. I'll be a good queen."

"And this information will never come out?" Lord Hampton said, folding up the paper.

"Oh, it will."

Lord Hampton let out a dry laugh. "Your machinations are exhausting," he said.

"But whip smart!" Carolina said. "Admit it old man, you're enjoying this."

"I have always been bored at weddings, but this one is and I hope will always be the most unforgettable one I have ever attended."

"You can do better than that," Carolina said. "How about the most surprising, the most intriguing, the most thrilling."

"I will accept your superlatives."

"Ready for the master stroke?"

"Oh, dear God," Lord Hampton said, "There's more?"

"Yes. There's more. Much more. The fate of the monarchy, in fact."

Fifty

One Year Later

"Are you ready?" Carolina carefully brushed the material on Christian's right shoulder with her gloved hand.

"Is she okay? How is she doing?"

"Don't worry," laughed Carolina. "She's not going to run. I'll keep her close to my side all the way down the aisle."

"I just don't want her to hate this day," Christian said.

"She won't. She doesn't. Will you lighten up? Start enjoying yourself for God's sake. This is your wedding day."

"I know," Christian said, his entire face lighting up as if he were a little boy given a serendipitous treat. "I'm going to have a wife!"

Carolina took a step back and examined Christian from the bottom of his feet to the top of his head. "My work here is done," she said, nodding approvingly. "Jack," she said, turning so she could talk to Christian's faithful detective, "It's all on you now. Get him safely to the altar."

"I will Your Majesty."

Christian looked at Carolina with true affection. "You really do like that title," he said. "It becomes you. But just know that I'll never be bowing to you."

"You're not going to lose your head about it only because of Xo," Carolina teased. "She's truly a wonder." There was a brief moment of silence, and then Carolina took a step closer to Christian. "I really love her, Christian," she said, her voice sober and intense. "You are to take care of her, always."

"That makes two of us. And I will. Always. Forever."

"Is he doing all right?"

Carolina laughed. "Christian asked the same about you. Xo, he's so in love with you. Now, stand up so I can take a final look at you before I walk you down the aisle."

Xo didn't say anything. She just stood obediently. Carolina stepped back with a critical eye and then she said softly, "You're beautiful, Xo. Christian won't be able to say his vows he'll be so overwhelmed."

"Then I'll kick him."

Xo's flippant response was so immediate and unexpected that it felt for a moment that the words lingered in the air, as if giving time for an adequate response. Carolina looked at Xo, and Xo looked at Carolina, and then the two of them started laughing almost hysterically.

Carolina was the first to control herself. "Enough!" she said. "We've got to stop. There's never been such a beloved bride to be – by groom or country – and we can't have you showing disrespect by giggling down the aisle. Decorum! We're royal remember!"

"One of us is, at least," Xo said, smiling fondly at Carolina. "I can't thank you enough for being here for me. I think I'm the first person ever to be escorted down the aisle by a queen."

"I was honored you asked me."

"I wasn't sure it was the right thing to do, but the thing is. . ." Xo hesitated before continuing.

Carolina looked at her with narrowed eyes, "Yes? The thing is that. . ."

". . .is that even though we didn't meet until really, not so long ago, and at first we weren't exactly close. . ."

"I was horrible to you!" Carolina said, unabashedly cracking a wide smile.

"Oh, there's that," Xo said, "And yes, you were, but never the less, out of all the people whom I've met apart from my original people, you're the person I feel closest to. Not in a falling in love way, like with Christian, but in a more familiar way. A chosen bond. I know that's strange, but. . ."

"Enough said," Carolina said. "I feel the same way. And now it's time. Your man is waiting."

Xo was radiant as she made her way down the aisle, and Carolina holding her arm, dazzled with tenderness as she kept catching Xo's eye and smiling warmly. Christian wasn't the only one whose breath had been taken away by the sight of the two women making their way down the red carpeted aisle toward him. It was the entire congregation, the entire populace of the country, the entire viewing world who all felt they were privy to something magical – a vision in white and an, albeit, very young, but adoring fairy godmother who just happened to be a queen.

Xo hadn't said a word all the while Carolina was by her side, but when they reached the front pew and Carolina leaned in to kiss Xo's cheek before taking her seat, Xo said something so softly that only Carolina could hear it. Carolina's face lit up, and the world could not help but take note. Everyone wanted to know what was said. People on talk shows made conjectures, scholars theorized, and comedians made jokes, but Carolina kept it only to herself. As for Xo, not only did she say it to correct Carolina but she said it to Christian, many, many times over because it was what it was.

"He is not my man. He is my love."

Fifty-One

Lord Hampton read the summons, and he quickly stood up, calling for his jacket and his car even before he moved around his desk. By the time he stepped out of the back of the building, his black car with dark tinted windows was idling at the curb, the chauffeur waiting ready by the door to open it for him.

"To the Palace," Lord Hampton said, tersely, as he sat upright in the seat. Once there, he made his way directly to the Queen's sitting room where she was waiting for him.

"Tea?" she asked, lifting a heavy silver pot off the tray off the small table in front of the couch she was sitting on.

"Only if I'm joining you, Your Majesty" Lord Hampton answered, seeing that there were only two tea cups and saucers on the tray.

"You are. It's just the two of us." The tea was poured and the Queen carefully handed over one of the fine bone china cups on its matching saucer to her guest.

Lord Hampton sat, militarily erect, until Carolina took a sip from her own cup. It was only then that Lord Hampton tasted his own.

"I can add something stronger to the tea, if you would like."

"Your Majesty?" Lord Hampton looked over at Carolina with a cautionary expression. He carefully placed the cup and saucer on the table. "May I presume, Your Majesty," he said slowly, "that you are playing a new game of chess with me again?"

"A new game?" Carolina asked, her head cocked inquisitively. "Why start a new one? I thought the current one is going quite well. Fantastic, in fact. I'm in complete control of the board. Do you think we need a new game?"

Lord Hampton's eyes came as close to twinkling as black holes ever could. "I can only watch with admiration," he said. "You are proving to be a master."

"Quite the complement," Carolina said, wagging a finger at him, "but I know what you've left unsaid. *So far.* That's what you're thinking. *So far,* I'm doing well. But that's okay. In fact, that's what I like about you. You are actually, quite good for the monarchy."

Lord Hampton watched in silence as Carolina daintily sipped her tea. Carolina didn't speak again until she had set down the dishes. "Castling," she said, "is the only move in chess in which a player moves two pieces in the same move. The rook and the king. We're going to do that now. Move two pieces at once."

Lord Hampton couldn't help himself. Instead of maintaining his vertical rigidity, he leaned forward. "Your Majesty, how are we going to do that?"

"It's already happening," Carolina said, a huge smile crossing her face. "All we have to do is sit back and wait." As if to give emphasis to her words, Carolina sat back against the couch cushions and continued to smile broadly at Lord Hampton.

When a few seconds had passed, she leaned forward and said, "She's pregnant."

Lord Hampton had to ask to be sure. "Princess Xo?"

"Yes, the incredibly popular Prince Christian of Norway and his most beloved wife are to be parents. A boy. I'm the first to know. And I've been asked to be the godmother. The only godmother. There will be no other."

"This means, of course," Carolina said, "that he will be spending many hours with me. Days in fact. Time to teach him all about the Commonwealth. Introduce him to all its wonders. He will be the world's darling."

"You mentioned castling, Your Majesty," Lord Hampton said pensively.

Carolina gave a mischievous giggle. "That's the grown-up way of describing what's going on."

"I am afraid to inquire," Lord Hampton said. He paused a moment and then added, "Your Majesty."

"Cuckoo birds lay their eggs in other birds' nests. Spares them the trouble of raising their own chicks. And they're really clever about it. Their babies often hatch sooner so they're bigger and stronger. Survival is a tough game.

"Xo's son will be the rightful heir of Great Britain and all of the Common Wealth. And I don't have to raise him! One could say I'm a cuckoo bird, but. . ."

"You are far too intelligent for that, Your Majesty," Lord Hampton said, understanding completely. "Too good of a chess player. Your move is to castle. The boy will be raised well. Unspoiled. Taught responsibility. Nurtured. And then, when you're ready, you will take him. Move him across the board – or should we say the continent – to take your place."

"Yes!" Carolina said, clapping her hands in glee. "He's going to be compared to King Arthur, you know. The legend will become real!"

"Have you given thought to when the boy and Princess Xo will be informed, Your Majesty," Lord Hampton asked.

"Not for years!" Carolina said happily. "We have to let Christian and Xo do their magic on him first. He's going to be the most down to earth, unpretentious, hardworking royal ever. And really smart. And good looking. I mean, just look at his parents."

Carolina leaned forward and continued, her voice earnest. "The monarchy will never be stronger, all because of him. He will be righteous. He will be a great leader. Probably able to run a marathon, before breakfast, no less. Yes, he will a mighty king."

"So do your work," Carolina said, sitting back and taking a sip of her tea. "Make sure all records show so if something happens to me unexpectedly there is no doubt as to who will take my place. Make it impossible for any usurper to even come close."

Lord Hampton looked gravely over at the young woman sitting across from him. He nodded, as if he had made a decision after weighing the consequences, and then he asked, "Your Majesty, may I have permission to speak freely?"

"I would have it no other way," Carolina said. She returned Lord Hampton's gaze without any sign of trepidation. She knew she was strong. She was confident of her moves.

"At your sister's wedding. After you informed me of Xo's bloodlines, I asked you if there was more. To be revealed, I meant. And you said, and here, I quote, 'Yes, There's more. Much more. The fate of the monarchy, in fact.'"

"Yes, and that was when I told you I was sterile," Carolina said. "And I didn't have to explain anything further to you. You knew instantly what that meant. I appreciate you not making me feel like less of a woman because I was/am barren. That is a chilling word, isn't it? Barren. As bad as sterile. I hate being pitied, and you didn't pity me. You didn't even say you were sorry."

"Maybe," and here Carolina made a wry grin, "you were relieved."

"No," Lord Hampton said with fervency, "I was not. Indeed, I don't feel pity for you. Empathy, but not pity. The truth is that I admire you. You took your fate and you carved it into your own. That is no small feat."

Carolina sat, deeply touched and so surprised at Lord Hampton's words that she wasn't sure how to react. She simply sat, motionless. It was the following words that Lord Hampton spoke that caused a reaction.

"Your Majesty, if I could have had a daughter, I would have wished she was you."

Carolina stood abruptly. "Dismissed," she said. Lord Hampton nodded acquiescence and rose from his seat. After making his respectful retreat, he stood outside the chamber door for a moment. He wanted to treasure the memory of what he had just witnessed.

Carolina had been so touched by his sentiment that she had cried. Not with any drama or histrionics, of course, but he had seen a single tear begin to trickle slowly down the side of each check as she stood upright and regal, watching his egress.

Fifty-Two

"He is the most beautiful creature in the world," Christian said, almost reverently. "I never thought I could feel this way. I've helped in so many births, but I didn't know until now how all those parents really felt. I think it's easier to be the doctor than the one in charge. You worry less. Xo, he's a miracle!"

"He is perfect, isn't he?" Xo said, reaching out so she could once again lay their baby on her chest. Christian handed the newborn over, but then he moved onto the bed so he could lay next to his wife and child.

"Can you hear it?" Christian asked after a moment. "The noise? Every bell in all of Norway must be ringing. My mother says the streets are filled with cheering people. It's a huge party. The celebration will go on all night."

"He has the whole world in front of him," Xo said. "He could be anything. And we get to see it – whatever it is he decides to do."

"At least we've spared him the weight of the crown," Christian said. "He's not even close to ever becoming king, not now with Oscar's three."

Xo laughed. "And you know Oscar's not done. He'll have at least one or two more to put our boy further down the line of succession."

"But what your brother doesn't realize," Xo said, kissing the top of her baby's head, "is that his insecurity just makes our son's future brighter. Our child can choose to be anything he wants to be."

"Indeed, he can, my love. He can be anything in the world," Christian agreed, "Anything, except a king."

About the Author

Ruth Foster did compete in an ultramarathon as part of a family bet. She did not even come close to finishing, but she had marvelous conversations with other contestants on the course. The other participants were an eclectic group, running the gamut from speed dynamos to plodding bucket listers. As bodies were challenged and nature's elements embraced, all were encouraging.

When Ruth Foster was given the opportunity to visit Leticia, Colombia, she found a vibrant mural of an indigenous woman amidst flora and fauna typical of the area painted on a wall. Next to the woman were these beautifully scripted words:

Mi Cuerpo
Mi Territorio
No se Vende
(My Body
My Territory
Not For Sale)

If you enjoyed this book, take a gander at Ruth Foster's other titles:
The Bike Messenger
The Water Witch   (written under the name Julie McLean)
The Sky Walker   (written under the name Julie McLean)

Made in the USA
Middletown, DE
17 January 2023

21933830R00168